Catch

I couldn't stop reading! Darcie J. Gudger has brought her coming-of-age series to readers with a special blend of pizzazz. *Catch*, the third and final book, is not only the cherry on top of the ice cream sundae, but also free additional whipped cream, chocolate fudge, and sprinkles! The plot is intriguing, the characters are relatable, the narrative is engaging... In essence, *Catch* is the perfect blend of suspense and humor, supplemented by a healthy dose of heart-string-pulling.

–Kayla Woodhouse
Co-author of *No Safe Haven* and *Race Against Time*, co-founder of The Write Nook

All of the books in this series are great, but Gudger saved the best for last. The characters shine—even the ones you love to hate. The blend of action, humor, suspense, heartbreak, and triumph is just right. These characters will steal your hearts as they learn lessons of maturity, friendship, and forgiveness.

–Becca Whitham
Award-winning co-author of *The Promise Bride* and *The Kitchen Marriage*

Darcie Gudger's last installment in the Guarded series will leave you breathless. Brilliantly woven together, the story had me sucked in from page one with all its twists and turns. And the characters! I wanted to hug them, strangle them, and cry with them as they journeyed together. With a signature blend of wit and suspense, Gudger is one to watch. Don't miss this terrific series!

–Kimberley Woodhouse
Award-winning and best-selling author of more than twenty books including The Heart of Alaska series and *The Patriot Bride*

Catch

Guarded Book 3

Darcie J. Gudger

Mountainview Books, LLC

ISBN: 978-1-941291-40-5 (paperback)
ISBN: 978-1-941291-41-2 (ebook)

This book is dedicated in memory of Doris "Mabel" Nielson (1931-2017) the founder of the Highlander program at Houghton College. She saw the writer in me long before I did. She also taught me I could push beyond my limits and survive. Because of her, I have a greater love of the outdoors and my Lord, Jesus Christ.

Acknowledgments

First and foremost, I give glory to God. He gifted me with the ability to tell stories.

Thanks John for putting up with all the writerly stuff I do. I know you don't have a clue about any of it, but you let me do it anyway. Kyle, dude, I love how you have the story bug. Your writing astounds me. I can't wait to see you in print someday.

I'd also like to give a HUGE shout out to my Bloodthirsty Crit Partners aka The Write Nook. I wouldn't be published if it weren't for our motto: *friends don't let friends turn in stinky writing*. I first submitted *Catch* to them at about 22k words in. All three of them said it stunk. I deleted and started over about 4 times, threw away over 60k words before they were satisfied with the direction in which I took this book. Kimberley Woodhouse, Kayla Woodhouse, and Becca Whitham – I don't know where I'd be without you. You keep me writing when it gets hard. (They also send death threats if I even think about quitting.)

Big thanks to my local WY Write group – Neva Bodin, Lauren Robinson, Jamie Barbe, and Deb Moerke (who is about to have a book launched by Tyndale in the fall of 2019!) You guys are my rock. My cheerleaders. Thanks for letting me read parts I struggled with. And for all the laughs, encouragement and prayers. Jamie, thanks for that amazing back cover copy!

Gayle Irwin, thanks for dragging me to the Lund ranch in Kaycee to get some writing done. I am grateful the Lund's allowed me to tag along to that amazing distraction-free setting. Look forward to more writing retreats with you.

My fearless, all-knowing Highlander leaders, Sharon Campbell and Jon Cole. Yes, I loosely based the leaders in the story off you guys. Jon, I had to make a Joan because of the all-girls thing. Both of you taught me to keep going when things get hard. You made me laugh. You pushed me when I just didn't want to (fill in the blank). To this day, you inspire me.

I'd also like to thank Marlene Bagnull of the Colorado Christian Writer's Conference, and the Greater Philadelphia Christian Writer's Conference. Marlene, your conference was really where it all began for me in the early 2000's. I went from shell-shocked conferee, to continual faculty member. You give me a chance to share what I've learned along the way – to pursue my dream of helping others write amazing stories. I look forward to the conferences to come.

And Jenn Carrasco, one of my best buddies who walked alongside me through the color guard years. I love how even though we don't live in the same state, that when we do get together, it's like time stopped. I can't wait to see where Malachi goes. Kisrie wants to spin on the world team so bad.

And C.J. and Tracy of the Mountainview team. I wouldn't be in print if it weren't for them. This Guarded trilogy has been a wild ride. You guys believed in this story. You determined it must be in print. I am forever grateful. You made me a multi-published author. This has been a long time coming. I still aim to spill coffee on Tracy again in the near future.

A stiff Colorado summer breeze blew long strands of dark hair across Wendy Wetz's face. She wrapped her arms around herself to calm the shivers despite temperatures in the high nineties. Kisrie Kelley and her weird little friends stood a few feet away on the newly made wheelchair ramp to the Kelley's new home. Any minute Mr. and Mrs. Kelley were gonna pull in the driveway with Kisrie's little sister.

Keri.

One of several Wendy left in Pennsylvania when she escaped the prostitution ring. It wasn't her intent to leave Keri or the others behind. Someone had to get away to get help, and her connection with the truck driver made her the best candidate. But the captors crashed the RV before any help arrived. Because of those dumb privacy laws hospitals have, Wendy could only hope the others kids were safe.

"They're coming!" Jacque Gonzales squealed, her dark hair flying in all directions as she flapped her hands. Kisrie pressed on the railing to lift herself higher. The wood creaked.

Great. Now they were all gonna die. That girl needed to go on a diet so bad.

A red van turned into the drive, wheels squeaking on the concrete. Zena Plank burst out of the house and jogged down the ramp to meet the van. It slowed to a stop and its side door slid open. Kisrie thundered past her, followed by the others.

Wendy held her breath. She'd seen Keri in the hospital back in Pennsylvania, but to see her home in Colorado, wheelchair bound, was a whole 'nother thing. It meant things were permanent. Keri wasn't getting better. It meant Wendy'd always have a reminder of those horrid weeks with the pimps.

Everyone crowded by the van door, blocking Wendy's view. None of them seemed to notice she was holding back—except for Keri.

The girl craned her neck, and her eyes seemed to skim over the group in search of something or someone.

Wendy.

Keri locked eyes with her and pressed her lips together. Wendy looked to her left to break the gaze. Did the sight of her cause all of the bad stuff to come rushing back in Keri's mind? Maybe it was a mistake to be here. Maybe she could slip away and trek back to Zena's house where she lived.

"Wendy, don't be a stranger, come on down and join us," Mr. Kelley called as he walked around the front of the van to open the passenger door for his wife. He always did things like that. Wendy's heart skipped a little as he pulled on the handle and Gwyn Kelley slid out. She tossed her curly red mane over a shoulder and squeezed through the group to the opening in the van.

Mr. Kelley closed the door and headed toward her. He was tall, fit, and incredibly handsome for a guy his age. The gray at his temples made him look smart. Life was so not fair. Why wasn't he her father? And how come someone as plain and dumpy as Kisrie could be born to those two?

"Keri was asking if you'd be here." His blue eyes flashed as he touched her arm. "I think you're the first person she wanted to see. Come with me."

She followed.

By the time she reached the van, Keri and her hot pink wheelchair were on the ground. Wendy's heart thumped so hard it almost hurt. What would she say? What could she say? This was *her* fault. Would Keri hate her guts? Is that why she wanted to see Wendy? To point a finger in front of everyone in accusation?

"Wendy." Keri's voice was soft.

The others moved back a little. Kisrie shuffled closer. Wrinkles dug into her forehead, and the corners of her mouth tipped down into a twisted frown.

Ignoring Kisrie, Wendy focused on Keri. But what should she say? A greeting would have to suffice. "Hey."

"I missed you." Keri's blue eyes locked onto hers.

Wendy swallowed hard, fighting the tears that threatened to break out of her eyes. "I missed you too."

Wendy stood on the back deck at Zena's house…er…home. Her mind whirled, and her heart ached as she tried to process all that happened earlier.

Keri came home today.

In a motorized wheelchair.

And Wendy's heart shattered into a million, billion pieces.

Strong, popular, invincible Wendy who, after winning that scholarship, was gonna conquer the world.

Life had a cruel way of ruining the best laid plans.

The glass doors between the house and the back porch slid open. Footsteps. A steaming mug of herbal tea hovered under her nose. "I thought I'd find you out here."

Wendy took the tea from Zena Plank, the woman who took Wendy in when her mother abandoned her earlier in the school year. And this happened *after* she falsely accused Mr. Plank of sexual misconduct and *after* he committed suicide. Wendy might as well've driven the car off the side of Lookout Mountain herself.

And yet...

And yet...

After all she'd done, Zena Plank took her in as if she were a daughter. What was with these people? What were they *really* made of?

Zena rested her elbows on the wooden railing and gazed up into the canopy of a large cottonwood that shaded them in the evening light. "Do you want to talk about it?"

What was there to say?

That the sight of Keri in a wheelchair stabbed Wendy to the core, stealing her breath and causing her legs to itch so bad she wanted to run and run to make it stop? That Keri's neon pink wheelchair reminded Wendy about what *she* did to cause it?

If only she hadn't banged on the car window when Marcus and Jorge kidnapped her.

If only she'd never got into that stupid car.

If only she was born into a normal family with a normal mother and a normal father. Instead, the Universe saw fit to have her born to a drug addicted prostitute. Her mother, Iona, had *no freaking idea* who Wendy's father was. Forget Ancestry DNA tests. Wendy was a girl without a legacy. Life was so unfair.

"It's not your fault, you know." The breeze picked up a strand of gray hair that fell out of Zena's bun. It stuck to her eyelashes causing her to blink rapidly. Zena looked much older than her fifty-eight years. Wendy tried to convince her that dyeing her hair would take decades off, but Zena insisted she was comfortable with how she looked. She wanted to age gracefully or some weird thing like that.

Wendy curled her fingers around the railing and leaned over. "It's all my fault."

"You can't blame yourself for things beyond your control."

"I could've said no to getting in the car. That was within my control."

"You didn't know Marcus had bad intentions toward you. You knew him and he never hurt you before. You had no way—"

Wendy cursed and spun to face Zena who sloshed tea down the front of her button-down shirt. "Would you cut the psychobabble, already? It *is* my fault. All you grownups say kids today don't take any responsibility for their actions...well here I am. I'm taking responsibility." Wendy slapped her chest with an open hand. "It's my fault Keri is in the wheelchair. It's my fault your husband is dead—"

"Wendy that's not—"

"Will you let me finish?" Wendy clenched a fist and pounded it on the railing. "You wanted to talk. You all don't think I know about how you guys blame me for everything. Kisrie said it. Mrs. Kelley's practically said it. I know deep down that all you people wish I'd never been born. I bet you guys threw a party when I disappeared. I also bet if Keri hadn't disappeared as well, no one would have bothered to even look for me. Am I right?"

Zena shook her head and took a step closer. "Wendy—"

"Am. I. Right?" Wendy moved out of reach. There was no way she was gonna let Zena Plank touch her and break further into her heart. Pressure built and surged in Wendy's chest, like an undulating ocean of unidentifiable emotions. She couldn't let it out.

She couldn't.

She wouldn't show she was weak.

She stared into the canopy of the cottonwood unable to look Zena in the eyes. "I don't get you. Why am I even here?" Wendy's throat ached. "What do you want from me?" Her voice echoed off the siding of the neighboring houses. Someone opened a window and peered out.

"I don't want anything from you."

"Everybody wants something from me!" Wendy grabbed a candle in a glass container from the table and threw it hard at the nearest tree. It exploded into a million pieces—much like her soul.

Zena stared at the sparkling glass littered around the base of the tree. It seemed like Wendy finally pushed the usually calm school psychologist to silence.

"You people can't fix me. You can't fix any of this. You can't undo anything that happened. You might as well save yourself the trouble and quit trying." Wendy stormed into the house and ran to her room. She made sure to slam the door hard enough to knock the family portrait off the wall in the hallway. Every cell in her body shook. Her heart hammered in her chest. She thought about calling Sabrina or Brittany, but they'd ditched her when they joined that stupid color guard. They were always at rehearsal. Running away wasn't an option— not after experiencing the living hell with Marcus and Jorge. And, those two were still out there. Looking for her. Looking for Keri.

Looking to kill them both.

Death wasn't the answer either. Wendy had stared it in the face once before and...never again. No, she didn't want to die. She had no clue what happened after and that was more terrifying than living through all this.

What did she hear those churchy people say when life got hard? This too shall pass? She scoffed. Such drivel.

Wendy eyed the books on her shelf. She needed to get her mind off all this until this too passed.

Ah! Stephen King.

Zena hated those books.

Which was why Wendy smuggled *all* of them into the house. Zena had no clue. Wendy grabbed *Misery* and cracked the cover.

Time to escape from her own horrifying reality into someone else's.

Kisrie Kelley wiped the sweat off her forehead with the back of one hand and chugged from the bottle held in the other. Why did they have to practice in this heat? It was like a hundred and forty-seven degrees. And why didn't the school believe in air conditioning? She didn't know which was worse, standing in the blazing sun on the field or in the sauna-like environs of the gym. Why couldn't color guard be a water sport in the summer?

Plus, it seemed like Gavin was punishing them for their team building escapade in late May that landed the entire guard in jail overnight. *That* created quite the scandal through the school. Gavin's leadership, along with band director Dr. Morgan's, was questioned. Aunt Zena came up with a solution of some sort of wilderness death trek, but none of the adults seemed to agree on the best punishment for eleven teens who were only trying to find two abducted girls. Some adults demanded juvie hall! It was a hot mess. Hotter than the day's two-*hundred* degree temps. And what was she doing complaining? Her sister was trapped in a wheelchair while she was able to walk and do a lot of other stuff Keri couldn't. A thought struck Kisrie in the head like a brick. What if Keri couldn't play her flute ever again?

"Hey, Kisrie, can I talk to you a minute?"

Kisrie pulled the bottle from her lips, water dripping from her chin. She turned around to find Sabrina, one of Wendy's goons—er...former goons—standing there, flag cradled in her arm. "Uh, yeah. Sure." Kisrie screwed the cap back on, tossed the water bottle to the ground, then folded her arms. "What's up?" Her heartbeat accelerated a tad. Just because Sabrina and Brittany helped with the disastrous search for Keri and Wendy, then joined guard, didn't make them safe in any way.

"Britt and I've been talking, an' we're kinda sorta worried about Wendy ever since she came back...and uh...even more since your sister came back. She just isn't herself anymore." Sabrina fished in her pocket and pulled out a lip gloss that smelled like watermelon. She swiped it over her lips.

Sabrina was right. Wendy *was* different. However, it was a change Kisrie kinda liked. Before the kidnapping Kisrie had dubbed Wendy The Queen of Mean. Wendy delivered a backpack to her face behind the bus when they were in elementary school. In middle school her insults were relentless. Then, in high school, her proclivity turned to shoving Kisrie's head into not-so-clean toilets.

But that wasn't all Wendy had done to make Kisrie's life a living hot place where snowballs can't live.

The list went on.

And on.

And on.

Wendy's ultimate act of terror was getting some thugs to beat Kisrie within an inch of her life for ratting Wendy out regarding the rumors about Uncle Evan.

But now?

Near silence. Sure, Wendy may have shot a barb here and there, but it was weak and often missed its mark. The Former Queen of Mean's heart wasn't in it. For the first time in her entire school career, Kisrie felt peace. She felt...free.

But she couldn't say all that to Sabrina. It wouldn't be right. "Yeah, she's…quiet."

"I bet you actually like that." Sabrina's eyes narrowed a bit as she shoved the lip gloss back into her pocket and picked up her flag.

"Can't say I mind much."

"Well, I'm worried. Britt and I think she might try…you know…uh, how do I put this?" Sabrina ran the red silk flag through her fingers and let it drop. "Uh, she might pull a Mr. Plank."

Kisrie's lungs seized. Her heart seemed to stop. Her uncle's death along with her sister's abduction were burdens of guilt she dragged behind her like hobble stones used on horses in the olden days. Sabrina had no right to fling it around as some sick euphemism. "How can you say that?"

Sabrina sucked in her lips, then blew out. "Sorry, Kiz. That wasn't a nice thing to say. Well, whenever Britt an' me try to get ahold of Wendy, she never answers. Like, she tried to be normal when she got back from that place, but since your sister came home last week, it's total silence. Your aunt can't even seem to get her to come out of her room. It's… it's…" Sabrina's eyes got all shiny and a tear slipped from the corner.

"You guys feel like she doesn't care."

Sabrina nodded. "Yeah. Something like that."

"Soooo?" Kisrie struggled to put herself in the girl's place. Sabrina and Brittany had caused so much pain in her life and the lives of her only two friends, forgiveness was a tad bit elusive.

"Britt and I were thinking we'd talk to your aunt about getting Wendy to join color guard."

Kisrie reeled back, blinked a few times, shook her head and coughed. No. Not just no, H-E-double hockey-sticks no. Did she just curse? Hot places no? Was that better? She didn't want to become like Wendy whose colorful vocabulary could make a sailor blush.

"Kisrie?"

"Uh…"

"She needs friends." Sabrina cradled her pole and made small circles with the silk by her feet. "You all have been nice to us. We never had friends who cared like you guys do. What if Wendy had it too?"

Wendy invaded Kisrie's classroom in kindergarten. Then, she invaded her family. Guard was the only Wendy-free zone on the planet. Now Brittany and Sabrina wanted her to invade the only safe place Kisrie had left?

"Kisrie, are you okay? You're looking a little pale."

Wendy wasn't *as* mean as she used to be, but earlier in the year, she accused Kisrie of trying to kill her with a sabre! Took it to the *police*. What if the old Wendy emerged meaner than ever? She'd been through a lot and her MO was to take it all out on Kisrie. Why would that change now?

"Ladies, grab your sabres and get into block." Gavin dipped his sabre, threw a hilt six, leaped, then caught solid on white tape. The blade didn't even vibrate. "We're gonna warm up with spins and stops."

Kisrie gritted her teeth and pulled her sabre out of her equipment bag. Aunt Zena may try and get Wendy to join, but there was probably a bigger chance she wouldn't. Kisrie pulled her sabre into a right flat and flipped a single. The steel blade stung through her gloves. She couldn't imagine Wendy doing this. There was probably nothing to worry about.

Or was there?

ou gotta at least admit, Sabrina has a point." Jacque spoke out of the side of her mouth as she rolled her flag and shoved it silk-down into her guard bag after rehearsal.

Kisrie stiffened. "Whose side are you on?"

"Jacque and I aren't trying to take sides or anything—" Tammie wiped the toe of her sneaker back and forth across the tops of the grass.

"Can either one of you imagine what guard would be like if Wendy joined?"

"You're assuming she *wants* to join, Kiz. This is Sabrina's idea, not hers. I think you're getting upset about nothing. But considering what she's been through, she kinda does need some friends." Tammie took a deep breath. "C'mon, Kisrie, you have to admit that's true."

"More ways to make *my* life miserable."

"That's not fair and you know it." Tammie moved in closer and put a hand on Kisrie's shoulder. Jacque did the same.

"Girl, I heard you say a buncha times how she's not the same. You actually seemed worried about her because she hasn't been so mean lately. I don't know a whole bunch about the human psycho—"

Tammie coughed. "Psyche—"

"Whatever. Anyhow, what I'm trying to say is Wendy is a person and people can change. Maybe what happened to her changed her. Maybe she's ready to become a nice person."

Kisrie highly doubted it. But Jacque had a point when she said people change... the question was, could Wendy? If Kisrie was honest with herself, her own feelings toward her life-long nemesis had somewhat evolved. Ever since Wendy became part of the Kelley-Plank family, Kisrie felt her hatred slowly dissolve. Wendy *had* been through an awful lot. Her mother abandoned her, she got abducted and who knows what happened while she was gone. All Keri would say was that, of the two of them, Wendy had it worse. And when she got back, her only two friends had joined what she perceived to be enemy forces. If Kisrie walked in Wendy's shoes, she'd probably be bitter and mean as well.

Jacque didn't let up. "Face it, Kiz, you'd be the make or break for her if she actually gives Sabrina's idea a thought."

"Remember the Bible says to love your enemy." Tammie hefted her equipment bag onto her shoulder.

Ugh. Didn't she go through the love-your-enemy thing after Wendy spread those horrid rumors then got hurt at the pageant? What about organizing the guard to look for Keri which meant they were inadvertently helping Wendy? It's not like Kisrie had done nothing while Wendy was missing. Heck, she spent a night in jail—the whole group did—in her attempt to find her sister and the *former* Queen of Mean. Kisrie sighed. "I guess you guys are right. And I don't have to like it. But I seriously don't think it's an idea she'll go for."

"Given the fact we all spent a night in jail, she may consider us her kind." Jacque examined the tips of her cobalt blue talon-like fingernails. "Which brings me to the next point of concern—that wilderness thing your aunt is gonna make us all do. I don't do woods, guys. Dirt. Animals. No hot showers…"

Tammie poked a finger into Jacque's shoulder. "If you don't do that trip, you'll have to stay in one of those juvie kind of places. I'd personally rather poop in the woods than share a cell with a serial killer or someone like that."

"This is all so dumb! Why are those policemen so upset?" Jacque's eyebrows lowered. "We were just trying to help Kisrie find her sister based on…based on…what Kisrie thought. Maybe Kisrie should've made sure we weren't messing something up."

"I had no idea there was an actual police sting going on—that was random."

"And the Aurora Police Department wants the consequences to send a message to other young people who think they know more than the experts."

Kisrie locked eyes with Tammie. "I did what I thought was best. It didn't seem like the police were doing anything. And after forty-eight hours—"

"Ya really need to back off the reality TV, there girl-friend."

Kisrie flubbered her lips. "Whatever."

"So!" Jacque clapped her hands once. "How do we fake our deaths so we don't have to go to the woods or spend a few weeks in a cell?"

"You know what, Jack? I'm done trying to interfere with things." Kisrie massaged her right shoulder. "I'm just gonna go on that wilderness trip and hope for the best."

Tammie looped her arm through Kisrie's. "I'm with her."

"Well then, I guess that means I need to start shopping for travel sized beauty products."

Kisrie felt a smile spread on her face. "You know what

guys? What if we all agree that this will be the most awesome adventure in our lifetimes. Aunt Zena said we'll be going with professional guides. After all that's happened this year, what else could possibly go wrong?"

"Aw, but Wen, it'd be so good for you. I'm even starting to get a six-pack from all them crunches." Brittany pulled up her shirt and pinched the flesh on her stomach. "See?"

Wendy smirked. Brittany's stomach used to look like dough. But it still wasn't enough to convince *her* to take on such a stupid form of exercise.

"It's also really fun. I especially like the swish of the flag when we prep for a toss and then it goes up, up into the air—"

"Shut it, Sabrina. You too, Brit. I'm not joining that stupid guard." Wendy pushed off her bed and crossed her room to be away from her so-called friends.

"But… but there's cute boys in the band." Brittany glanced at Sabrina then continued talking. "Those drummer guys, they are hot." Brittany drew out the last word and fanned herself.

"No." Wendy folded her arms.

"You can't stay locked in your room and be a mopey butt," Sabrina said.

Wendy cocked her head and blinked. "Did you just say mopey-butt?"

Sabrina snickered.

Wendy flung her hands up and sighed. "You two are becoming like them."

Both girls adjusted their sitting positions on Wendy's bed. Good. They were squirming. Maybe her message *was* getting through.

"Whatcha thinkin' Wendy?" Sabrina ran her lip gloss over her lips in a giant circle.

"I'm thinking no. Nope. No way."

"It'd be a blast to have you join. I learned to toss a double in a week. You're so smart, I bet you'll be the best on the team in no time. Better than Kisrie."

Better than Kisrie? Ha. Probably wouldn't be too hard. "No."

Wendy closed her eyes and rubbed her temples with her fingers. Images of dark hotel rooms and over-the-cab bunks crowded into her mind.

Stop! Stop! Stop! Don't go there.

She tried to picture something else. A gown she'd seen on the cover of *Vogue*. It was a deep mauve with a plunging V neckline that was a tad short of what might be considered inappropriate for a teen girl. Perfect for a pageant. There. One crisis averted. Maybe if she kept her eyes closed long enough by the time she opened them again Sabrina and Brittany would be gone, and this asinine idea of joining the guard would be a bad memory. She felt a sharp jab in the ribs. Her eyes flew open in time to see Sabrina's retreating finger.

"Believe it or not, Wen, color guard is actually kind of fun…if you can get past the painful parts."

Wendy huffed her disbelief. "Fun? Fun? What kind of drugs did you both take while I was gone? Don't you remember when Kisrie tried to disembowel me with that…that…sword of hers—"

"Sabre." Brittany cut in.

"Spelled s-a-b-r-e. Not –er." Sabrina grinned from ear to ear.

Wendy roared and jumped to her feet. She grabbed a shoe from the floor and threw it against the wall. What else would be taken from her? It was clear her only two close friends, if she could even call them that, decided to become a bunch of traitors.

"Everything all right in here?" Zena Plank's voice filled the room. Great. Just what she needed. Britt and Sabs better keep their fool mouths—

"Hey, Mrs. Plank. Me and Sabrina here were trying to get Wendy to join—"

Wendy whirled around, fists clenched. Ready to pound Brittany into the carpet. "Shut up! Just. Shut. Up."

Brittany's eye's quadrupled in size. Sabrina's mouth hung in a wide 'O'. Zena, who was leaning against the door jamb, arms folded, didn't flinch. "Brittany, as you were saying?" An eyebrow raised as if challenging Wendy to say another word.

Brittany looked from Wendy to Zena then back at Wendy. "I was just saying we think Wendy should join color guard."

Wendy closed her eyes and felt her nostrils flare as she fought to control her breath and her body. *Breathe. In. Out.* Last thing she needed was more therapy for unresolved anger issues.

"That's not a bad idea, Brittany, but it doesn't appear Wendy is quite open to it at the moment."

The moment? That was it. "I will *never* be open to that idea. I would rather die than be a part of that..." Wendy gritted her teeth. The only words that came to mind were quite foul, and Zena made it clear such language was not welcome in her home. After the blow up with her on the deck last week, Wendy didn't want to stoke the fires farther.

"Why don't you girls head on home."

Britt and Sabs pushed off the bed, nodded and backed out of the room. Wendy watched the traitors go, picturing throwing a pillow at their cowardly, retreating backs. Now she had to spend the rest of the afternoon being psychoanalyzed.

"So." Zena put her hands on her hips. Her sleeves were rolled above the elbows, and a strand of hair hung above her left eye. Wendy searched but couldn't find a trace of anger on Zena's face. "It's been quite a while since I've gone on a shopping spree."

Wendy stepped backwards. Confusion filled her chest. Shopping spree? That was a totally random segue.

"I had a conversation with Michele Field, the pageantry coach I told you about before...well, she wants to work with you. In fact, she has an opening in September after school starts. I have a list of wardrobe items from her. Thought we'd head over to Park Meadows and see what we could find."

It felt like a fully loaded RTD bus slammed into Wendy's chest. She gasped and stumbled backward until she hit the wall. Zena stood over her smiling like she had some incredible secret.

Zena Plank was so unpredictable Wendy couldn't figure out how to throw up her defenses.

After all she'd put Zena through, the woman was *still* determined to help Wendy achieve her dream of competing for the Miss America title someday.

But...

But...

Would she even qualify? Pageants were for girls of high moral character. Her character had been torn from her bit by bit during each encounter the pimps forced her into. If any of her friends knew what she'd done... Wendy shuddered. She was used up. The idea of getting close to a guy made her sick to her stomach. Sometimes interview questions got personal. What if she was pressed about her experiences? What if one of the johns turned up on the judging panel? Someone who *knew*?

"Wendy?" Zena smoothed the tops of her capris and knelt by the bed.

"I...I...don't know what to say." Her voice was little more than a whisper. All that rage exploding inside was gone. Gone! This was so unfair. Sometimes the rage masked the pain. It gave her a reprieve from having to face reality.

"How about a yes?" Zena offered her a hand.

Wendy stared at it as if it were a gun pointed in her face.

Was it possible that someone could have pure motives? Wanted to do something for her...just because?

Who knew? At least she'd get some new clothes out of the deal.

"Sure."

"Excellent! We'll go after my meeting at the high school."

Marcus watched the front door of the Plank house open. He slid low into the seat of the old pickup truck parked a block away. Wendy and the woman stepped onto the front porch. After she escaped, Wendy fell off the radar—for a while, but she came back on. They all did. As the old saying went, there was no place like home. And to make it even better? An ignorant home. Idiots had no idea how committed business men like him took back what was theirs, especially if that item had potential to make serious bank.

He'd bring Wendy home again. All he needed was one slip up. One time she was left alone. And then he'd be back in business. Several clients didn't like the fact she got away. Stupid Jorge. If he hadn't been so heavy-handed...

That was all in the past. Jorge was fish food at the bottom of Chatfield Reservoir.

Marcus needed to bide his time.

Patience in such matters always paid off.

Kisrie shivered. It felt like the air in the band room was near freezing. All members of the guard sat on chairs in a circle. No one moved. They were a bunch of scared statues waiting for dreaded news.

The color guard was given two days to choose between a torturous jaunt in the wilds of some wilderness and two weeks at some low security reform center for teen girls all because Kisrie and the other guard kids took it upon themselves to see if they could find clues about what happened to Keri. Who knew their sting operation would interfere with a real one? Both options for obstructing a police operation involved six weeks of community service of some kind. The adults wanted to make sure nothing like this would ever happen again.

The band director, Dr. Morgan, entered the room and made his way to the middle of the team along with Aunt Zena, acting in her role as school psychologist. Dr. Morgan shuffled though a stack of forms as he stood, feet slightly apart. After a few moments of furrowed brow, he looked up, then looked at each member of his guard sitting on the floor. "Well. It looks like *all* of you are choosing the wilderness trip?" His statement sounded more like a question.

Silence.

"It means you will miss two weeks of rehearsals."

Rehearsals. Always rehearsals.

Gavin, their guard instructor, had refused to attend this meeting. He was still angry they'd given up a first placement at WGI world championships because of infighting. He was even angrier when their little "team-building" exercise—the one meant to find Keri—landed them all in jail. Kisrie overheard him telling the band director that for him to stay with Mountain Ridge he wanted to move forward as if nothing happened. He was *not* going to be a laughing stock in the competitive arena because of silly teen girl behavior.

Whatever.

"Mrs. Plank is here to, uh, fill you in on the details." Dr. Morgan cleared his throat. "We were able to find a program that would get you out and back before the first round of band camp." He set the papers down, picked up his water bottle and took a swig. He set it down so hard it rattled. "That means the trip leaves next week."

Audible gasps peppered the room.

Next week?

Aunt Zena, a stack of papers cradled in her arms, stepped forward. "I've personally spoken to all of your parents and guardians. They agree this is the best course of action—"

"But we were going to Maine to see Acadia!" Leigh-Ann wailed, breaking the guard-silence. She craned her neck left and right so fast her sunglasses fell from their perch on top of her head.

"All behavior has consequences," Dr. Morgan said, a stern look pressing into his face.

"I am not here to discuss what your family vacation plans

were." Aunt Zena adjusted the papers so she could peel the packets off one at a time. "I am here to disseminate information to prepare you for this program which commences in exactly one week from today. This," she began to pass out the packets, "is all the information you need. Your parents already scanned the permission forms. Here you have a general itinerary and supply list."

"This says Wyoming!" Miranda, one of the captains, held her papers tight with both hands until the edges curled. "There's nothing up there! That's the end of the world."

"And there are bears," Zoe, another senior, added.

Kisrie looked down at her round belly, and then at all the concave bellies in the room. If there were bears, she'd be prime pickings.

Jacque raised her hand and fluttered her manicured nails— why she had those things and spun weapons escaped Kisrie's understanding. "Uh, what if we have never been in the woods before and then there is the um… bathroom thing. There are bathrooms with showers and toilets and stuff like that, right?"

"Gonzales, how can you be so stupid?" Chrissy shook her head.

"I am not stupid. I'm merely looking out for the hygienic welfare of this group of fine young women who don't like to stink."

"Two weeks. Am I hearing your right? I've never been gone from home that long," Brittany said.

"It's not that big of a deal. I go hunting up in Wyoming with my grandfather every now and then. It won't be as bad as you guys think," Sabrina added.

Brittany rocked on her bottom toward her friend. "Whoah. Sabrina, I didn't know you hunted and we've been BFFs all this time."

Tammie eased her hand up and waited until Aunt Zena called on her. "Um. Are we just going to be let loose out there to fend for ourselves? Like, *Man vs. Wild?* That kind of thing? I don't know if I can learn all the survival techniques we'd need in a week."

Aunt Zena shook her head. "Ladies, let me explain this to you. You are *not* going out alone. It is not a survival situation. You will be accompanied by highly trained wilderness experts. Dr. Morgan and I hope you will learn how to work together and make better decisions." She rested her gaze on Kisrie. "Being in the wilderness, there are some risks."

"Exactly what kind of risks, Aunt Zena?" Kisrie felt as if her insides turned to pudding.

"Well, you know...the elements, wild animals—"

"Bears! I *knew* it! I am so utterly terrified by bears!" Zoe shrieked.

"Are you sure this is a good idea, Mrs. Plank?"

"Jenn, you can always choose the other option."

"And get knifed in my sleep by a serial killer? I'll take my chances with bears, thank you very much."

"This program has an excellent track record for safety. I went over that with your parents. They haven't lost a participant yet. You will all be fine, and hopefully learn some lessons about what happens when you make choices without considering the ramifications. You are dismissed unless Dr. Morgan has anything else to add." She looked at the band director who shook his head without looking at the group. If he had his way, he would have cut them all and started over with a new team. But Gavin threw a fit. Can't compete world class with a new team the first year.

Chrissy raised her hand. "Do we need to like, start running ten miles a day or something to train for this?"

"Your conditioning program from color guard should be adequate enough," Dr. Morgan said.

For about thirty more minutes Aunt Zena and the band director fielded questions. Finally, Dr. Morgan looked at his watch. "I have a tuba lesson coming in shortly."

"Anything else?" Aunt Zena looked around the room. "Well. It's settled then. Have your parents email me with questions about the packing list."

Kisrie huddled with Tammie and Jacque. "Well, this should be fun, right?"

Jacque turned and waved her hand over her shoulder. "Whatever you say, Kiz."

"In all actuality, I would like to see a bear—from a distance that is."

"Tammie, you are so weird."

"I know. That's why we're friends."

A double knock sounded on Wendy's door. "Hey, you need to come out and eat something." Zena's voice was muffled through the solid wood. Ever since they returned from yesterday's shopping trip, Wendy had stayed holed up in her room.

Because she saw him.

Marcus.

At the mall.

Watching.

Not wanting to alarm Zena, Wendy held it together through several high-end stores and a coffee shop. How did he know where she was?

Unless...

He was watching her.

Now.

Outside.

"Wendy, I am worried about you. You haven't even had water."

Not true. Unable to sleep for fear of more nightmares, Wendy made sure all the lights were out and snuck into the kitchen for a piece of cheese and a glass of water which she brought back to her room. She also took care of bathroom business. But every time she tried to close her eyes, images of Jorge standing over her undoing his belt filled her mind. The nightmares persisted whether it was day or night. And now she *knew* for sure he was out there.

Watching.

She had to move about in the dark.

Because if the light went on, he could see in.

See her.

That could *not* happen.

If Marcus were here and found her, that meant he knew where Keri was.

Wendy's heart pounded against her chest in time with the pounding on the door. Dear God, if there was one, she had to do something to get Marcus away from Keri! She'd been through too much to worry about those horrid men again.

Wendy stuffed her fist in her mouth. What to do? What to do?

Her memory lit on Brittany and Sabrina complaining about the wilderness trip the guard was being forced to go on—the guard! That was it! Two days ago her used-to-be friends asked her to join guard. And she threw a fit.

But what if that was the one way to lure Marcus away from Keri? Going to the police could spell disaster. If Marcus got wind of it, he'd go after Keri before Wendy had a chance to protect her. And the police, according to Kisrie, moved too slowly. No. Wendy wasn't gonna get them involved. That would also upset Zena. Things were starting to get better here. Wendy didn't want to mess that up. She had to lead her former captors far away from Keri. Besides, once Wendy was in the woods there was no way he could find her. Maybe he'd even give up. He didn't seem like the woodsy type.

Wendy rolled off the bed and opened the door as Zena

raised her hand to knock again. "I want to join color guard and go on that trip."

"What?" The shock on Zena's face was priceless.

"I want to join—"

"I heard you the first time. But why?"

"You know, my friends are there, my pseudo cousin is there, and I could use some help with my decision making process."

"I... don't know what to say."

"How 'bout a yes?" Wendy grabbed Zena by the hand and pulled her into her room. "I'm gonna need some gear, but I want to just order it all online. I am not a fan of those outdoorsy kinds of places. I also want to surprise everyone."

"I'm not sure that's a—"

"Sure it is! This will be fun! Look. I'm smiling." Wendy pointed to her mouth. "How long has it been since you've seen a genuine one of those, huh?"

"It's been quite a while."

"Exactly! So. Can I use your computer? Do you have that list of gear? This is our secret. Operation Backpacker. No one can know. Deal?" Wendy held out a trembling hand. She hoped Zena didn't notice or passed it off for sheer excitement.

Zena grabbed her hand and squeezed. Questions floated around in her gray-blue eyes. "Are you sure about this?"

Wendy gave the hand a hard shake. "I've never been so sure about anything in my life."

Two days later the first package from Amazon arrived. Wendy hoped Marcus didn't get suspicious over the brown UPS van. Maybe he'd assume Zena was ordering books or kitchenware. She made sure only Zena retrieved the packages. It had to appear they were not for her.

When the boots came in, Zena stood nearby as Wendy opened the box and pulled them on her feet. "Don't you think you should put on the suggested socks and go for some walks to break them in?"

"They fit so perfectly! I don't think they need that like the old leather kind did." There was no way she was gonna traipse around the neighborhood in hiking boots with Marcus out there waiting to snatch her. And if he didn't, he'd be clued in on her plan—a risk she wasn't willing to take.

The day finally came for the guard to depart. Zena came into Wendy's room and grabbed an armful of items.

"Hey, Zena?"

"Yes?" She paused, pack straps and long underwear trailing to the floor.

"Can we load up the car in the garage…with the door shut?"

Zena blinked a few times. "It's quite stuffy in there, and we'd have to squeeze around some of my husband's old woodworking tools."

"I just want to maintain the element of surprise—that's all. You know, in case Sabrina or Brittany happen to drive by."

"Wendy." Zena tossed a pair of boots in the trunk. "What's really going on?" She wiped her hands on her gray capris.

"Nothing."

"I don't believe you."

Of course she didn't. The fact Wendy was shaking didn't help. She squeezed her hands together to keep them still. If she told Zena the truth, Zena would freak out and call the cops and then the cops would whisk Wendy away to another one of those safe house things. No. As nice as the people were in the last one, it wasn't the kind of place she liked. She didn't want anyone in her business. She also didn't think Zena or anyone else knew how dangerous guys like Marcus and Jorge were.

Wendy never told Zena what happened and didn't plan to. The woman had suffered enough awful things in her life—some caused by Wendy.

Zena folded her arms and raised an eyebrow. "Talk."

"Okay, so I'm afraid Marcus and Jorge are watching me, waiting to… to…" Her throat clogged. She gasped as a vice tightened around her chest and squeezed all the air out. Tiny pinpricks of light danced across her field of vision.

"Wendy?" Zena rested her hands on Wendy's shoulders.

"I'm hoping he won't…find me in the…woods."

Zena pulled her in, holding her tight. "Is that why you are doing this?"

Wendy nodded against Zena's shirt, smearing snot in a vertical line.

"No one has seen them since the accident. The police are keeping close watch and patrolling the neighborhood several times a day."

"I saw Marcus at the mall." There. She said it.

Zena gasped and put a hand over her mouth.

"Please, I need to do this. I need to get…get away and I don't care if it's with the color guard. The truth is, I don't want him to find Keri. I don't care so much about me." Wendy pulled back and searched Zena's face, trying to get a read on the woman's thoughts. Tears burned her eyes as emotions swelled inside of her. "Keri is like the sister I never had. I'd never forgive myself if something happened to her." Wendy's voice rasped and she felt hot tears trail down her cheeks.

"You really care about her."

Wendy nodded. "I… love… her." Never in her life had Wendy uttered those words and meant it. In the past, they were either tools or weapons depending on her motivation. Surviving all the horrors of the abduction together, Wendy and Keri formed a bond—which evolved into love.

Zena cupped Wendy's face and wiped the tears with her

thumbs. Wendy didn't recoil as she would have under any other circumstances. Was she starting to feel something for the Plank woman?

"All right. But I'm calling the police and telling them you saw Marcus here in town." Zena pulled out her phone and poked at the screen.

Wendy let out a sigh and blinked the tears out of her eyes. Time to refocus on the business at hand. "Oh, one more thing. Could we…" She swallowed then looked Zena in the eye. "Could you use evasive maneuvers to get to the school just in case?"

"What do you mean?"

"Take a route with as many lights as possible. Run a few, cut into neighborhoods, double back on the route. Speed a little, but don't get pulled over."

"You're asking me to break some traffic laws."

"He could be following me."

Zena sighed. "Let me call Detective Arbuckle and let him know. Maybe he can send somebody to check the route between here and the school."

Wendy climbed into the passenger seat then slumped into the foot well. "It's so it looks like you're alone."

"I don't like that you're not wearing a seat belt." The garage door cranked up and Zena backed out into the street. She took off in the opposite direction she normally took to the school. The car zigged and zagged through the neighborhood until they got to one of the major streets.

"Do you see anyone?" Wendy's legs cramped from the crouch.

Zena glanced at the rear view mirror. "I don't."

Wendy slid up into the seat and buckled in. She couldn't take the pain anymore. "He's there. I just know it. Hurry, that one's about to change!"

"The police are looking around for suspicious drivers." Zena pressed her lips together and Wendy fell back against her seat. The light turned red right before they shot over the cross walk. Wendy turned and looked out the back window. An old pickup skidded to a stop to avoid hitting a biker walking through the intersection. The figure in the vehicle seemed to slam on the steering wheel again and again. *Marcus!* He really was following her.

"I saw him. Oh, God, I saw him, Zena!"

The car picked up speed. The speedometer read sixty and the limit was forty-five. Zena believed her. "Grab my cell. I'm calling the police to give the location." Zena stared ahead, knuckles white on the wheel as Wendy grabbed the phone off the arm rest. "Hey Siri, dial 911."

"911, what's your emergency?"

Zena explained the situation, asked for Detective Arbuckle to be informed, then cut into and through neighborhoods without using her signal. "Why did you wait until we were ready to leave to tell me about this?"

"I hoped my mind was playing tricks on me?" Wendy paused. "I didn't want you to worry? Okay, I didn't want to cause more trouble than I already have. I thought going on this trip would take me away and lead him away from Keri."

"Even more reason why I needed to know the moment you thought you saw him."

"But what if I was wrong?"

"Well, given the current evidence, you weren't." The school appeared on the right hand side. Zena pulled hard into the entryway. "Look. I don't know if the cops found him or if he got away. I'm pulling behind the school, out of sight. We'll go in the back entrance. I'm going to make sure you are with the group, but I need to meet with the detective. I wish I could stay for the send-off." The car stopped.

"I know." Wendy looked down at her hands, folded in her lap. A hand squeezed her shoulder. She looked up to see Zena's face, tears streaking down her cheeks. She lifted her other hand and cupped Wendy's face.

Before Wendy could react, Zena pulled her into an embrace—she'd never done this before today, and this was the *second* one. Wendy's first reaction was to yank away, but the moment those arms encircled her, something inside melted.

But as soon as it happened, it was over. Zena gently moved Wendy away. "We need to get you unloaded and inside." Zena's phone buzzed. She glanced at it. "Detective Arbuckle. He's on his way to the house."

"But what if Marcus sees you? What if he follows you home?" They both got out of the car. The trunk popped open from the remote.

Zena hefted the over-loaded pack into her arms. "You let me worry about that. Move."

Wendy grabbed whatever was left. A swipe of her card, and Zena had one of the backmost doors to the school opened. "You go in first. I'll be right behind you. I want to make sure the coast is clear."

Squeezing through, Wendy lumbered down the dark hall. She heard the door close behind her. Footsteps beat a quick tempo on the tile floor. Then she felt a hand on her back. "I'm here, Wendy. I need to let the Kelleys know Marcus is in the area."

"Okay."

Excited voices bounced down the locker-lined corridors from the gym. This was it. No one knew she was coming. Wendy tried to push thoughts of Marcus and Jorge out of her mind. "I hope Britt and Sabrina will be happy to see me." It took all her effort to keep a tremor out of her voice.

"I'm sure they'll love it that you're there."

"The others though."

"They'll get over it." Zena paused. She guided Wendy to face her. "Give the others a chance. Show them who you really are—that you are someone worth knowing."

Wendy stumbled back a bit. No one outside of therapy ever said anything like that to her before. But Zena *was* a psychologist. Wendy narrowed her eyes. "You're just saying that because it's what therapists say."

"No, Wendy, I mean it. Look, we'd better get in there. The send-off is about to start and I need to grab the Kelleys."

Together they hurried down the hall to the gym entrance. Wendy took in a deep breath.

Here goes.

The light flashed green and Marcus peeled out of the inter-section. He was sure they saw him. The Plank woman suddenly started driving all erratic after she blew the red. He didn't expect her to break the law.

If it weren't for that stupid guy in spandex with his ten-speed or whatever speed bikes were these days.

He pounded the steering wheel and let off more than a few choice words. He had to get out of here and fast. The cops would be on the lookout. A few blocks away he pulled the old truck up to a curb and took care to wipe the inside as clean as he could.

He jogged down the block and looked back. He'd always wanted a truck like that. It was an old soul from the 1980s. Maybe he could lift another one. Whoever owned that one would be happy to get it back. But more pressing was the possibility that the Plank woman reported seeing him in Denver. He needed to get away and fast. Lie low for a few days.

A stray dog ambled in front of him looking like it had not

a care in the world. Marcus gave it a swift kick. It yelped. He was so close. Even had a plan to break into the house in the middle of the night and take Wendy.

She was too valuable. He had one client in particular that offered a six-figure contract for regular appointments. One. Contract.

He didn't care what it took. Wendy Wetz—the poor, orphaned beauty queen—was worth *millions*. It was time to bring her home.

Kisrie stared at the pile of clothes on the gym floor next to her backpack. They'd already been through Purging 1-point-oh, and were on Purging 2-point-oh. What was up with this purging? Seriously? They were gonna be out in the middle of nowhere Wyoming for two whole weeks, and she was down to not enough clothes for five days. And Joan and Sharon, the "fearless, all knowing, all understanding, and resourceful leaders" wanted her to purge more? Didn't they believe in the power of clean underwear?

Joan and Sharon. What a pair. Joan was what Kisrie imagined an Amazonian woman looked like. She was as tall as a professional basketball player and had crazy wild dirty-blonde hair hanging in a braid from the side of her head. She was nearly as thin as Tammie.

Sharon, on the other hand, was short and muscular. Her dark hair was curly like Kisrie's and held off her face by a wide colorful hair band. When she smiled, her teeth flashed and her eyes sparkled.

"Oh my! Wendy!" Brittany's voice echoed above all the grumbling in the gym. Kisrie looked up and saw Wendy Wetz standing in the double doors, backlit like some scene from a movie. She had a pack slung on her shoulder as well as an armload of other gear.

"What's she doing here?" Miranda, Zoe, and Chrissy looked up from their packing. Kisrie thought she heard Miranda snarl.

"Hey, Kiz, look who walked in the door." Jacque sidled up to her, a tankini dripping from her fingers.

"Really, Jack? I can see perfectly fine." Snippets of the conversation with Sabrina wiggled into Kisrie's brain. Holy moley. The hottest place in the universe must have just frozen over. "She must have decided to join guard." The words fell out of her mouth like they were made of stone.

"What? You gotta be freaking kidding me!" Jacque jumped back and started flapping all around. "This is great!"

Kisrie put her face in her hands for a moment, shook her head, then looked up toward Wendy.

Sabrina finished lashing a pot to the exterior of her pack—she kind of seemed like she knew what she was doing—and raced to Wendy. "I can't believe you're here! Are you serious?"

Wendy nodded. A small smile quirked the corner of her mouth. "Yeah, I decided I needed a new challenge in life and color guard seems to fit. Besides, I couldn't let you two venture into the wilds of the wilderness without little ol' me, now could I?"

A ripple of something shivered through Kisrie's core. That was the Wendyest Wendy had sounded since coming back from Pennsylvania. What kind of trouble was she planning for them all? Was this a revenge stunt?

"Nope! No way! I'm not going if she is." Miranda threw a handful of underwear in the air and stomped toward the exit doors of the gym. Fearless Leader Sharon intercepted. "Get out of my way." Miranda tried to push past.

"If you leave, you are choosing the alternative—two weeks in—"

"I know, I know. Just give me a minute, okay?"

"Hey, Kisrie, where's your aunt? I thought she was going to do the send-off ceremony. My parents wanted to ask her something." Tammie's breath was hot in Kisrie's ear. Where was Aunt Zena? How did Wendy get here? Did Aunt Zena even know about this?

"I don't know." Movement at the corner of the gym caught Kisrie's eye. Aunt Zena and her parents stepped through a side door leading to a hallway.

"Oh, man, this is turning into us getting on the Hot Mess Express!" Jackie bobbed around on her toes. "Guys. Can you believe that Joan chick? She told me I had to leave my straightening iron. How am I going to keep the frizz out of my hair? This trip is gonna be nothing but a gargantuan trage-dy—and Tammie, before you say anything, I *have* been reading the dictionary every night before bed. So there!"

Tammie crossed her arms. "Who said anything about your vocabulary?"

"Guys, now's not the time to argue over word usage." Kisrie put both hands on her head.

Jacque pursed her lips and blinked a few times. "You're not impressed with gargantuan?"

Kisrie rolled her eyes and looked up at the ceiling. "We have bigger issues here—like Wendy. I want to know her motives for being on this trip. I can't imagine Aunt Zena would allow this. She's not on the team."

"I am now." Somehow Wendy managed to creep up behind her.

"Lovely."

"And Kiz, may I call you Kiz since we are to be teammates,

I hear you are really good at teaching people how to throw one of those," Wendy twirled a finger in the air. "...things. I want you to teach me."

Be nice. Be nice. "I don't think we're taking any equipment on this trip."

"Well. Maybe after we get back." Wendy sauntered away with a wag of her tail-end.

"She's just trying to get to ya." Jacque patted Kisrie on the back like a mom burping a baby.

Before she could respond, Sharon stuck her fingers in her mouth and blew an ear-shattering whistle.

Tammie slapped her hands over her ears. "I hope she doesn't do that in the woods. I may have to stuff my ears with moss."

"Everyone! May I have everyone's attention please? By now you all should be finished with Purge two-point-oh. Joan? Do they look like they are ready for Purge three-point-oh?" Sharon paused and let out a giggle. "It's the last one, I promise."

"What is this? A nudist hike?" Jenn dropped to her knees and started rifling through her pile under Joan's watchful eye.

"No, my darlings, it's a decision-making process. Think about it this way. For two weeks you will be carrying your home on your back. Like a turtle. We will be hiking a few sections of the Continental Divide trail in Wyoming, ending in Yellowstone National Park. That means hills! Glorious hills! And do you want a home that weighs too much to carry up those hills?"

No one said a word. Each member of the guard, including Wendy, looked around and made eye contact before finding someone else. It was as if they all hoped someone had a better idea.

"Well." Sharon paused and trotted over to Kisrie. "The goal of Purge Three-point-oh is to reduce your current clothing pile by half. That does *not* include thermal and outwear. I see some of you have fourteen pairs of underwear."

"But I have room for it." Kisrie pointed to her pack.

"Ah!" Sharon pointed a finger to the sky. "That's where you are wrong, my dear. You *think* you have room for it. But you don't. We have yet to distribute the group gear that needs to be divided amongst you all. Things like tents, tarps, ground cloths, stoves, pots, pans, first-aid kits, and most important …food."

Joan, who towered over them all, raised her arms high. "Youse guys have four minutes. Make good choices…and three…two…one…go!"

Sharon put an arm across Kisrie's shoulder. "Now, why do you think you need fourteen pair of underwear?"

"I like a clean bottom?"

"Don't we all. But, here's the thing. You don't *need* fourteen pair. I bet you can get by with two."

Kisrie choked on her spit. "Two?" She coughed out.

"You can get two day's wear out of each. Wear it one day, turn it inside out. Wash that pair, hang to dry on your pack while you wear the other and—"

"That's gross."

"I get four days out of mine." Joan called from where she was helping Jacque reduce her pile. "Right side out to the front, then turn them backwards, then inside out, front and back."

"I'm gonna hurl." Chrissy moaned.

Sharon slid away and gave Kisrie a pat. "Trust me. You don't have to do it Joan's way. Plus, you'll be glad you didn't bring all that on the harder hikes."

"No! Not my makeup too!" Jacque held onto one end of a hot pink zebra patterned bag the size of a small train case, and Joan latched on to the other. They tugged back and forth. Joan smirked. Jacque scowled.

Kisrie wadded pair after pair of underwear into her hands.

"Hey, if I have to give up twelve pairs of underwear, you can give up your makeup."

"I like the way you think." Joan winked at her.

Jacque stopped pulling and the case popped out of her hands. "See what you made me do? Kiz." Jacque trotted over and leaned in real close until her nose touched Kisrie's. "You know I can't be seen without makeup. It's who I am. Without it I'll scare even the bears!"

Kisrie tried to hide her smile, but it didn't work.

"Kiz, that's not funny. Why're you smiling? Stop it!"

"Jacque, if ever there was a person on this planet who didn't need makeup to be beautiful, it's you. You're one of those exotic natural beauties."

"Must be the Inca and Aztec in me. But Kiz, you don't understand."

"Jack. Look at me. Girls like me are the reason makeup exists in the first place."

"Heh. Got that right." Wendy hovered nearby.

"Shut it, Wendy." Tammie snapped from where she culled her sock collection.

"Ooh. The bookworm speaks."

"Time's up! Step away from your packs. Sharon and I will be around to gather all the extraneous items and put them in garbage bags labeled with your names for when we return. We'll also evaluate your selections to make sure you'll be safe."

"Oh, no, she's gonna touch my underthings." Tammie lurched forward. Kisrie grabbed one arm, Jacque the other.

"It's okay. Really." Jacque cooed.

Tammie plopped to the gym floor. "I'm starting to wish I chose jail. All of this plus now Wendy? I'm having a bad feeling."

50

Wendy wobbled under the weight of her pack. She feared a single step would send her plunging backward onto the hard gym floor. The leaders, after having packs fully loaded, herded everyone into a circle in the center of the gym for a send-off. Parents and guardians were supposed to join their student. A deep ache swelled in Wendy's chest. Zena would have been here, but she had to meet with Detective Arbuckle. No matter. Being alone wasn't new. Not once did her own flesh-and-blood mother, Iona, attend anything. The only time she involved herself with Wendy was the sabre incident. She smelled a lawsuit and a lawsuit meant money. Money was more important to Iona than anything. That's why she up and left Wendy to fend for herself. Well, she just had to suck it up and not let on she was feeling alone.

Something heavy landed on her shoulder, and Wendy jolted, her pack sending her sideways. She spun, arms whirling for balance, until someone grabbed her. Mr. Kelley.

"Hey, there. I figured I'd stand with you seeing my sister-in-law had to meet the cops." A concerned look softened his face. "Are you okay?"

Wendy looked down and fiddled with a strap hanging from her pack. Why would he want to do that? Especially since Keri's disappearance and sentence to life in a wheelchair was her fault. What did Mr. Kelley *really* think of her? Was he secretly hoping she'd be eaten by a grizzly bear or mountain lion in Wyoming?

"Wendy, is everything alright? You seem distracted."

Wendy cursed. "Sorry, Mr. Kelley." Was she that easy to read? She needed to think of something that made her feel like her normal self. But what? Nothing felt normal anymore. "Just a little nervous about being out there with the bears and other things that could eat me." She laughed, hoping it sounded sincere.

"All right everyone, I think we are ready to get this party started." Sharon stood in the very center of the circle, Joan by her side. "I thank you for putting your trust in us as leaders. Our objectives for each student is that they learn to experience joy in hardships, build self-confidence through the skills they will learn, develop deep and meaningful friendships, and become better problem solvers, as well as discover some truths bigger and beyond themselves."

Joy in hardships? What kind of crack were they smoking? It almost sounded as if they were gonna make this thing harder than necessary. A flash of anger flared in Wendy, which actually felt good. She was sick of hard things.

But on the other hand, *nothing* could match what she and Keri suffered at the hands of those half-brained, brutal pimps.

Nothing.

So. Maybe this would be a piece of cake.

Joan cleared her throat. "Now, if youse will all make one big circle, let's put our hands in the center and on the count of three, yell 'that which does not kill me makes me stronger'."

Mr. Kelley sidled up to Wendy. "You ready?" His eyes

crinkled at the edges and his smile was real. Kisrie had no idea how lucky she was to have a dad. Wendy had never, ever in her life called anyone by that title. She feared she never would. Another little shiver shot through her soul. Enough! She had to stay strong.

It was safer that way.

"These questions are kinda dumb since we've practically known each other since birth." Jacque whispered over the seat to Kisrie.

"Shut it, Gonzales," Miranda snapped. "We're not supposed to talk for two hours, which is now up to three and a half thanks to you."

Sharon's brown eyes appeared in the rear-view mirror. They flashed a warning. This wasn't the first time Jacque violated the two hours of pondering and writing answers to questions in journals. Every time Jacque spoke, the timer started over. She even tried announcing she was bored—in pig Latin. And Sharon proved to be quite proficient in that strange language, threatening to stop the van if Jacque uttered another word. It was like they all got into the Tardis and traveled back to kindergarten.

Tammie cocked her head back until it rested on the seat, her mouth opened, her eyes rolled around and she made it appear as if she screamed.

Before loading into the vans for a seven-plus hour trip to the campground, Joan and Sharon talked about something called group dynamics. Stuff about how every member was critical. Therefore, what one person did affected the group. Any misbehavior affected the group, hence, group consequences. Kisrie tossed up a silent prayer thanking God she wasn't in Wendy's van. But Jacque was pushing everyone to the point of murder.

True, most of them had known one another for years, but they hadn't always been friends. It wasn't until Keri disappeared that the guard stopped being a bunch of bickering biddies and started treating each other like human beings. Jealousy and cruelty were rampant until then. Maybe they all realized that what happened to Keri could happen to them. And Miranda sharing about the death of her sister?

Things changed.

Kisrie had hated the captains before. But now, she saw them differently.

If she were honest, she saw Wendy differently as well. She just needed to try to forgive and push all that horrid stuff behind her.

"Okay, ladies, time's up."

"Thank goodness! I thought I was gonna die." Jacque opened her mouth wide and let out a wolf-like howl. "No one has ever asked me to not talk for *two whole hours* before and when I'm told I can't do something, I feel I *have* to do it."

"Jack?" Tammie swatted her over the seat. "I have a roll of duct tape and I'm not afraid to use it."

"Can we have a conversation about what we think will be most challenging on this trip?" Zoe asked, then continued after a beat. "Because in spite of bears and mountains, I think Jacque's mouth will be my biggest challenge."

"That's not fair!" Jacque huffed and grabbed the back of the seat in front of her.

Sharon laughed. "We all have an area we need to grow in. Personal goals are coming soon. Jacque, take note. Thinking before speaking may be one of yours. And Zoe? Patience with others is something for you to consider as well."

Zoe slumped. "Ouch."

"As your fearless, all knowing, all understanding and

resourceful leader, I'll be fair. Count on that. Now. I want to hear discussions about what you wrote in your journals."

"I'm a bit curious." Jenn strained against her seatbelt and twisted around to look Wendy square in the eye. "I want to hear what you think your worst enemy would say about you."

Was that a smirk? Wendy wished she could wipe it off the chipmunk-cheeked girl. Aside from Brittany and Sabrina, all the other members of the guard projected this icy attitude toward her. She had to admit, she brought it on in making fun of them ever since she entered high school. What was she expecting? A warm and fuzzy reception?

"We're waiting." Leigh Anne wrapped her brown hair around itself to form a bun on the back of her head. She kind of reminded Wendy of a mouse. Her face was a little too narrow and her eyes a bit close together.

"Give her some time." Joan's voice held a note of worry. Did she sense they were ganging up on her with these questions? Why couldn't they ask her about her favorite joke? Or about her dreams for the future? No one seemed to laugh at her response to 'How do you deal with your anger?' She answered that she crushed people. Even Britt and Sabs looked at her in an odd way.

"I bet she's having a hard time answering because she has too many enemies to consider." Chrissy's voice held a sneer.

"All right. You guys want to know what my enemies yes let's go ahead and make it plural—will say about me?" Wendy paused for dramatic effect hoping her answer would shut them up once and for all—*they* all, with two exceptions, sure fit the description of an enemy. "They will say I never back down and I don't lose. Next question." If they want to play this way, bring it on.

Sabrina flashed a weak smile. "Uh, Wendy, what do you most often dream about?"

It was as if someone poked a hole in her lungs with a knife. The air wooshed out. She knew her friend was trying to move the discussion to "safer" territory, but there was nothing "safe" about this question. Oh, she knew what she dreamed about all right, but it was something she never dared to share for it would show her weakness—a chink in her armor.

Think! Think! Think! Wendy rubbed her temples and tried to come up with a more flippant response rather than the one clawing its way into her consciousness—a desire for a real family—a dad. Maybe to actually fall in love someday and get married and have children of her own. If the Universe wouldn't give her a family now, she could create one of her own someday, but even then she'd never know what it would be like to call someone Dad.

And that hurt.

It's what drove her vitriol against Kisrie.

Kisrie had everything she didn't.

Life was *not* fair.

"Wendy?"

"Oh. I dream about becoming the CEO of a major fashion design corporation." Her participation in beauty pageants should make that one believable, and it wasn't out of the range of things she saw herself doing. "Don't you think it's my turn to ask the questions now? I feel like I'm being grilled."

After the question and answer session was over, Joan instructed them to journal about their impressions of their vanmates for the next hour. Wendy decided it was a great time for a real nap. Who knew when she could sleep again with both eyes shut?

It sounded like the van's tires were running over a road made of potato chips. And the jostling... Ugh. Kisrie's brains were probably scrambled from it all. And did anyone even live in Wyoming? It seemed like every time she looked out the window she saw nothing but a vast expanse of...nothing. Open places with grass waving in the wind.

The wind.

It was relentless, battering the van as it drove along two-lane highways to more desolation. If there ever was a place to disappear, this was it. What if something went wrong? What if the group was attacked by a grizzly bear? It sure wasn't like much of Colorado where even the mountains were crawling with people.

"Hey, wake up. We're almost to camp. When we stop at our sites, Joan and I will do a quick how-to on setting up a tent. Then grab your packs, put on your headlamps, and find the tent parts. Then we'll pull out the stoves and do a late supper."

"I feel like we're on the moon." Jacque stretched and let out a long, rather smelly yawn.

"Ew, Jack, did you have to do that in my face?" Tammie clambered for the door.

"It's dark enough out there, that's for sure." Zoe squinted.

Getting in and out of the van wasn't the easiest thing for Kisrie. She knew she was practically cemented to the vinyl seat. She dreaded the pain of peeling her thighs away, and unlike the others, she had to work her way out sideways. Hashtag fat girl problems.

"Oh. My...." Zoe's voice trailed off.

Miranda hopped out of the van and tipped her head back. "Wow."

Kisrie wondered what was leaving the others speechless. It was just a sky, right? They saw the sky in Denver.

Tammie poked her head in the van. "Hurry, Kiz, you gotta see this! The sky! It's like…just get your butt out and take a look!"

Kisrie gritted her teeth and rocked to the side. The sucking sound of her thighs coming off the seat filled the van. Tears sprung into her eyes. *Note to self: on the ride home, put something under the legs or grow enough hair to not stick.* She kneed her way across the bench, turned sideways, popped out from between the seats and hopped down out of the van. Everyone, including the leaders, stared at the sky. She looked up.

Oh.

It was as if her lungs were stunned into paralysis.

Gadzillions of stars filled the sky. Some glittered, others blazed white or even red-hot. Also, there was a huge, milky white band in the middle. "Is…is that the—"

"Milky Way," Sharon answered. "Yes. From up here, we can almost see into the center of our vast universe." She pointed straight up. "Hercules is high in the summer sky. And there, there and there are the three stars of the Summer Triangle. Get used to it ladies. This is our view for the next two weeks."

"I've never seen anything like it." Jacque's voice was breathy.

"I get why you girls are so amazed. There's so much light pollution in Colorado you have to go far from the cities to see it," Sharon explained. "The city lights are visible from over a hundred miles away, and it drowns out most of the stars."

"I just saw a shooting star!" Miranda shrieked.

"Oh! Another one!" Someone else squealed.

"Likely part of the Perseid Meteor Shower. Anyway, as much as I'd love to stand here all night and star gaze, we need to set up camp and get a good night's sleep. We have a ten-mile hike tomorrow just to get to the trailhead. And, here comes the other van."

Ten miles? Never, ever in her life had Kisrie hiked ten miles. Or even walked ten miles in one trip. And she had to do it carrying a pack that weighed sixteen hundred pounds.

Occupants of Joan's van were star-struck too when they exited the van. Even Wendy seemed stunned into silence over the shocking stardust in the sky. Sharon clapped her hands rapidly and called everyone to a circle. "Kisrie, why don't you and your tent mates grab your tent parts from your packs. You should have a ground cloth, fly, tent, poles and stakes. One minute. Go."

Kisrie, Jacque, and Tammie ran back to the van and grabbed their packs. Kisrie wrapped her arms around hers like it was a huge toddler and waddled back to the circle where it slipped from her grip and fell into the dirt. All blinding headlamps turned toward her. "Hey, can you not point those at me. I can't see." What part of the tent did she have? And where did she put it?

"I have something that says it's a footprint." Tammie held a stuff sack in her hands.

"That's the ground cloth." Joan moved closer. "It's the surface you put the tent on to protect the bottom, and in case of rain, keeps it from taking on water."

"I must have the poles." Jacque held a long slender sack in her hands.

"Kisrie, you must have the tent and fly. They are usually folded up together."

Kisrie turned her pack upside down and shook it until everything fell out. Of course the tent had to be at the bottom. "Found it." All of her clothing lay in the dirt. A gust of wind whipped along, picking up one of the two pairs of underwear, sending it airborne. It billowed out and flew toward the group like a Chinese lantern. Kisrie dropped the tent and went on the chase. She was *not* going to go two weeks with only one pair! They swirled and twirled and…

…plastered themselves on Joan's face.

Joan swiped at her face. "What's this?" All lights lit her up like a spotlight.

"Kisrie's underwear!" Brittany pressed her hands on her tummy, bent over and howled.

"Can we say granny panties!" Someone called out.

Joan wadded them up in her hand and looked around. Face burning, Kisrie grabbed the wad, stuffing them in the pocket of her shorts.

"I recommend keeping tents toward the top, so when we set up camp, you don't have to dig. Jacque, hand me the poles." Joan then turned and winked at Kisrie.

Good thing at least one leader seemed to have a sense of humor.

Kisrie slunk to her pack and shoved everything back inside before more items blew away. She should have taken some zip lock bags when they were offered. Maybe Sharon had some more in the van.

Sharon and Joan took turns showing them how to set up a tent. Lay out the ground cloth. Match the colored loops of the tent to the loops on the footprint and lay it all flat, expand poles, make sure the fly is tight to keep water out should it rain.

Fly was optional on clear nights if they wanted to star gaze. And stake, stake, stake! Wyoming winds could take the tent into Montana or Idaho.

It didn't look all that hard. Seriously.

Joan stretched her arms wide, then brought her hands together in a clap. "You know, back in my day, when I was a freshman going on my first wilderness adventure at Houghton College, we had these green Eureka! tents. They were A-frame with a ridge pole. The thing with those was that you had these two T-joint pieces. Lose one or both... no tent. Let's just say, my tent mates and I had quite a wet week."

"How'd you lose them?" Leigh-Anne asked.

Joan chuckled and flipped her braid over her shoulder. "You would have to ask. Well, I put them in my pocket and forgot about them. We had the great fortune of coming across an outhouse on the trail and when I pulled my shorts down, I heard *plop! Plop!* I looked just in time to see the second T-joint fall into that black hole of ultimate nastiness."

"Which is why we have *dome* tents." Sharon slapped her partner on the back. "Go set up your tents."

Everyone scurried off except Jacque. She stood frozen in place, biting on her lower lip, fidgeting with the bag of poles Joan handed back to her after taking the tent apart.

"Come on, Jack." Kisrie touched her friend's elbow. "We have ten minutes to be set up."

"But I have a question."

"Can it wait?"

"No."

"Are you guys coming or what?" Tammie yelled from their tent site.

Jacque looked at Kisrie, her expression morphed into one of near terror. "How in the world are we supposed to poop out there? I know there are outhouses here, but when we get on the trail?"

"Don't worry about it now. I'm sure our all-knowing, resourceful leaders will tell us."

Wendy had hoped she'd feel far removed from Marcus and Jorge in the remoteness of Wyoming, but that wasn't the case. Millions of square miles didn't seem big enough. What if he caught up with Zena as she went to talk to the cops? Wendy shook her head. She had to get her mind off this or she'd go crazy.

She looked up into the sky. Never in her life had she seen so many stars! Gazing up into the vastness of space made her feel quite small. It was almost as if she felt the presence of something bigger than herself.

"Hey, youse guys, circle up." Joan stood by the campfire which flickered and glowed so bright Wendy had to squint to look at it. She pointed her headlamp to the ground and made her way in. Sharon told them to never point lights in anyone's eyes. It blinded them and was actually painful. At first the concept didn't make sense, but considering how dark it was, and after Brittany shined her light in Wendy's face, it did.

The group gathered, bringing along their sit-upons—small squares of closed cell foam to keep their bottoms dry and warm against the cold ground. Moments later everyone sat in a tight circle. The fire popped and crackled.

"So far things have been pretty fun and chill, right?" Joan nodded looking at each one of them. "But after tomorrow things are gonna get pretty hard. This hike isn't easy. Even if you are the star athlete of your school you will find yourself being pushed to your limits. You're gonna reach the end of yourself and have to dig deep to keep on going because, as you experienced on the drive in, we're in the middle of nowhere.

By the end, all of you are going to discover you did things you thought impossible. You are going to learn you are more capable than you think. You're also going to learn cause and effect. Every decision you make out here in this vast awesomeness will either help you or hurt you—and potentially everyone else in the group. Consider the possible outcomes before acting." Joan paused and rubbed her hands together. "So, tonight, I am going to give youse guys half an hour to write some personal goals. What do you want to get out of this trip? Maybe write down who you are now, and who you'd like to become. What do you hope to discover about yourself? What are you afraid of? Grab your journals, find a place in sight of the fire, and use your headlamps to jot down those goals. Thirty minutes. Go!"

Sitting by the fire made Wendy feel safe and warm. After grabbing her journal and a pen, she plopped down as close as she could get without setting herself ablaze. At first her thoughts drifted. This whole journal-writing thing seemed stupid. But maybe it could help her figure some things out. If something happened to her out here, she could leave a record that she'd changed. She wasn't as horrid as everyone thought.

She tapped the pen against her lips. Her reasons for being on this trip—or whatever it was called—were different than anyone else's. The less anyone knew, the better off. Her goal was to elude Marcus and Jorge and make them think she disappeared off the face of the earth. But, she inhaled sharply, what if when they realize she'd gone missing they took things out on Zena? What if they broke in, ransacked the house and...? Zena was smart. She knew those guys were watching. The woman did own a gun. And maybe Detective Arbuckle and the police caught them already.

Wendy stared at the blank page as she tapped her lips some more. Weird things were going on inside that she didn't understand. For one, she couldn't conjure up the resentment she felt for Zena taking over her life. True, if it weren't for her, Wendy would be living in a refrigerator box on the street—or worse—but the stupid rules and expectations were a bit too much. On the other hand, if something happened to Zena, Wendy'd be devastated. She couldn't bear the thought. So what happened inside?

Back to goals.

The unspoken goal was to get through this experience and go home and start pursuing her dreams of becoming Miss Colorado and eventually Miss America. After that, the opportunities would be endless.

The next question haunted her. What was she afraid of—really afraid of outside her circumstances. She drew little triangles on the page, connecting one to the next waiting for something to come to mind.

The pen stopped moving.

Death.

She was afraid of death. And that was mostly because she didn't know what happened after. Would she just stop existing? Would everything go black? Would she come back as a camel or a hippopotamus? According to the church people she'd go to hell because she didn't know the secret password, or so it seemed. She scribbled over the triangles. That religious stuff was just a fairy tale to make people feel better about life.

The sound of crunching gravel broke Wendy's concentration. Joan stood next to her. "You finished?"

She nodded.

"Good. I'm going to call the group over here so we can all share our goals."

"Do we have to share?"

"Sharing our goals is part of the accountability process. If our goals are out there, we can each help one another achieve them."

"Huh. I never thought of that before." Wendy hoped her

comment made it sound like she was buying into all this psychology crap. A few more taps to the lips. She clicked her pen and put the tip to the paper. Her goal was to understand what was going on inside of herself.

That should be vague and psychological enough to share. She stared at her words as Joan whistled and everyone scurried to the fire.

"I love this part!" Joan looked at Sharon. "Don't you?"

In the firelight, Wendy saw Sharon's mouth turn up in a grin. "I sure do."

"And why is that?" Joan put a finger to her chin and tweaked an eyebrow upward.

"I love this part because it's where we get to know each of you better. It's also the baseline of your character development. After a few days on the trail we'll revisit our goals and make changes if necessary. And guys, it's the goals that let Joan and me see your growth!"

"Who wants to go first?" Joan bounced on her toes. Because she was unnaturally tall, it looked awkward.

"Me! Me!" Jacque Gonzales thrust her hand up into the sky over and over again like an eager preschooler. Wendy shot a sideways glance at Sabrina who tucked her chin to her chest trying to hide her laughs.

"Ooh, this should be good." Brittany had rolled up onto one butt cheek to whisper in Wendy's ear.

"Go ahead Jacque." Joan made a sweeping gesture toward the twit.

"Okay. This is my goal. My goal by the end of these two weeks is to achieve the perfect Brazilian Butt Lift."

Sabrina made a sound like she just spit out a mouthful of water. Wendy clamped her hands over her mouth. She. Did. Not. Just. Hear. That.

Joan opened and closed her mouth like a fish.

"Aw, you guys, don't tell me you don't know what I'm

talking about. Brazilian Butt Lift? It's where you work out your butt muscles so they get really round and lifted? All the celebrities are doing it, and I figured with hiking I could—"

Kisrie slapped a hand over her friend's mouth. Wendy mouthed a silent cheer—*way to go, Cow Pie!*

The entire group burst into laughter. Wendy swore Jacque's head was full of helium at times.

Jacque peeled Kisrie's hand away. "I'm serious." She made a ridiculous pouty-face. Wendy rolled her eyes and groaned.

"I'll go next," Miranda shouted over the noise. Her goal was something about becoming a better leader.

Others had goals of making better friends. Not complaining when things got hard. After a while, only Wendy and Kisrie were left.

"Some interesting goals. Some may evolve a bit on our trip, but interesting nonetheless. We have what? Two left? Wendy? Kisrie? Who's next?"

"I'll go last." Wendy ran her hand over the cover of her journal. "Kisrie, you go."

Kisrie stared at her, then glanced at her paper. She blinked a few times. When she finally spoke, her voice was barely audible over the sounds of the fire. "I just wanna know I can be strong."

Well, that was unexpected. Wendy was sure Kisrie'd have something about losing weight. Truth was, nobody would really care if she herself didn't focus on it so much. She practically drew a target on herself, a target Wendy couldn't resist.

"Wendy?" Joan flipped her braid over her shoulder.

She looked around at the faces bathed in a warm orange light. No one sneered. No one looked threatening. "I know none of you expected me to be here. I didn't either. I've been through some hard stuff. I also did a lot to hurt some of you. My goal is to try and understand myself better." She paused. "And learn to be a better person, if that's possible."

Ugh. That was *not* what she intended to say. TMI. What made her get all mushy all of a sudden? Everyone was sure to laugh. But…

No one moved.

It seemed like no one breathed.

Kisrie stared at her, head tilted.

Sharon broke the spell. "Wendy, that's wonderful! I bet it took a lot of guts to say that. I'm so proud of you."

Heat crept up Wendy's neck. She wished the woman would shut up. Everyone looked at her as if she glowed in the dark. "Whatever," she mumbled to try to avoid more discussion.

"I don't know about youse guys, but I'm feeling a wee bit sleepy." Joan stretched her arms above her head and yawned. The woman looked like an albatross. She dismissed the group to go get ready for bed. Tomorrow was the first official day on the trail, and compared to the others, it was low mileage.

As if that was to make anyone feel better.

Up and at 'em!" Sharon's voice rang across the campground. Kisrie moaned and tried to sit up, but the sleeping bag hugged her so tight, she could hardly move. The sound of zippers peppered the quiet of the morning. It seemed like only ten minutes ago she finally got her bag zipped up and stopped shivering. Now she had to figure out how to get out of the Chinese finger trap bag.

Jacque was already out and pulling a sweatshirt over her head. "C'mon Kiz, we only have three more minutes to be outside.

"I think I'm stuck." Kisrie wiggled until one arm popped out. She reached across her body and tried to pull the zipper down.

It didn't move.

"Can one of you help me?"

Tammie crawled over. She grabbed the pull and tugged. "I think it's stuck on the fabric." She bent down real close. "Yep. Some of the material is snagged. Since time is short, why don't I hold the bottom and you wiggle out the top."

"I don't think it will work. I'm practically vacuum sealed in here."

"Tam, you hold the bag, I'll try and pull her out from the top. I am sure we can get her out."

"Two minutes!" Sharon yelled.

Kisrie heard the crunching of feet on gravel and the whispered expletives as other guard members squealed and shrieked, "It's so cold!"

Tammie grabbed fistfuls of the down bag at Kisrie's feet. Jacque slipped her hands under Kisrie's arms. "Ew. I'm touching your arm pits."

"On the count of three," Tammie said with a tug, "one...two...three!"

Jacque grunted and pulled. Tammie flopped forward onto Kisrie. The tent rocked and the stakes tore out of the ground. There was a *plunk* as Jacque fell backwards into the wall. Kisrie wiggled and thrashed like a mad woman.

The tent billowed down on them. "Well, that didn't work." Jacque pulled her hands out from under Kisrie's arms.

"What's going on over here?" Joan's voice sounded from above the mess of material. Great. How was Kisrie gonna explain this?

"We're okay, just, uh, having some technical difficulties," Tammie called out. "Jack, we need to try again. Take the sleeping pad out from under her so she doesn't slide."

Kisrie twisted and sucked in her gut, but she had pulled the zipper up so high, the opening wasn't much bigger than her neck. It was all she could do to get one arm out, but the other was pinned to her side. Why did they make these things so dang small?

"I hope you ladies are decent, because I'm coming in. We don't have much time to spare." There was a rustling of fabric, the zing of a zipper, and Joan's face hovered over Kisrie's. "Zipper stuck?"

"Yeah, ya think?" Jacque huffed, repositioning herself to allow room for the very tall leader.

"You and Tammie should go on ahead. I've dealt with this before and will have her freed in no time."

"But I want to keep these clothes clean for sleeping." Tammie wrapped her arms around herself.

"Grab a sweatshirt and head on out. You can change in another tent while breakfast is being made."

"But my makeup wore off and I can't be seen without it. And my hair! I can't believe you, of all peeps, are seeing me like this." Jacque put her hands on either side of her head and moaned.

"Jacque, perhaps you need to stop worrying about your looks all the time. Consider learning to accept yourself the way you are. You don't need to hide behind all that stuff." Joan looked down at Kisrie. "Now, to get you out of here." She found a way to lie down in the partially collapsed tent and pinched the zipper with her left hand and the fabric with her right. "You really got this jammed in here."

Kisrie grunted. Heat washed over her face and the sleeping bag become more claustrophobic than it had been. Everyone was gonna figure out what happened. Truth was, she was too fat for the sleeping bag. It seemed like it was made for pre-pubescent girls with no curves. This was gonna be a looooong two weeks if she had to go through this every single morning.

"I think I almost have it." Joan tugged and Kisrie heard a small tearing noise. "Oops. I put a small hole in it, but that shouldn't affect the insulation at all." She pulled the zipper down. Cool air rushed in, chilling her now sweaty body. "You know what? I'm gonna go ahead and trade sleeping bags with you. I bought an extra-long bag to accommodate my height and it has more room in it than these."

Kisrie sat up and rubbed her eyes. "But what about you?"

"Fugeddaboudit. I'll be fine. I had to do a bunch of trips

in a standard bag. I also have extra layers I can put on if I need them."

"Thanks for rescuing me." Kisrie rolled out of her nylon prison and Joan grabbed it. "Where's the stuff sack?"

"It was in one of the mesh pockets on the side of the tent that collapsed."

"Okay. Why don't you get on out there? Sharon is assigning camp duties."

Emerging from the tent, a cool breeze dried the sweat on Kisrie's body. Zoe, Leigh Anne, Tammie, and Chrissy had one hand tied behind their backs and were struggling to open some packets of pancake mix. How weird. What was up with that?

"Ah, Kisrie! Glad you could make it." Sharon beamed at her. Kisrie couldn't detect an ounce of disgust in the leader's voice or body language for her lateness. Sharon put a hand on Kisrie's arm and led her to where a pile of cookware sat waiting to be used for breakfast. "I've assigned you, Brittany, and Sabrina to dish duty. I've already explained this to them, but I need to go over it with you." Sharon rubbed her nose, then continued. "This is gonna sound strange, but you are going to go at least two-hundred yards from camp and put a handful of dirt and pine needles in each item that needs washing—"

"Dirt?" Kisrie scratched her head. Her fingers got stuck in the tangled curls.

"Sounds silly, right? The dirt and pine needles scour out debris and absorb grease. It's pretty amazing. When you bring them back to camp, we'll rinse them in cold water, then dip in boiling water to sanitize. It's a leave no trace way to doing dishes. No chemicals or soaps are put into the environment. Cool, huh?"

"Uh, if you say so."

Sharon patted Kisrie on the shoulder. "Once you do it, you'll see how it works and it won't sound so icky."

Kisrie looked at the breakfast crew. Zoe held the bowl,

Leigh Anne poured, and Tammie mixed. Chrissy was trying to find a good, balanced spot on the fire for the skillet. "You know, we'd be eating by now if they could use both hands."

"Ah, my friend, you are missing the whole point! Your fearless, all-knowing, all-caring leaders are here to help you ladies learn to cooperate and problem solve in constructive ways. I promise you, meal prep will always be somewhat interesting out here."

"I'm afraid to ask what you'll have us doing for dinner."

"For me to know and you to find out!" Sharon patted Kisrie on the shoulder. "Looks like they're going to be done soon. Why don't you tell everyone to meet here with their cup, bowl, and spoon."

Kisrie headed toward Miranda and Jenn who were rolling up a tent. On the way, she saw movement deeper in the woods. Joan moved from tree to tree. Flashes of her hot pink fleece appeared and disappeared. She seemed to be making something strange with rope. What in the world could it be? Kisrie shrugged and went on to fulfill her mission.

After breakfast, which was some sort of reconstituted egg goo, Joan ordered everyone to pair up with someone who was not a tent mate. Everyone ended up with a partner except...

...Wendy.

The former Queen of Mean wrapped her arms around herself looking sullen and—dare she think it?—alone. Compassion tugged at Kisrie's heart. Where did that come from? Probably the same place the compulsions to pray for Wendy did back in the fall. Kisrie turned to Jenn, her partner.

"Hey, do you mind seeing if Sharon would pair with you? I am going to go to Wendy. It's something I feel I need to do."

"Ummmmm... okay. If you're sure. I'm not going to stop you." She appeared to think for a moment. "Looks like she needs someone to choose her rather than be stuck with her."

Kisrie looked everywhere but directly at her nemesis as she

approached. She felt Wendy's obsidian eyes boring into her. "Mind if I join you?" Her voice came out in a squeak.

"You want to partner with me?" Wendy cocked an eyebrow and backed away a few steps.

"Look, Wendy, we're all out here in this wilderness for the next two weeks. We can't always avoid each other, and to be honest, I kind of sort of want to get along. It's not like I'm asking you to be my BFF or anything."

"I tolerated you when we had to share my room at Zena's. Wasn't that enough for you?"

"And I felt I always had to sleep with one eye open because I didn't know if you'd slit my throat in the middle of the night." It was true. Kisrie never felt she could fully relax at her aunt's house. Wendy's presence electrified the air with painful tension.

"I thought about it." Wendy's face remained stone-hard. Not a muscle twitched. Kisrie believed her.

Joan loped toward them holding out a bandana. "Okay. I want one of youse guys to put this over your eyes. The other gets to keep her eyesight."

"I'm not wearing that thing." Wendy's face drained of color and she shrunk back as if Joan held a python rather than a rainbow colored bandana with little monkeys on it.

"Give it to me." Kisrie grabbed it from her, rolled it up and tied it around her head good and snug so she couldn't see. "Now what?"

"Looks like Wendy will be your eyes. Without touching you in any way, she needs to use words to guide you to my Web of Doom about a hundred yards from here."

"Web of Doom?" Kisrie shuddered as images of millions and bajillions of spiders flooded her imagination. Was that what Joan was working on? Hopefully there weren't any spiders involved.

"It's a team building exercise. I'll explain later. Wendy, see where I'm pointing? You can see some of the rope on the trees...that's where you're taking her." Joan took a breath. "Ladies, this is a trust exercise. Kisrie, you need to trust Wendy to lead you safely to the web. Okay?"

What the heck did she just get herself into? Knowing Wendy, she'd have Kisrie stubbing her toe on rocks and whacking her head through a bee hive or something.

"Kisrie?"

"Uh, yeah. Sure." But she was far from sure. Her 'one eye open' was taken away. "Joan?"

"Yeah?"

"C...could you keep an eye on us?"

"Do you think I'm gonna kill you or something?" Wendy snapped.

Joan let out a belly laugh. "Kiz-a-roo, if I may call you that? This activity is about trust. I believe you can trust Wendy in this circumstance. Right, Wendy?"

"Whatever."

Kisrie could almost hear Wendy's eyes rattle around in her skull.

"See you at the Web of Doom in a few!" A thumping crunch of pine needles signaled Joan's departure.

Wendy snickered.

If Kisrie ever got there.

Wendy sighed. This was almost too good to be true. Kisrie Kelley totally dependent on her to navigate blindly through the woods. There were plenty of sticks, stumps, fallen trees and rocks to make things interesting.

"Uh, Wendy? Where do I go?" Kisrie held her arms out in front of her like Frankenstein—whoops—Frankenstein's *monster.*

Mr. Plank always corrected kids in his lit class for messing that up. Kisrie toed the ground with her hiking shoe.

"Go on and take a few steps toward me. Be careful of rocks because you're on your own if you fall."

Three tiny steps were all Kisrie took.

"It'll take until next week to get there at that rate. Bigger steps, *Kiz-a-roo-oo."* Wendy stretched out the last vowel sound. She then burst into laughter. It felt good to laugh—especially at Kisrie's expense. Like old times.

"How do I know you're not gonna march me into a tree or off a cliff?"

"Did you see any cliffs within a hundred yards or so?"

Kisrie remained silent.

"I didn't think so. As Joan said, you have to *trust* me. And besides, *you* are the one who chose to be my partner."

"I didn't know it would mean placing my life into your hands," Kisrie mumbled and listed off seven ways Wendy could kill her here and now.

"A few minutes ago you were all about teamwork and getting along. Now you're all like, 'Oh! Wendy, is gonna kill me!' You either mean what you say or you don't."

Kisrie hesitated. "You're right. Now how many giant steps can I take?"

Along the way, Wendy guided Kisrie over a fallen log, around a mud puddle, and through a thicket of dense shrubbery. Much to Wendy's surprise, she and Kisrie were not the last to arrive at The Web of Doom. When Joan peeled the bandana off of Kisrie's face, Wendy couldn't help but smile at the girl she spent most of her life hating. "We did it. You only stumbled once on that log."

Kisrie examined all her extremities as if making sure Wendy didn't cut something off while she was blinded. "Yeah. And you didn't kill me." The corner of her lip twitched upward. A sense of accomplishment swelled in Wendy's chest.

"All right, ladies, the last duo is tripping into the zone. Well done Zoe and Jacque."

"We'da been here sooner if this twit didn't worry about her manicure so much and shriek every time something brushed against her face." Zoe glared at Jacque with squinty eyes.

"The trees were pulling at my hair, and I finally got it up in a perfect French Twist, plus, I have these really neat camo nail wraps, plus—"

"Okaaaaay, moving right along, welcome to the Web of Doom! Muwah ha ha ha!" Joan spread her arms wide and let lose a deep-throated evil laugh. "You are on a quest to find lost gold hidden up in these here hills by a deranged pirate who wandered far, far away from the sea. In spite of his lack of sanity, this pirate was smart. He hid his treasure in a land infested by gigantic man-eating spiders!" Joan reached toward the group and wiggled her fingers. A few girls squealed.

"The spiders are alerted to prey when something touches a fiber of their web, so they cast gargantuous webs *everywhere*, making passage through their territory impossible. So here you are, on your quest, and there is a web. You can't cut it down or you're Purina Spider Chow. You must go through the web without touching." She stopped talking and walked over to the web and rested a hand on a supporting tree. "I see you all eying that larger hole along the bottom. You can use it, but only once. In fact, you can only use any of the openings once. It's like they magically close. Should you touch the web, the entire team has to return and start over. How late we arrive at camp tonight depends on how quickly you all get through the web. Happy questing!"

Kisrie stared at the web, calculating the size of each opening. From what she could tell none of the openings were large enough to accommodate her size. Unlike most of the girls who were barely out of training bras, she had to special order hers on the internet. And Joan said *all* of them had to get to the other side. What were they gonna do? Catapult her? That wasn't likely. No one could lift her. Ugh. Kisrie wished she could strangle Joan the Amazon. Maybe she'll call the leader Amazon to get some revenge.

She backed away from the group as they huddled together, pointing and planning.

"Hey, Kisrie, the team needs your brains." Sharon appeared alongside her, arms folded, head tilting, as she appeared to examine Joan's masterpiece.

"I can't do this."

"What do you mean?"

Hot tears stung Kisrie's eyes. She framed her body with her hands. "Look at me. There's not a single hole in that web I could fit through. Because of me, the group will have to go back again and again, and then they'll be mad at me because I'm the one that—"

"Stop." Sharon held up one hand like a traffic cop. "Joan and I have been doing this for years and years. We work with all kinds of people. We've even worked with NFL teams, and believe me, some of those guys are twice your size. Eventually, they figure it out. You have to trust your team to come up with a solution."

Trust.

The only person Kisrie really trusted was herself.

"You know, the last time you didn't trust your team ended up in a jail cell."

Kisrie whirled to face the leader. "Are you reading my mind or something?"

Sharon's brows rose up under her headband, and her eyes widened. "I've been doing this a long time. Human behavior has patterns. I see the patterns in you."

Kisrie scoffed. "So you can read me like a book."

"A little bit." She put a hand on Kisrie's back and pressed her toward the group. "We're wasting precious time. Part of the strength you need requires you to learn to trust others."

For the first half hour or so, getting through the web was nothing but trial and error. At first, the group decided each girl would choose a hole and crawl or dive through it.

No one succeeded without touching the web.

"Looks like there's no way to do it on our own." Miranda squatted low looking from the web to the guard.

"What if we pass people through like pizzas on a conveyor belt?" Chrissy held both hands flat in front of her and moved them horizontally to the web.

Zoe flicked her braid behind her back. "Could work, but how does that work on the other side?"

"We need to get people over there first. People who can crawl under. We may have to press on them and flatten them so they don't touch." Tammie's suggestion got a bunch of nods.

An idea popped into Kisrie's head. What if she went first? That way work wouldn't be wasted if she hit the rope. It would also allow her to burrow a bit into the dirt to widen the gap if it were too narrow. The others could press and squish her as flat as possible. "I'll go first."

After a few tries, a Kisrie-shaped channel scored the earth. Good thing it was pretty soft under the trees. But, she only got so far before her back or butt touched. She needed someone on the other side to pull her.

"How're we gonna do that? We need to leave something open on the ground for the last person to crawl through."

"You can launch me over the top," Jenn said.

"That's crazy!" Zoe paced back and forth, hands behind her back.

"When I was at Pomona, my coach, Jenn, she had us do

all kinds of weight sharing lifts and throws. Being one of the smaller kids, I became the flier."

"I'm not thinkin' we should throw her. What if me mess up and she gets hurt?"

Sabrina had a point.

"I have an idea."

Everyone froze at the sound of Wendy's voice.

Jacque adjusted the twist in her hair with both hands. "And what would that be?"

"We could make a human staircase. She climbs up on us and drops to the other side."

Could it work? The members of the Mountain Ridge color guard looked around at one another. Some shrugged. No one said anything. Probably because there weren't any better ideas.

"I say we give it a go." Miranda walked around the team assigning positions. No surprise that Kisrie was one of the bases.

Jenn practiced climbing up and jumping off with a drop-roll a few times to have her technique down.

Joan looked at Sharon, shoulders nearly touching her ears. "Never saw anyone practice strategies before."

"They're guard kids. It's in their nature to rehearse everything before doing it for real."

Kisrie couldn't help but hear the comments. "Yeah, we're guard kids and *proud* of it!"

"I'm ready. Let's do this thing!" Jenn hopped up and down shaking her arms.

Zoe held her hand out, palm down. "Let's do our cheer."

One by one, every girl put her hand in the middle—except Wendy who stood about two yards outside the circle. "C'mon Wendy, this was your idea."

"I don't know what you're doing."

"Just go with it, Wen. It's not hard." Brittany squished closer to Tammie to make room. Wendy added her hand to the pile.

"Alright. Here we go." Miranda closed her eyes, pointed her face toward the tree-covered sky. "Five...six...five, six, seven, eight, MRCG wooooooo!" Hands flew up into the air, then everyone took positions in front of the web.

The Jenn launch was successful.

She perched on top of the guard pyramid, then sprang over the top strand. Her feet hit the ground, her legs folded and she rolled twice before bouncing up. Everyone broke into a loud cheer, including Wendy.

"Way to go, Wendy." Jacque slapped her on the back.

"I'm ready to pull Kisrie through. I think I can keep her upper body pressed down as I pull."

Forty-five minutes later, the guard conquered The Web of Doom.

Wendy couldn't help but smile. So this is what it felt like to be part of a team. Once faced with the challenges of figuring out how to get team members through the middle holes and higher holes, personal conflicts were shoved aside. Wendy forgot how much she didn't like the color guard, and it seemed like they forgot as well. The pressure of starting over kept them focused and intentional.

Would it last?

"Great job, youse guys! Once you guys got a rhythm going, you knocked that problem into Alaska! Finish packing up, and let's hit the trail."

Wendy hefted her pack over to a picnic table. All attempts of getting it on her back failed. Joan and Sharon stood away from the group watching. They wanted everyone to figure out how to get their pack on without someone else holding it. They had to do it alone. Why couldn't they use teamwork now?

First, she tried kneeling in front of it and putting the straps over her shoulders. That didn't work. She couldn't stand up. Rather, she ended up flopping over onto the ground and having to worm her way out of the thing. She tried putting it against a tree trunk and slithering up, but the pack got stuck on branches and she ended up rolling in the dirt. She needed to start from a higher vantage point. Picnic tables. If she could get it to sit up on the table top, she could lean it onto her back and already be in a standing position. From there?

The picnic table idea was a success. She hoped all campsites had one of these things or she'd be in trouble.

She gazed around camp. So far she was the only one with a pack on her back. A smile worked its way onto her face. Others stopped struggling and stared.

"She used the table!" Sabrina cried out.

There was a mad rush for picnic tables as the rest of the group tried to figure out her method. Within a few minutes, the whole group stood around, teetering for balance.

"Well, well, I see youse all figured out how to get packs on. Good job! But I have some bad news for you. This is the last site for a while that has picnic tables. Tomorrow, we'll give ya another opportunity to figure it out. If you don't, Sharon and I will show you a trick. But I promise you this, the longer you're out on the trail, the easier it will be to shlep that thing onto your back." Joan walked over to Miranda, grabbed the back of her pack and pulled down. She yelped and buckled at the knees. She did the same to Sharon, who stood unfazed. "The difference, my friends, is that Sharon has the weight of her pack in the hip belt. Poor Miranda's shoulders took the brunt of it all. She wouldn't last more than ten minutes on the trail."

Wendy looked down at her hip belt. It was buckled. But her shoulders and upper back felt like someone was stabbing them with a dull bladed knife. There must be a trick.

"I see several of you looking at your belt wondering how

this works. Well, you gotta cinch it tight. Best way is to bend forward, adjust it so it sits above those protruding hip bones, then pull, pull, pull on the strap. Make sure you don't unbuckle, or you may go for a tumble."

Wendy followed instructions and stood back up. There was slack in her shoulder straps. All the weight was on her hips. She felt more balanced, and ready to take a hike. Maybe this whole thing wasn't gonna be so bad after all.

One by one, the others got their packs adjusted—all but Kisrie. No surprise there.

"I need help. I can't seem to grab the end of the strap. It's partially under the buckle. It also feels like it's cutting me in half when I lean over."

A nasty remark surfaced in Wendy's mouth. Oooh, she wanted so badly to make a comment about Kisrie's weight but what good would that do? That goal about trying to be a better person came to mind. She decided to bite her tongue. Isn't becoming a better person part of why she came on this trip in the first place?

A shiver ran down her spine as the *other* reason wiggled into her mind. She also came to get away from her captors. What were Marcus and Jorge up to now? Was Zena okay? Where was Unique, the pimps' "manager"?

Relax. There is no way they know where I am. Wendy shook out her arms, rolled her head a few times to ease the tension.

"Yeah, that's pretty jammed under there. Can you hike it up a bit? Maybe we can grab the end of the strap to pull it tighter." Sharon bent down to help Kisrie.

Brittany tottered by. "I wish we could get moving already. Standing here is starting to hurt. It's like the pack wants to pull me forward."

"Looks like backpacks weren't made for…plus sizes." Sabrina nudged Wendy and tipped her head toward Kisrie. "I kinda feel sorry for her. It doesn't seem easy being that big."

Wendy laughed. There was a reason Kisrie was fat. She ate too much. The girl could polish off an entire pizza by herself, and then there was that habit of hiding peanut butter cups from her mother.

"We sure didn't help much when we made fun of her all the time." Brittany sighed. "She's actually not such a bad person. She helped me get some of my tosses."

No comment. Wendy wasn't ready to go there yet. Curbing her remarks was one thing—liking someone she spent most of her known life cutting down was another. Something about Kisrie still irked her in a thousand ways.

Shards of plastic exploded the moment the phone slammed into the bricks. The battery skidded to a stop and spun at Marcus's feet. How could Unique do this to him? Marcus slicked his hair back and paced in the alley behind a liquor store.

Unique blamed him for getting sloppy and bringing the whole operation to a screeching halt. She got it into her stupid head that she could do better on her own.

She told him to give up on Wendy and find some other girl.

That wasn't going to happen. There was no way he'd be able to score another bona-fide beauty queen. Such titles brought bigger bucks. He kicked the battery under a dumpster. It was his fault she got away. He slipped up and she saw him at the mall. Then he lost them when they left the house. That girl was smarter than he realized.

But he had to remove a new obstacle—Unique.

Like Jorge, Unique needed to be taken care of. He couldn't risk leaving any witnesses. With her out of the way, he could alter his appearance, get a fake ID, then start all over again watching the Plank house. He'd act quickly. Take the first opportunity to nab her—especially since Wendy and that woman probably assumed he ran from the cops.

Which he did. He cursed.

In the meantime, he needed to wait until things settled down in Denver before doubling down his efforts to find Wendy and make sure Keri never talked.

Wendy caught her breath as she stepped into the clearing at the end of the torturous ten-mile hike. Jagged mountains wrapped around a lake that reflected the cobalt blue sky. As she hiked closer, she could see the smooth rocks on the bottom and all kinds of fish wiggling around. Never in her life had she seen water so clear.

"We're in Middle Earth!" Tammie yelled, stretching her arms out to the sides and spinning in circles. "Hobbits, and elves, and orcs, oh my!"

"You are so right. I wonder if Peter Jackson shot the movies here." Leigh Anne raised her eyebrows as though she were asking a question.

"The Lord of the Rings movies were made in New Zealand." Joan positioned herself in front the of the group. "Here we are—at the trailhead of the Continental Divide Trail. In my opinion, the section we are doing is one of the most beautiful hikes of the thru-hiking trail systems. And I've done the Appalachian, the Pacific Crest, Finger Lakes, Colorado, Susquehannock Trail System—"

Sharon moved in and socked her on the arm. "Braggart."

Joan shrugged as if there weren't a heavy pack on her shoulders. "Youse guys gotta understand. I get all excited about the trails. It's my jam."

Joan had to be the dorkiest person on the planet. Wendy couldn't believe that woman was for real.

"Well, we have a lot of material to cover before bedtime since we are now in the wilderness and the real hiking begins tomorrow."

Real hiking? What was today, pretend? The ache in Wendy's muscles sure didn't feel like pretend.

"Take advantage of the late afternoon sun and get those tents set up, your bedding and packs situated, and we'll meet back here in twenty minutes." Sharon turned to join Joan.

Wendy unbuckled her hip belt, pushed her shoulders back, and let her pack drop. She couldn't tear her eyes away from the scene before her. Whatever she expected, this was not it. Aside from sleeping at the campground last night, this was the most time Wendy had ever spent in the woods. How come her life kept her from discovering the magic of life outside the city?

"Come on Wen, we need to get set up," Brittany called from somewhere behind her. Letting out a deep sigh, Wendy trudged over to the tent and crawled in.

"Ladies!" Sharon's voice echoed as Wendy got her sleeping bag laid out so it could fluff up after being stuffed tight into a compression sack. It was amazing she could squeeze it down to the size of a loaf of bread.

"We better get over there." Brittany unzipped the tent and peeled back the door. They all crawled out.

Joan stood in the middle of the circle, her arms spread wide in her weird way, and a grin on her face. "Welcome to the poop talk. I waited until we were away from pit toilets and the vans in case some of you tried to bail."

The group let out a collective groan. Joan made everyone groan.

She dropped her arms and clasped her hands. "I know many of you are feeling a tad bit anxious about this, but I gotta tell youse guys, one of my favorite things about being on the trail, is taking care of business. Where else do you doo with a view? This place is epic!"

What? There weren't any outhouses here like at the last place? The thought never crossed Wendy's mind. She shuddered. The thought of going out in the open made her skin crawl.

"I see the panic on many of your faces, but going to the bathroom is nothing to fear."

Joan launched into a lecture on leave no trace practices. Basically they had to pack out...*everything.*

Brittany leaned in close. "I think I'm gonna try and hold it until we get to Yellowstone. There's no way I'm carryin' out that stuff."

"...cover the bag in silver duct tape so I don't confuse it with anything else..."

"You can't hold it for almost ten days." All of a sudden, Wendy's newfound affection for the backcountry deflated like a balloon with a slow leak.

"If you make it a game, it's not so bad. My personal favorite is 'bombs away'. I draw a target on the ground with a stick, grab onto a tree branch above..."

"I really want to go home. I am thinking if I spent time in that juvie jail, I'd at least have a flush toilet and a shower." Brittany wrung her hands and chattered over Joan's narrative. "I'm starting to stink."

"If comfort is your thing, you can hang your bottom end over a log—closest thing to using the commode in the privacy of your own home—but with a view."

Brittany jumped up from where she was seated. "I just

can't. I just can't." Her skin had a greenish tint, and she held her stomach as if it ached.

Joan looked from one girl to the next. She spoke slow and deliberate. "Why do I get the feeling no one is excited about this?"

Jacque shuddered and joined Brittany in the hysterical display of disgust.

"How do we…wipe?" Jenn asked, her voice weak.

"Personally, I like to use sticks, rocks—not sandstone, mind you—leaves, and bury them. If you *must*, you can use a few squares of toilet paper as long as you pack it out with your poo."

"I think it's important to mention we have a separate bear bag for hygienic waste," Sharon added.

"It's not like I told youse all ice cream is extinct. You can't be that worried about this?"

Actually, Wendy was worried about this. The wilderness was rather open. It wasn't like there were private copses of trees or anything. How did she take care of business without anyone seeing her? After her experience earlier in the spring, she'd gone to great lengths to stay concealed. She could try and go as far away from the others as possible, but what about other people? What if she was sitting on a log and some guy came traipsing along? This going to the bathroom in the woods thing was too much. Maybe she'd give Brit's idea a try and hold it.

Joan and Sharon sent everyone to bed early because the hike tomorrow, despite being the same distance as today, would be very challenging due to ascents and descents. Wendy snuggled down into her bag, Sabrina and Brittany on either side of her. She insisted on being in the middle. Her friends didn't know it, but it was one way she could remind herself where she was in case she had more nightmares. If she felt her trusted friends on either side, she could mentally anchor herself in the tent. Anchoring herself in her present reality was something one of the therapists at the rescue house talked about.

It didn't take long for Brittany to fall asleep. The girl snored so loud it sounded like an army of chainsaws ripping through a mature growth forest. Sabrina on the other hand tried to sing in her sleep. Old country songs. Which were severely off-key. Wendy tried to calm the anxiety building in her chest by attempting to name the song and artist, but Sabrina's apparent tone deafness made it hard.

At some point in the middle of "Elvira" by the Oakridge Boys, Wendy dozed off. At first, her mind filled with visions of sparkling stars, diamond surfaced lakes. Tall evergreen trees stretching to touch the indigo sky.

Then...

Jorge loomed over her. He tore off his belt, unzipped...

Wendy screamed.

A scream tore through the night. Kisrie bolted up in Joan's sleeping bag. "Tam, Jack, you guys hear that?"

"No! Get off me! Stay away! Noooo!"

"Wendy, what the—"

"Touch me and I'll kill you, I swear!"

"Guys, it's Wendy," Jacque said.

Kisrie unzipped her bag, then the tent. "I hope it's not a bear."

There was a sound of a skin on skin slap. "Ow!" Brittany yelled. "Someone come help us, Wendy's trying to kill us in here!"

Kisrie scrambled out of her tent on her knees and almost knocked into someone running. She couldn't tell who because the light from the headlamp blinded her.

"I'll kill you! I will! Stop touching me!"

In the dark, she saw two forms explode from Wendy's tent. Sabrina and Brittany dove as far away as they could, and sat on the ground panting. "She's freakin' crazy," Sabrina announced to the entire campground.

"Wendy, you're okay. It's me, Joan." The circle of light on the tent grew smaller as Joan inched closer.

Wendy ranted and screeched like she was in a fight for her life.

Tammie plopped next to where Kisrie hunched. "I had no idea nightmares could be so bad."

Air froze in Kisrie's lungs. If Wendy was having such bad nightmares about what happened to her, what about Keri? What kind of torment did her sister suffer in the dark of night?

"Hey, why don't the rest of you all head over to the fire ring and give Joan and Wendy some space." Sharon shoved her arms into a heavy fleece. The light on her head bobbed.

"I can't say I ever cared about Wendy before, but this is scaring me," Miranda said from somewhere in the darkness.

"Wendy, I am coming in. It's me, Joan. I'm not going to hurt you."

Pray.

That voiceless voice popped into Kisrie's head. She shot up a quick prayer for her life-long nemesis.

Everyone gathered around the dark fire ring, huddling in the chilly night air. Sharon turned her light off, and Kisrie's eyes adjusted to the dark. The stars blazed and sparkled overhead. A thin moon cast a faint glow on the water of the lake.

"Sabrina and Brittany, you guys were in the tent with her. Do you know what happened?"

"Nuh-uh. Sabs and I were sleepin' and all of a sudden she started yelling and stuff. We tried to get her to wake up and she went all crazy on us."

"Pretty much. I thought she was gonna kill me."

"I think some pretty bad stuff happened to her when she was...gone." Brittany looked toward the tent.

"What can you tell me about what happened? I know a little bit from reading the intake forms, but I don't know details," Sharon said.

"Kisrie, why don't you tell it? Your sister was taken with her."

Even though it was quite dark, Kisrie could feel all eyes on her. Waiting. Why did Brittany pass the buck to her? It's not like she knew any more than anyone else. Keri only got home a few days ago. "Earlier this spring, some guys grabbed Wendy and my sister off the street. They were human traffickers." She paused as revulsion worked its way up her throat. She swallowed hard. "But we didn't know that at first..." Kisrie went on about how she and the guard put pieces together after a trafficking ring was advertising in the Denver area trying to lure students looking to raise money for activities. She brought up their rescue attempt gone wrong which landed them on the wilderness program. "So Wendy was rescued by a trucker guy who is in a group that looks for girls being sold and frees them. Keri was still with the pimps who crashed their RV. She was..." Tears bit into her eyes. Oh, what she wouldn't give to have that annoying bush baby behavior back. "She was hurt real bad. She's in a wheelchair now."

"I'm so sorry," Sharon said.

"We're all out here because we didn't think the cops were doing anything. Kisrie came up with this idea to go undercover in a really bad part of town," Leigh Anne explained.

"Wendy won't talk about what happened," Sabrina cut in.

"Keri hasn't said much since she came home."

No one else said a word. The only sounds were night critters and breathing. Even Wendy was quiet. Joan must have gotten through to her.

"Well, I think the best thing we can do for Wendy is to

make her feel safe. I don't care what your history is with her, she is a broken person in a world of hurt and needs to know she is safe here with all of you. As you go back to your tents, and as we hike tomorrow, I want you all to be thinking of ways *you* can get beyond the past and give that to her."

"I can't imagine," Jacque whispered in Kisrie's right ear.

"Neither can I," Kisrie responded.

"D'ya think she'll ever get over it and go on to live a normal life?"

"I don't know. I hope so."

~10~

endy's throat ached. She squeezed her eyes shut to block Jorge's hideous face, and fought with all her might. Not this time. She was *not* going to allow him to rape her again. She would kill him first or die trying.

"Wendy, it's Joan."

A familiar voice that didn't fit the context cut though the cacophonous racket in her head. Someone grabbed her arm, but it was gentle. She grunted and lashed with the other one.

It was caught. And not crushed.

She popped her eyes open.

She was in the dark.

Voices peppered the night air somewhere beyond… the…tent…walls.

Tent.

She was in a tent.

She was in a tent!

So much for those anchoring techniques.

She felt like she'd been run over by a train and cooked over an open fire.

Joan let go of her arms. She sat quiet as if waiting for her to say something, or maybe she was afraid Wendy would attack her again.

"I'm okay. It was just a bad dream." Last thing she wanted to do was speak aloud of the things that happened.

"That was some bad dream. I hope it wasn't based on a real experience." Joan flicked on a small flashlight.

To tell or not to tell. Could she trust Joan? If she lied about it, she doubted Joan would believe her. There was no explanation for such nightmares aside from awful things. "It was real." Her voice was hoarse. How much noise did she make? Did *everyone* in camp hear her? Heat flushed over the surface of her skin.

"Do you wanna talk about—"

"No." She cut Joan off, venom dripping from her voice. She wanted to forget what happened. Talking about it would only cement it in her memory.

"But—"

"I said no. I won't talk about it with you or anyone else. Ever."

"That's fine, but when it affects the entire group, it becomes something we all—"

"Leave me alone!" Wendy moved away and started fluffing her sleeping bag. Joan's presence made her feel safe, but this was her battle and she needed to fight it herself.

"Wendy, it's not doing you any good holding all this in, carrying that burden alone."

"I don't want anyone else. People always let you down. I've had enough." She flopped around to face Joan. "And why would I spill my guts to you when after this trip, I'll never see you again? I, we…" Wendy made a sweeping gesture with her hand to imply she included the other girls, "…are nothing more than a paycheck for you, right?"

Joan shook her head. "Believe me, I'm not in this for the

money. I'm in it because I care. Because I've come through some pretty rough storms of my own."

"No one's been through all the stuff I have." Wendy crossed her arms and looked down, hoping to end the conversation.

"Look, Wendy, I'm not gonna press you to tell me what happened if you don't want to. I just wanna encourage you to tell someone you trust. When I shared my deep, dark secrets with a trusted friend, it was the difference between life and death."

Wendy popped her head up. How could this always laughing, goofy woman have been in such a dark place?

"I'm assuming you're wondering about what I just said. Believe it or not, when I was in college, I hit such a low I didn't think I could go on. I even came up with a plan to end it all. Wrote a note to my roommate. By the grace of God, she found it and found me. She knew me well enough to know where I'd go." Joan blinked a few times and swallowed hard. "I don't usually share this story—as a counselor, we're supposed to keep to things about our clients, but I feel you need to hear this." She stopped and tilted her head as if inviting Wendy to let the conversation go on.

"Tell me." Wendy's voice cracked. She felt her lip tremble.

"That night I told her everything—things I never told another living soul. It was like a weight lifted off my chest. I know that sounds cheesy, but I don't know how else to describe it. She then went on to tell me about faith, how I could have—"

Wendy put her hand up. This is where she was getting off the train. "I don't want to hear any more. I don't believe in God. He, she, it—not real. If God was real, none of this stuff would've happened to me. Bad things wouldn't happen to innocent people."

"I wish you'd give Him a chance—"

"God had every chance to keep those pimps from grabbing me and especially Keri." She stopped. She was going too far. "I'm done talking. I'm tired. I need some sleep."

~11~

Pain seared its way up Kisrie's calves with each step, and she took one about every thirty seconds. It was getting harder and harder to convince her body to keep going—and it was only the *first* day of real hiking! The rest of the group was far ahead, out of sight. Joan hung back with her as it was decided the group had to make camp before it got dark, yet it was unsafe for Kisrie to be left alone. Too many wild things about. And the trail was steep and rocky. A fall could be life-threatening.

Stopping on a flat rock the size of one of her feet, Kisrie leaned forward, but not enough for the weight of the pack to topple her. Her lungs heaved, fighting to get enough air to stop the dizziness. The altitude shouldn't be a problem. She was from Colorado! Mount Falcon was over eight thousand feet. Ten to eleven thousand shouldn't bother her so much, should it?

"Come on, Kiz-a-roo, you can do this."

"Need...a...break. Hurts."

"I know it hurts. This is a strenuous trail. Some seriously steep ups and downs."

"How…much…farther…ow!" It felt like someone stabbed her right calf. "Ah, it hurts so much!" She stumbled forward, grabbing at her leg. Some rocks under the one she stood on broke loose and she slid into Joan. Joan braced herself with a wide stance and leaned into the uphill as they rode the mini rock slide about fifteen feet.

"You probably have a Charlie horse. Are you drinking enough water?"

Kisrie shook her head. The group took water breaks, and by the time she caught up, they were done and moving on. She didn't want to fall further behind. The pain gripped and grabbed and twisted the muscle so much, she thought it would come off the bone.

"First off, we gotta stretch that muscle. It's spasming. Here, let me help turn you around. Reach with your right leg, and lunge into the hill until you feel the painful area stretch—"

"Ah that hurts! It hurts!"

"Keep at it Kisrie, back off a little, take a deep breath and as you let it out, sink into the stretch even more. Give it some oh-two."

She flared her nostrils and pulled in large quantities of the thin mountain air. She tried to imagine the oxygen making its way to her calf. It wasn't too long before the pain eased up. She sighed and shook her leg. Now her hip was cramping from the lunge.

"Water time. Where's your bottle?"

"In one of the mesh side pockets."

"Got it." Joan slid it out and handed it to her. She looked at her watch, then looked up the eternal slope of the mountain.

Kisrie chugged and chugged, water dripped from her lips, ran down her chin and onto her chest. It felt so good.

"Drink up now. We can refill you here at this lake."

She drained the bottle and handed it to Joan. "How much farther?"

"I think these are the Jean Lakes so about six miles give or take."

Six more miles of this? There was no way. Kisrie stared down at her aching feet on the rocky path. Joan moved in close and lifted her chin. "Hey, good news is that our climb is only two of those six. What goes up must come back down. After that, there is a little climb up to camp, but by then, compared to this…" she paused and gestured to the panoramic view of a variety of mountain peaks, "…that last climb will be a piece of cake."

Kisrie groaned. "Why did you have to mention cake? I love cake."

"That's my girl. Now. I'm gonna be with you all the way, okay? We're gonna take this slow and steady. Slower if and when we have to walk through some snow fields. I'm also gonna do my best to distract you as you place one foot in front of the other."

"Clearly, backpacking wasn't made for us fat girls. The gear doesn't fit right, and trying to lug all this weight up the—"

"Beating yourself up isn't gonna help get you up that hill."

"Whatever." Kisrie rolled her eyes. *If* she ever got up that hill. Joan was tall—really tall—and thin. The woman took one step to every sixteen of Kisrie's. She could probably outrun one of those pronghorn antelope things that Wyoming had. Why couldn't these programs have leaders shaped like her? It would be kinda nice if *someone* understood her struggle.

"You coming?" Joan was about forty yards ahead. Kisrie had yet to move.

All right here goes. Step up. Put hands on thigh. Push. Swing back leg alongside the front. Switch legs. Repeat. Kisrie focused on those motions to keep her mind from wandering into a dangerous pit of self-loathing. She sensed Joan wanted her to talk about it, but what good would that do? Talking about it wouldn't change the fact that she was fat. That she couldn't fit into a normal sleeping bag. Nor did it change the fact she couldn't properly adjust her hip belt, therefore carrying much of her pack's weight on her shoulders. The chest straps barely fit over her boobs, and she couldn't get the stabilization strap to connect. Yeah. She couldn't feel more out of her element.

Step up. Hands on thigh. Push. Wave to the stick thin couple coming down toward them.

"You're doing great!" The stick man trotted down the steep slope like a mountain goat.

"Keep on going, you can do this." Stick woman gave a rapid fire of little claps.

What was up with this? Did the fact she was fat make other people think she needed extra special encouragement? Kisrie puffed her cheeks and blew out hard. This proves she probably was the first fat girl ever to be seen on a backpacking trip.

"Seems like there is a lot of history between you and Wendy." Joan's voice interrupted her thoughts.

She had to bring up that. Her other least favorite subject. "Uh. Huh."

Step up. Hands on thigh…push. Oh great. Snow. A trail of deep footprints stretched across about three hundred yards. She lifted her right foot and put it in the first footstep, then shifted her weight forward.

Her foot dropped through the snow, trapping her thigh deep. Her skin stung and tingled from the scratchy, icy snow. She felt her foot soaking through. "I'm stuck! Get me out of here!" As she rocked forward and back, side to side, she felt the snow close in on her leg. Images of Everest climbers with black extremities and amputations filled her mind. Why didn't she choose the incarceration? Doing time would have been so much easier than dying a horrible death up here.

"Unbuckle."

She did. Joan put her hands under her arms and pulled. "I need you to relax."

Relax?

Kisrie tried some deep breathing as the Amazon woman pulled. She felt her spine grow a few inches—or it felt like it stretched that much—and finally, she popped out. Joan's fingers snapped away, and Kisrie twisted in time to see the leader land on her butt. Being on this trip was putting everyone in danger. "Maybe I should go back and do my time." Kisrie pushed up out of the snow. She was soaked. Relentless blasts of mountain wind tore away her body heat.

"You girls need to stop saying that. You made your choice. This is where you are and will be."

She sucked in her lower lip then blew it out. Crossed her arms and moved away from the edge of the snow field. The mountains stretched as far as the eye could see. Lakes glistened in the sun, hurting her eyes. Why didn't she think to bring sunglasses? Birds chirped, causing her head to hurt more. The wilderness was more beautiful in pictures because there was no wretched pain from looking at a picture. "Aren't I putting you and the rest of the group in danger by being such a fat blob that can't keep up? I'm not cut out for this. Like I said before, even the gear lets me know my kind is not welcome." Tears rolled down her cheeks. She swiped at them with the back of her hand. "This was a mistake." Her teeth chattered, making her head hurt more. "I hate this cold!"

"No, Kiz. It's not. This is why you're here." Joan reached for Kisrie's pack and unzipped some of the outer compartments. She pulled out a fleece and draped it over Kisrie's shoulders.

She took the jacket and shimmied into it, then let out a bitter laugh. "What? To prove to myself and the rest of the team that I really and truly am nothing but a failure?"

"Failure is a choice."

"Is it? Kind of looks like all the odds are stacked against me."

"Which is why you of all people must press on."

Kisrie bent over and picked up a palm sized rock. She cocked back her arm and launched it as far as she could. "But I can't do it."

"That's all in your head. I believe you can."

She picked up another rock and whirled around to face Joan who flinched. She opened her grip and it dropped next to her foot. "You saw what happened when I tried to step on that snow field. I can't cross that. I'm too heavy."

Joan put a hand on her braid and twirled it around. She stepped onto the snow and pushed. Then pushed harder. "I think we can make it across."

What was she gonna do? Have her lie on her side and roll her? No way. Nuh. Uh. "How?"

"Come here and step into the tracks without your pack on."

"Are you crazy? And fall through again?"

"Kisrie, what was your goal?" Joan's brown eyes flashed in the late morning sun.

She said nothing.

"What. Was. Your. Goal?"

This was so not fair! She tucked her chin to her chest and looked away from Joan.

"It was about wanting to know you are a strong person. Well, strong people aren't born, they're made. And they aren't made in a factory full of ice cream and glitter-farting unicorns. They're made by facing and tackling hard things. You wanna know my take on you Kisrie Kelley? I think life *has* been hard for you. Unfair. I bet your mantra is, 'it's not fair'. And somewhere along the line, you gave up. You gave into it rather than—"

"That's not true! When my sister disappeared and the cops and FBI and all the people who were supposed to be finding her didn't, I did everything I could to try and find her. I got my friend Leigh Anne in trouble for driving illegally, and we... we..." The words formed a jam in her throat as the sobs forced their way to the front of the line.

Joan moved super close and just stood there. Kisrie threw herself at her and let her emotions flow. Joan put her arms around Kisrie—a cocoon of safety on this exposed mountain-side.

"And things still didn't turn out well from what I hear. You feel defeated. Why bother if nothing's gonna work out? I get that. I may not look like it, but I get that."

Kisrie pulled away to look up at Joan, questions working through the muscles on her face.

"Trust me when I say life hasn't been easy for me either. But between my faith, and some mentors who wouldn't let me settle into the victim role, I learned I didn't have to depend on my own strength to be strong. I don't know what you think of Jesus, but He is my strength."

"I can do all things through Christ who gives me strength," Kisrie whispered.

Joan's face split into a wide smile. "Ah, so you do know! That's awesome." She moved away and examined the snow field again. "So, kiddo, this is what we're gonna do. We're gonna trust," Joan pointed to the sky, "for our strength and make our way to the other side. You are *not* going to wear your pack. I'm gonna use some rope and tie it to you so you can drag it. I bet these tracks in the snow will hold just your body weight. Come here and let's try."

Joan held out her hand. Kisrie took it. Squeezing tight, she stepped into a track near the one she fell through. She leaned forward and expected to fall...but didn't. The snow held. Excitement bubbled up in her. She looked at Joan who was grinning, mouth open. She nodded and pulled Kisrie back to dry ground. "See, it worked? You didn't fall through."

It didn't take Joan long to rig up Kisrie's pack so she could drag it behind. Plan B was for her to either drag it, slide it, or roll it along in front of her.

"Okay, Kiz-a-roo, you ready? Once we get going, we're going to the other end without stopping. Got it?"

"Got it." Butterflies fluttered in her stomach as she led the way. One step. Then another. And yet another. Step by step, Kisrie picked her way across the snow field with Joan close behind. Pulling the pack wasn't easy, and she needed to catch her breath often. But she did go from feeling chilled to sweating like it was the middle of an August day during band camp.

"We're almost there. Looks like you have about five yards to go."

Five yards.

Eight steps.

Every muscle in Kisrie's legs trembled. Seven… six… five…the snow held!

Four…three…two…a giant leap…dry ground! Kisrie lunged forward, letting the pack drop off the snow. She dropped to her knees and kissed the ground. Success!

"Feels pretty epic, doesn't it?"

Yeah. It did. Hard as it was, there was something… satisfying. But she was so tired. Her mouth couldn't form words. A nod had to do.

"Yay us! Now it's time to get that thing on your back and keep going. We really need to get to camp before dark."

"Yeah." Kisrie grabbed her pack by a top strap, braced it on her thigh, then shrugged into one shoulder strap, then the other.

"Nice! You figured out the secret."

"Huh?"

"You figured out how to put the pack on without help.

Look at you, wilderness girl. I don't wanna hear that you don't belong out here come out of your mouth again. Mind over matter. You've got this, Kiz-a-roo."

Now if she could get her body to agree with her head.

"This isn't wind, it's a frickin' hurricane." Wendy wadded the tent-turned-kite under her arm and stomped back to where she, Sabrina, and Brittany struggled to put it up. Even balled up, the fabric whipped and snapped as if it were alive and trying to get away.

"Miranda and them are putting stakes in the ground thingy and tent part at the same time. Maybe we should try that?" Sabrina held out her palm full of small metal tent stakes.

"But we can't open any of this up without it taking off into space." Irritation burned through Wendy's veins. She was tired. Sore. Hungry. No, scratch that. *Hangry*. Why did they have to wait until that stupid fat cow arrived at camp to eat? When Kisrie showed her face, she'd have to pay for making everyone suffer. Hah. So much for becoming a better person. Maybe if things weren't so hard she'd have better luck at making progress on her goal.

Brittany extended some loops toward her. "Wen? Hello? I have the yellow loops of the ground cloth. I need you to find them on the tent so we can—"

"I'm not stupid. I know how to set up a tent."

Brittany and Sabrina exchanged looks. "You don't have to be so mean about it."

"I hate this wind!" Wendy screamed and threw the tent on the ground where it took off rolling across the open meadow.

Sabrina dropped the stakes and took off after the tent.

"Calm down, will ya? We're all tired and hungry, but we're not being jerks about it."

Wendy clamped her jaw until it hurt and glared at her friend through narrowed eyes. "What's wrong with you and Sabrina? It's like they," she cast a glance toward the other groups, "rubbed off on you."

"After all we've been through, being mad all the time just isn't worth it anymore."

Sabrina returned with the tent. She thrust it toward Wendy. "Here. Let's try this again."

Wendy folded her arms. Sabrina pressed the tent against her. "Come on, Wendy. It will take all three of us."

She didn't move. They could take that tent and—

"Fine." Sabrina threw it down. It wrapped itself around Wendy's legs.

Brittany stomped over and added the ground cloth.

"Do it yourself. I am sure we can find room in the other tents." Sabrina's voice sounded more like a growl.

"Yeah. And I hope you like sleeping in the wind."

"Traitors! That's what you are! I don't want you in my tent."

"Well no one wants you in their tent either. I don't know why we ever thought you were so cool, Wendy. You're just mean because you like to be mean." Sabrina grabbed Brittany on the arm and they marched to the first group of girls. After a few seconds of conversation, heads nodded, and Brittany helped that group finish with the tent. Sabrina finally attached to Jenn's group. Wendy looked down at all the nylon thrashing around her legs, then looked at their chosen camp. They were pretty high up and at the mercy of the wind. There wasn't even a rock she could hide behind to escape its ferocious blasts. She powered through a really tough hike only to be undone by wind. She had to be tougher than this. She had to find a way to prove to everyone else that she didn't need them—that she could take care of herself.

"Your tent's not gonna do you a whole lotta good like that." Sharon stared at the nylon flapping around on the ground.

Wendy stooped to scoop it up. "I don't need it."

"Suit yourself." She shrugged and jogged to her backpack.

That was it? Suit yourself? She hugged the tent closer to her body. "I'm going to sleep under the stars." She said it like it was some kind of public service announcement. That should make them think she was in control all along—that this was her choice.

"Wendy, Leigh Anne, and Kisrie are on for making dinner," Sharon read from a small notepad.

"Kisrie's not here," Leigh Anne called from inside her tent.

"When she gets here."

Tammie and Jacque trotted up. "There's not much in the way of firewood." Tammie opened her arms wide and twisted at the waist. "Hardly any trees."

"We'll be using the camp stove. This wind is a bit much for a fire." Sharon looked around the campsite. "Why isn't your tent up?"

"Kisrie has it in her pack. I have poles and stakes." Jacque said.

Tammie added, "And I have the ground cloth."

Sharon tapped her check with her fingers. "Then why don't you two make a windbreak for the stove. Find some rocks and make a wall to keep the wind out. My stove is about this big." Sharon curved her hands and showed them an approximate dimension. "Make sure we can fit two of these. Joan has a pack stove as well—oh, and there needs to be room for the fuel bottle which is about…this big." Another hand measurement. "And the pots. We can't forget about the pots."

"Tam, you got that? I didn't do too well in geometry."

Tammie tugged at Jacque's sweatshirt. "It's not gonna be that hard. Come on."

Wendy shoved the tent parts back into their respective stuff sacks and put her backpack on top so they wouldn't blow away. No use in putting her sleeping bag out until she could get in it. Sleeping in this wind was gonna be near impossible. Maybe she could build a windbreak.

"While we wait, I want you ladies to pull out your journals and write about the hike today. It was a doozie. I'm sure there were times in which you didn't think you'd make it, but you did. Write about pushing through what you think are your limits. Hopefully by the time you're done, Joan and Kisrie will be here."

It wasn't until the bellies of the clouds to the west were seared crimson that Joan, followed by a limping Kisrie, entered camp. It was about time. Wendy's stomach was tying itself in knots.

"We made it!" Joan hopped around in little circles, arms open wide in celebration.

"Kisrieeeee!" Jacque threw her journal, which tumbled a few times in the wind before hitting the ground, and ran toward her friend. "Tam an' I were starting to think you were dead. Eaten by wolves or...bears."

"Can we not talk about bears?" Zoe slammed her journal shut.

"I feel like I've died a thousand deaths and will probably die five thousand more." Kisrie tipped forward onto her friend.

"Oh, girl, you stink." Jacque scrunched up her face.

"You don't smell so hot yourself." Kisrie popped the buckle on her hip belt and her pack dropped.

"Kisrie, you are on dinner duty with Wendy and Leigh Anne. Better hurry because everyone is starving." Sharon held a small stove in her hand. "You three, follow me. Just because we're eating late doesn't mean you get off easy." She led them to where Tammie and Jacque built up a small rock wall. "Who has the grilled chicken and mashed potatoes in her pack?"

Leigh Anne stuck out her tongue. "Oooh. I can't wait to see what dehydrated chicken tastes like."

"My, my, youse guys are in for a treat tonight." Joan plopped down next to where Sharon was setting up her stove. "It's gonna be the ultimate stove-off. WhisperLite versus Jetboil."

"Oh, brother." Sharon rolled her head back.

"My stove doesn't lose efficiency in the wind and is much easier to set up...*plus* it can boil water in around two minutes."

"Joan, have I ever told you what a braggart you are?"

"Girls, look. My stove is just this! Everything I need, including fuel is in this one litre container. Hers is in an awkward bag, and her fuel is separate."

"My fuel is bigger, therefore it lasts longer."

"Does yours have push-button ignition?"

Sharon glared as she pulled the legs out on her little stove.

"Didn't think so." Joan dropped her voice to a near whisper. "She has to actually prime her stove to light it."

"What's that mean?" Leigh Anne looked from one leader to the next, squinting in the dimming light.

"Who cares. I'm hungry." This was the dumbest argument Wendy had ever heard.

"Which is why I have the better stove!"

"Here's the grilled chicken stuff." Chrissy dropped five bags of Mountain House on the ground.

Joan had her stove together and was pouring water in the container. "I'll have all these reconstituted before she boils her first pot of water. You watch."

"I thought we were supposed to make dinner?" Kisrie asked.

"Shut up." Wendy whacked her on the arm. If this who-has-the-bigger-stove contest got her out of extra work, so be it. What were they gonna do? Tie them together back to back and make them prepare the meal with their feet?

Sharon unscrewed the lid on her red fuel bottle and attached some contraption to the top. A click and roar startled Wendy. She turned and saw blue flames glowing from under Joan's stove. Her teeth glittered in the twilight.

"Can we get our headlamps?" Leigh Anne asked.

"Sure." Sharon started pumping away on her bottle.

"By the time you girls get back here you'll see my heat indicators changing color."

Leigh Anne and Kisrie left, but Wendy stayed. This was getting too good. The others were gathering around.

"I see all youse guys are coming over here to see Sharon and her WhisperLite stove go down in flames! Pun intended."

"Zip it, Joan." Sharon chuckled and attached a silver tube from her stove to the fuel bottle and turned a dial on the stove itself. There was a squirting sound. She twisted it off and flicked a lighter at the bottom. Apparently gas filled a little cup under the stove. Orange flames leapt up and she turned a knob. Within seconds the flames shrank and turned blue. Her stove was louder than Joan's. "My stove may take more to set up, and may not boil water as fast, but I can *control* my heat. I can cook eggs and bacon while she can only boil water."

"Not fair! I have an attachment for larger pots—"

"To boil water!"

By the time Leigh Anne made it back to the stove area with Kisrie dragging a few feet behind, Joan turned her stove off and grabbed the pot with her *bare hands* holding it up in triumph. "Boiled! And do all you guys see I can pick it up sans hot pad? Neoprene shell! Sharon can't do that." She set it back on the Jetboil. "Wendy, Kisrie, Leigh Anne, I want youse guys to open all the meal packs…wait for it…without using your hands."

What the—

"Looks like we gotta use our teeth." Leigh Anne said before dropping her head and biting the top of a bag of Mountain House grilled chicken and mashed potatoes. She shook her head like a dog shaking a rabbit. "Umoddy elfff eeee."

"This is gross. You guys are on your own." Wendy scooted away.

"That's not how it works." Sharon's legs appeared within her peripheral vision.

Kisrie moved in and put the top of her head against the bag, pressing it into Leigh Anne's chest. Talk about personal space violation. There was no way.

"I can't hold it still. Wendy, I need your help."

"I'm not putting my face near yours."

"What about your foot?"

"Have you thought about using rocks to hold it down? Or, better yet," Wendy paused and chuckled to herself, "you can sit on it and I bet that would pop the bag."

Kisrie gave her a look that could kill a weaker woman.

Leigh Anne spit the bag out of her mouth. "I like the popping the bag idea, but not that part about Kisrie sitting on them. That's mean and you know it."

"Whatever."

"But if we pop the bags, won't all the stuff inside blow everywhere? Kind of like what happens when you try to open a bag of chips and the bag pops causing chips to explode all over the room?" Kisrie picked up a rock and tossed it in the air and caught it in the same hand. "Is there a way to contain the mess?"

"Zoe has a large pot hanging off her pack. What if we lay it on its side and put the opening of the bag in the pot then drop the rock on the bag?" Leigh Anne hopped up. "I'll get the pot."

"But how do you two geniuses expect to drop rocks without using your hands?"

"Why don't *you* figure that one out." Kisrie folded her arms and lowered her eyebrows.

Joan spread her arms, palms up. "The whole point of these challenges is to get youse guys to work together and solve problems."

"These are stupid problems," Wendy muttered. Really. They were stupid. Everyone was hungry because *somebody* couldn't hike at the speed of normal. To add to misery, they had to figure out how to open the bags while the water cooled and stomachs shrunk.

"If you choose not to participate, then you are choosing not to eat." Sharon's voice was stern.

"This isn't fair. None of this is fair!" Wendy scrambled to her feet. "Fine. Then I *choose* to go to bed without my supper." She made sure the last part was in a high sing-songy voice. Then her stomach rumbled and cramped. She really needed to eat. But she already took a stand. She couldn't back down now and let anyone think she was weak or vulnerable.

All headlamps pointed at her, blinding her. The only sound was that of Sharon's dumb stove and the freaking wind. And she had no tent to retreat to.

Great.

She sniffed as loud as she could, pointed her nose to the now starry sky, and marched to where she stashed her bag. She'll show them she was invincible. Even if she felt like her whole world crumbled around her and there was nothing she could do to stop it.

~12~

As Wendy stomped off into the darkness, Kisrie looked at Leigh Anne and shrugged her shoulders. "I'm hungry, so let's do this."

By now everyone gathered around, tummies making all kinds of grumbling, squealing, and gurgling noises.

Leigh Anne positioned the bag of food in the pot as they discussed and held it in place between her feet. "Don't drop that rock on me. I need these for hiking."

Kisrie nodded then placed a heavy rock under her chin. She aimed carefully and dropped the rock. The bag burst open, a poof of freeze dried food wafted into the air. The whole group cheered. Joan grabbed the bag and poured some hot water in, handing it to Chrissy to mix. Kisrie and Leigh Anne had all the bags opened within a short time. Some bags blew out the sides, so the food had to be reconstituted in the pot. But hey, it was food! Never in her life did mush look so appetizing.

At first the food was distributed sparingly to make sure

everyone had some. Then Joan called for seconds. Kisrie still felt like she could eat an entire herd of wild horses, so she went for more. When she sat on her sit-upon and held her spoon over the bowl, a thought about Wendy popped into her mind. Wendy hadn't eaten at all. Sure, it was of her own doing, but still.

All of a sudden, her stomach settled. It actually felt so full that if she took another bite she'd barf it all up. Wendy was out there somewhere. Kisrie wondered if anyone would notice if she slipped away to find Wendy and offer her the food. Her nemesis would probably refuse to eat after her, but she felt she had to at least make the gesture.

She looked around the group. Joan was telling some goofy jokes and funny wildlife encounters while pooping. She rolled to her knees and forced her aching muscles to stand. She crept away in the dark not wanting to turn on her headlamp. And it wasn't like she needed it. The stars were so bright that once her eyes adjusted she could make out the tents and rocks and finally Wendy who was in her sleeping bag with a tent and fly wrapped around her.

"Hey, Wendy?" Kisrie crept closer.

"Go away."

"I brought you some food."

Nothing.

"I figured you might be hungry."

Wendy rolled over and cursed as guy lines and fabric wound tighter around her. "What do you care?"

Kisrie didn't have the energy to argue. Her body felt like a train ran over it. Every movement brought tears to her eyes. She wasn't sure how much more she could take. She set the bowl and spoon on the ground next to Wendy then walked away.

The smell of the food caused Wendy's stomach to seize so hard her knees pulled up toward her chest. Last thing she wanted to do was eat after Kisrie Kelley. Who knew what kind of germs that girl had? But she was desperate—desperately hungry.

Wendy grabbed the bowl and shoveled the chicken chunks and mashed potatoes in her mouth in five huge bites. It wasn't as much as she'd have liked, but it was enough to quell the gut-stabbing pains. What was up with Kisrie? Why did she of all people give up food?

Exhaustion washed through every fiber of Wendy's body. Maybe it was part of Kisrie's weight loss plan or something. Or maybe she was trying to be nice? Wendy was too tired to think much about it.

She stared at the center of the Milky Way until her eyes blurred letting the wind song block out all thoughts until sleep swallowed her whole.

A drip.

Then another.

And another.

Then…

…lots of them.

Wendy bolted upright as it felt as if someone turned on an ice-cold shower over her. She thrashed around with the tent, which served as a cover over her sleeping bag, trying to pull the nylon over her head for protection, but the wind seemed to mock her efforts. Shivers ran up and down her spine. She needed to get in a tent and fast, or she'd freeze to death.

But it was so dark.

What happened to the stars?

Where were the tents?

"Sharon? Joan?" she called into the wind, hoping they could hear her over the now torrential rain. Icy, cold rain.

She fought out of the tangled mess of her sleeping bag and strained her ears for the sound of rain on a tent.

It was no use.

She tried to imagine in her mind's eye where she plopped down in relation to where the tents were. They were spread out a bit in the meadow, and in her anger, she really didn't pay much attention.

Stupid, stupid, stupid!

Her fingers and toes started to lose feeling. She had to get out of this and fast.

Think, think, think!

"Sharon!" She screamed as loud as she could. The leader had a tent to herself and would probably offer refuge rather than let one of her students die, wouldn't she?

Through the blur of rain, a yellow glow appeared about fifty yards away. Sharon's tent was yellow. Wendy raked her wet things to her chest and hobbled toward the light in her socked feet. Stones and sticks bit into her tender soles, but she didn't care. She had. To. Get. Out. Of. The. Rain.

By the time she reached the tent, salty rivulets joined the water running down her face. Her body shook so hard it took all her strength to stand. The tent flap opened and the light of a small lantern blinded her for a moment.

"Drop your stuff and get in here quick." She felt a hand on her arm and a tug. Wendy tumbled into the tent and pulled her legs through the opening. Her eyes adjusted to the bright LED light while Sharon wrestled with the flap. The wind tried to tear it out of her hands.

Once the tent was closed, Sharon turned to look at her. "We need to get you out of those clothes."

Wendy's heart stopped. Images of men leering in anticipation filled her mind. Her lungs refused to expand. She stopped feeling the cold.

"Wendy? Can you hear me? Wendy?" Sharon's hands were on her shoulders and she was shaking her gently.

The leader's face came into focus. "No! No! Please don't make me. No!" She tore away and swatted in all directions.

"Wendy, I need to get you out of those wet clothes or you're going to have hypothermia. This is serious. It can kill you. Your skin already feels like ice."

"Get away from me!" Wendy lunged for the tent door, her fingers scrabbling every which way looking for the zipper.

Strong arms circled around her and held her tight. "I'm not trying to hurt you," Sharon said. "I don't know what kind of abuse you've been through, but you are here in Wyoming with me and I am trying to save your life."

Wendy gave a hard wiggle, then found she couldn't muster up the strength for another.

"That's it. Calm down. I will turn off the lantern if you like. But I need you out of those clothes and into my sleeping bag."

She was so cold her bones ached. She had no idea bones could ache so much. Her teeth chattered with such violence Wendy feared the thousands of dollars Iona spent on braces would be lost. "C...could...w...we...l...leave the light on." Last thing she wanted was dark. Bad things happened when she took her clothes off in the dark.

"You are safe. I will turn away if that will help." Sharon let go of her. "Here, let me hold up the sleeping bag between us if that will make you more comfortable."

Wendy tried to bend her fingers to grab the edges of her shirt, but they didn't seem to respond. She fumbled and fumbled as the chill worked its way deeper.

"You need to move quicker," Sharon said.

"I...c...can't."

"Do you want me to help you?" Sharon's voice was so soft, the pounding rain nearly drowned it out.

Help? It was bad enough Wendy had to strip naked in front of another person she didn't know, but to have said person help? Whenever someone "helped" her... No. She couldn't let those memories take over. But she was so cold. And Sharon was a woman.

So was Unique.

"I promise I will not do anything that makes you uncomfortable, but Wendy, every second you stay in those wet clothes is a second closer to hypothermia. You are at a stage where we can reverse this, but give it a few more minutes—you'll stop shivering and we'll be in serious trouble. Please trust me."

Trust.

Never in her life had she trusted anyone. The only person Wendy knew beyond a shadow of doubt that she could trust was herself.

But her fear of death was greater than her fear of getting naked in front of Sharon. She tried to make her head nod amidst the tremors.

Wendy imagined a huge hammer in her mind as Sharon peeled the clothes away. Every time a leering face appeared, Wendy smashed it with the hammer.

When she felt the cool air on all parts of her body, she whimpered.

"I need you to slide in here. I'm going to pull it up and put the hood over your head. Then, I'm going to pull you into my lap so my body heat can insulate you from the outside as your body starts warming the inside. I'm not going to do anything to make you uncomfortable. I promise."

For the first time in her entire life, Wendy accepted her vulnerability and allowed someone to hold her close.

However, she couldn't allow Sharon to think of her as

weak. She needed to prove she was in control—but that had to wait until she got through this crisis.

~13~

"Oh what a beautiful morning, oh what a beautiful day!" Sharon sang at triple forte and a little off-key.

Kisrie managed to open only one eye. She didn't have the energy to open the other. The sun hadn't quite come up yet, so it was a little less than dark. Plus, it was honkin' *freezing*. Crawling out of the sleeping bag seemed like a bad idea.

"Get up, get up, we have a long hike today, but I'm so excited because we will be trekking down to the Green River. Oh my gosh, you guys, the next few days on the trail will be magical."

Sharp pain shot up Kisrie's spine as she reached for the zipper of Joan's sleeping bag. It was a miracle she made it to camp late last night. Every step was excruciating, and if Joan hadn't been with her she probably would have dropped on the trail and let the wolves and bears eat her.

"Sooo, Kiz, I didn't get to ask ya last night, but what's it like hanging out with Joan? Is she always so weird?" Jacque let out a lion-like yawn at the end of her question.

Did she have to answer? Kisrie feared opening her mouth would send more pain coursing through her beat-up body.

"Five minutes to get your clothes on and be ready for breakfast."

"I like her weirdness. She makes me laugh and forget about my pain—sometimes."

"I don't know. I just don't understand how someone could be so happy all the time. And have you ever seen a girl so tall? What is she? Like, seven feet tall?"

"Jacque, you're pathetic!" Tammie slapped Jacque up the side of the head with a pair of underwear. "I agree with Kiz. I like how she makes everything fun."

"Ew! I hope those are clean."

"Three minutes!" Sharon's voice cut through the wind which was still knocking the tent around like a punching bag.

"Kiz, you're not even up yet."

"Jack, your command of the obvious never ceases to amaze me. Of course I'm not up. I don't think I can move."

"Oh, but you gotta. We have to go about *seventeen* miles today. Can you believe that? Seventeen? That's more miles than I am old."

"How are those two related?" Tammie asked.

"I better see bodies crawling out of tents."

"C'mon, Kiz. You need to get up, or we're all gonna have to suffer again."

Taking a deep breath and holding it, Kisrie pulled the zipper down and rolled out of the bag. It took pushing with both arms to get into a sitting position. No matter how much she hurt, from now on, she would be the first out of the tent. She'd show them.

Tammie yanked a wool sock onto her foot. "We had to wait for you to get to camp to eat. No one was happy about that. I'm not gonna lie."

"I've never known you to lie, Tam. Jack, can you grab my

socks over there?" She tried to reach, but came up three inches short.

Jacque crawled to the door and grabbed Kisrie's socks between her thumb and pointer finger. "I hate touching people's socks." With a flick of the wrist she flung them onto Kisrie. They didn't exactly smell like lilacs.

"Aren't you gonna change? Tammie zipped open the tent. A blast of arctic air blew in, causing bumps to break out on Kisrie's skin.

"Time's up!"

"I don't have time." She pulled on her socks, rolled onto her knees and crawled to the door. Every muscle in her body protested. How in the world was she gonna make it through the day? Jacque and Tammie were running toward Sharon and Joan by the time Kisrie figured out how to get her feet into her boots without bending her knees too much. Thank goodness for flexibility. She stuffed the laces in the tops figuring she could tie them later.

Once erect, she lumbered stiff-legged toward the rest of the group, who waited on her—again.

"Looks like someone needs a lesson on how to be on time." Wendy grumbled from behind the circle. Her usual goons seemed to stay as far away from her as possible. What happened?

"Starting tomorrow, I'll be the first one up and out." Kisrie put her hands on her hips and gave a little "so there" wiggle.

"Because we have a long day, we're just gonna eat Pop-Tarts for breakfast, break up camp, and get on the trail." Joan handed out one silver packet to each girl. "If you don't like the flavor, trade with a friend."

"For lunch, we're going to be eating the bagels, pepperoni and cheese. Whoever has those ingredients in her pack needs to make sure they are accessible in a side pocket." Sharon tore open her Pop Tarts, scooted one out and took a bite, trying to keep all the crumblies in the silver wrapper. "We have a long descent this morning. We're gonna lose over two thousand feet. Key thing will be to keep your center of gravity low. When packing, put the heavier objects in the bottom. You really don't want to be top-heavy for this trek."

Sabrina and Brittany snickered, gesturing toward Kisrie with their eyes.

"Ladies. Please focus." Joan's usually cheerful face dropped into a serious scowl.

Sharon picked up the narrative. "When we get to the descent we're gonna take it easy. We will spread out in case someone slips. We don't want someone taking another person with them. But hopefully, if you watch where you put your feet and take your time, you won't fall. Any questions?"

No one said a word.

Sharon gave the tail on her hip belt a tug. "Good. Looks like most of you are done eating. Pack up, and let's get going."

Wendy couldn't bring herself to look at Joan's pack. Her wet sleeping bag was spread all over it with the hopes that if the sun came out, it would dry.

If that wasn't bad enough, the tent and fly had to be stretched over Brittany and Sabrina's pack, while Wendy's clothes hung from her own. Nothing like signaling to the whole world that she was an idiot. Everyone, save Sharon and Joan, stayed away from her—especially Brittany and Sabrina. They yowled in protest over having to drape wet tent parts on their packs.

Sharon's voice echoed in Wendy's head. "One person's choice can heap consequences on others."

Yeah, yeah, yeah. Whatever.

Staring at the ground, Wendy placed a foot and tested the hold before shifting her weight onto it. More than once she slipped on loose rock causing her heart to jump into her mouth. The ledges were narrow and it was a long way down from where they descended from Summit Lake toward the Green River. She wasn't sure which was harder: climbing or going down. Going down was scarier, for sure.

After a few excruciating hours trying not to die, Wendy's brain could think of nothing but bagels and cheddar cheese. With every step her quads trembled. It took every ounce of her concentration to stay upright. And the fact that it rained last night didn't make the going easier. The rocks were slippery, and what was dirt was now mud.

A scream split the air, jarring her thoughts, causing her to stumble. Her arms whirled through the air as she fought for and finally regained her balance.

"Oh my God! Miranda!"

"Help me!"

"She's gonna die!"

Shouts echoing off the hard surfaces peppered the air. A couple of through hikers came skidding down the slope from behind her to see what happened.

Sharon called for the group to huddle up. Wendy squatted low and slid down on her feet to where they gathered. Joan and the two strangers peered over the side of the trail. Miranda lay a far way down, her leg twisted in a gruesome, unnatural angle. Good thing breakfast was long gone or it would have made a reappearance.

"Dude, you got any rope?" One of the hikers asked Joan who ran a hand along her long braid.

"I'm not a dude and I do have some rope, but it's for bear bags. Not sure it's strong enough to support her weight plus mine."

The guy's face turned beet red. "Uh, sorry about that. I tend to call everybody dude. And I have some climbing rope. Also have some 'biners and harnesses."

"Alright. Can you pull your gear out while I scope a good triple anchor point? You got enough for me to do a triple? I like the extra measure of safety."

"We're gonna do Gannet. We have plenty. Use all you need. We'll help in any way we can."

Miranda tried to sit up, then let out another scream. "My leg! Something's wrong with my leg."

"Hold tight, sweetie, Joan and I are trying to figure out the best way to get you up here." Sharon moved in close to Joan and spoke into her ear, but her voice carried. "That break looks bad. May even be a compound. We're gonna need to splint it before we move her."

"You're right. But it's pretty barren out here. No trees."

An idea formed in Wendy's mind. "Uh, what about tent poles? You can unfold them as long as you need and keep the rest together for support." The words were out of her mouth before she had a chance to think.

Joan twisted to face her. A grin split her face. "Why that's a great idea. Go get me two of the long poles. I have some Ace bandages in my first aid kit."

Sharon reached out and touched her arm. "Thanks, Wendy."

By the time she turned around Jenn held out some tent poles. "Here. Take these. I never would have thought of using these. I probably would have hiked for miles and miles looking for sticks long enough."

"I hope she's gonna be okay." Zoe covered her face with her hands. Her body shook.

"She will be." Chrissy put a hand on Zoe's shoulder.

Joan approached the group rubbing her hands together. "Okay, ladies. We're gonna need a few of you to be anchors to lower me down to Miranda safely. Then you'll have to help pull us back up in increments she can tolerate. Seems like one of those guys has a sat phone. He's gonna see what kind of help we can get in here for her."

"Why can't you just wait until a helicopter comes in or something like that?" Brittany asked.

"I'm afraid she may go into shock, if she hasn't already. I also need to splint that limb to help cut down on her pain a bit. We gotta do what we can out here to help her until someone comes along, or until we can get her to a safer rescue spot."

"I don't see no electricity out here. How's she gonna get shocked?"

Wendy slapped her hand over her face at Brittany's question. The girl really did have rocks for a brain.

Tammie made her way to Brittany. "It's when a person's blood pressure drops dangerously low after a traumatic event— such as falling and breaking a leg—blood flow is restricted to the heart and brain and if not treated, it can kill that person."

"That's my girl, the walking encyclopedia." Jacque did a fist pump in the air.

"I need anchors, now." Joan paused. "Kisrie, Zoe, Jenn, Leigh Anne, would you all come with me?"

"Of course she'd take Kisrie," Wendy muttered under her breath.

"I heard that." Jacque was all up in Wendy's face.

"I just mean it's a good thing she's here to help?"

"You said it to be nasty, and you know it."

"Now's not the time to argue, ladies." Sharon glared at them.

Joan and the two men wrapped a neon green and purple speckled rope around each anchor girl who sat on the ground. Joan asked each one how much they weighed. Kisrie's face lost all color. Wendy crept in closer. She wanted to know the answer.

"It's okay Kiz-a-roo. I need to make sure the anchor weight exceeds the combined weight of Miranda and myself plus any gear."

Kisrie toyed with the metal clip thingy on the rope circling her girth. "Two...two forty-one."

The other girls gave their weights.

Satisfied, Joan stepped into a harness and tied some fancy knots with the rope to another clip thing. She backed over the steep edge of the trail and leaned back. Kisrie and the others grunted as the rope tightened on them.

"Ooh, this hurts," Jenn moaned.

"I know. I'll get down there as quick as I can."

"Hey, dude—I mean, miss—I got a hold of the rescue people. They will send a chopper, but we gotta get her down to the river. It's too windy up here right now for a safe rescue."

"Well, that means we're gonna need to make a litter of some kind." Sharon dropped her pack to the ground. "Ladies, it's up to us to figure this out. Once Joan and those guys get Miranda up here, we need a way to safely get her down. The ground is too rough to drag, so we need to figure out how to make something similar to what they used forever ago to carry royalty in parades or some kind of stretcher."

"I think we're back to tent poles and maybe a tent itself. Or a raincoat or something like that," Tammie suggested.

"Yeah, we need to make a sling-like thing for her to sit on, but do you think tent poles are gonna be strong enough?" Zoe sloughed off her pack and zipped it open. "I have a pretty heavy-duty rain coat. I think the tent or fly may be too much material to work with."

As good as the idea seemed, the fact they still had some steep hill to go down bothered Wendy. "But how are we going to actually carry her down? It's hard enough going down alone. But carrying her with poles? What if she slides off?"

Chrissy put a hand to her cheek. "I didn't think of that."

"What if we lash her to Joan or one of those guys and they all stabilize each other on the way down?"

All eyes pointed at her. She didn't see any hostility, only wonderment. "What? Did you all think I was stupid or something? It's common sense."

"I think it's worth a try. We need to minimize our risk as much as possible," Sharon said before heading back to where the anchors sat.

"I need several fleeces. She's not shocking yet, but I fear it's not too long. I need to get her warm before I look at the leg."

Miranda's whimpers and cries rose on the wind to where everyone stood.

"I hope she's gonna be okay," Zoe chanted over and over again.

Sharon hustled around catching warm layers tossed her way.

"Here, I'll take them down." One of the hikers balled them under his arm and practically surfed down the hillside to Joan and Miranda. He seemed like he was part mountain goat. Wendy'd never seen anyone so sure-footed.

The guy rolled one jacket up and put it under Miranda's head while Joan draped some of the others over her body. She pulled a knife out of her pocket and pressed a button. The blade popped out. In one swift motion she slit Miranda's pant leg from ankle to upper thigh. It was the thigh that was all weird colored and bent at an odd angle.

"No broken skin, but it's the femur for sure. I'm gonna have to do an in-line traction splint, Sharon."

Wendy felt her pulse quicken when she saw the color drain from Sharon's face. Was that in-line thing bad? Was it worse than anyone thought?

Joan pulled off her shirt and a boot. She shoved the shirt in the boot, then put a bundle of tent poles in it. Hiker dude handed her some long pieces of webbing. Joan tied some here and there, but when he put the boot in Miranda's crotch, Wendy turned away. Her knees felt like deflated balloons.

"Miranda, this is gonna hurt like nothing you've ever felt before, but when I'm done, you'll feel tons better."

"I think I'm gonna get sick! I can't do this! I can't do this!" Jacque flapped her hands around and had her face all squinched up.

"You're not the one—" Tammie's words were cut off by the most unearthly scream Wendy ever heard. It was so primal it sent goosebumps up and down every inch of her flesh. She slapped her hands over her ears as Miranda's screams morphed into Keri's screams when the pimps tortured her to break Wendy. Her knees buckled, and she thought she was gonna be the next one down that hill.

But as soon as the screaming started—it stopped.

"All done. Feel better?"

Wendy heard Miranda reply with a weak "yes".

When the leg was splinted, Hiker Dude and Joan helped Miranda stand up on her good leg. Hiker Dude turned so he and Miranda were back to back. The duo locked elbows. Joan made sure both were tied into the rope and clip things. Joan gave a thumb's up sign to Other Hiker Dude at the top who then helped pull the pair up to the trail. Once at the top, the rope was sent back and Joan made the steep ascent.

Now to head down to the valley.

Except for the men helping Miranda down the mountain-side, no one said a word. The going was slow, and the weather vacillated between snow, rain, and sun. Wendy lost count of how many times she had to add or subtract layers of clothing along the way.

Miranda's frequent cries of pain kept pulling Wendy back to that dank room in Denver. The feelings of helplessness as someone suffered was something she hoped never to experience ever again—yet here it was. Her body shook. The urge to scream punched its way up into her throat.

She didn't know how much more of it she could take. The images that crowded her mind threatened to take over and cause her to have another embarrassing freak-out attack like she did last night.

She was gonna lose it—again.

Ugh.

If she fell apart now, Joan and the hikers might drop Miranda. Sharon would have to try and calm her down in front of everyone. Then everyone would want to know what her problem was. Logically she had no reason to freak out.

Focus.

She had to focus. Keep thinking about solutions to help Miranda. Maybe that would distract her from her own inner demons.

"Hey, Joan, there's some paramedic kind of people coming with a stretcher!" Jacque called up the trail.

"They must've landed near the river and hiked up," one of the men helping Joan carry Miranda said.

"I waved at them, and now they're running uphill toward us. We better get outta the way."

Since when did Jacque become the team leader? Wendy was behind Miranda so she stayed put as the rescue team—or paramedics or whoever they were—reached Joan.

"That's quite an ingenious getup you got there," one said as he gently detached Miranda who hovered between this world and passing out.

"It was her idea." Joan pointed to Wendy and flashed a huge smile full of teeth.

A strange feeling rose up in Wendy's chest—a feeling that caused the ugly images to vaporize in an instant. Whatever it was, it felt...nice.

"She also came up with the idea of using tent poles as

splints, and wouldn'tcha know, it's her first time in the back-country."

The paramedic holding the board thingy looked at her and dipped his chin. "I'm impressed." He, along with all the other men, plus Joan, lowered Miranda onto the board. Her head rolled from side to side and her skin was a pale grayish color. "You did a good job with that splint. Where'd you learn that?"

"I first learned it when I was a student at Houghton. There were these guys that came down from New Hampshire. Anyway, Sharon and I go back east for Wilderness Emergency Medicine training whenever our cards expire."

Wilderness Emergency Medicine...Wendy never heard of such a thing.

There was a short debate on whether they should drag the board or carry it. Carrying it won out even though it put the men taking turns to carry it at greater risk. They didn't think Miranda would be able to handle all the bumping around over rocks.

It seemed like a long time before the valley below came into view. The Green River was just that—green. A helicopter sat in a grassy area along the riverbank.

"Probably'll take her to Idaho Falls. We'll need all her info so we can contact the family."

Sharon fished in her pack, pulled out a zip-lock with papers in it, found what she was looking for and handed it over.

Joan switched places with a through hiker as a paramedic took a pulse while they hiked.

When they were down, Wendy watched in fascination as they transferred Miranda to the bed in the chopper. There wasn't a whole lot of room in there, but it seemed to have everything an ambulance would have. She hoped Miranda would be okay.

"Last chance to say goodbye before we turn on the rotors."

Everyone gathered at the helicopter's side door.

"Oh, Miranda, I wish I could go with you." Zoe wiped

tears from her cheeks with the palms of her hands, smearing dirt across her face.

"If you see a bear, take a picture for me," Miranda answered in barely a whisper.

"I wish we were allowed to have our phones, because I'd put this on Insta for you. It would go viral and you'd be famous." Chrissy made like she held up a phone for a picture.

"Thanks, Chrissy."

One by one, the girls said goodbye.

It was Wendy's turn. She approached the chopper as one of the paramedics started an IV. What would she say?

She didn't have to say anything. Miranda spoke first. "Hey, I was really angry about you coming with us. But...you're really not all that bad." She winced as the needle pierced her skin. "Thanks for the ideas. I don't know how I would've made it down here."

Whoa. Where did that come from? Wendy blinked a few times. Her eyes felt hot and sticky. "Y...you're welcome." No one had ever really thanked her for anything.

"We're ready to go! Need all you lovely folks to back far away." The door was pulled shut. Everyone in the chopper shifted around and the blades started to turn.

Whomp!

Whomp!

Whomp!

As they picked up speed, dust, dirt, rocks, and a few small critters peppered the group. Then, when they stirred up a full-blown haboob, the chopper lifted off then darted to where the sun was lowering itself in the sky.

Joan looked at the group one girl at a time. She let out a deep sigh. "No one is allowed to hurt themselves for the remainder of the trip. Got it?"

The sky blushed with the oncoming night by the time the group, minus Miranda, reached their target camping area. Every jarring step sent rockets of pain up and down Kisrie's legs. Her back ached as if someone had beaten her with the butt-end of a rifle. Joan and Sharon pointed out aspects of the incredible scenery, but Kisrie hurt too much to appreciate it. All she could think about was getting the pack off her back and the boots off her feet. After that long, steep descent, her hot spots had hot spots, which gave way to blisters having blisters. She practically had to use a whole sheet of mole skin—hope it wasn't made from real moles…ew—to minimize the friction on her feet.

Everyone, including the leaders, kept quiet as tent city arose along the river in the lush grasses exploding with wild-flowers. The downside?

Mosquitoes.

Every. Stinking. Orifice of Kisrie's body was invaded by swarms and swarms of the nasty bugs.

"So, what kind of challenge will we have for dinner tonight?" Jacque asked Joan.

"I think we're gonna go ahead and have the assigned persons make dinner the normal way tonight. I want to make sure we have enough time for a good debrief around the fire before bedtime." Joan seemed to look over and around Jacque like a mother hen taking count of her chicks. She seemed on edge.

"It's like I don't even exist." Jacque plopped down on her bottom with a huff. A wisp of black hair fell into her eyes. She failed to swipe it into place.

"Oh, you exist all right." Kisrie rolled her lips in against her teeth to keep from saying what was *really* on her mind.

"So what did you think of those helicopter rescue guys?" Jacque rolled up to her knees and grabbed Kisrie's shoulders, giving her a little shake. "Cute, huh? Don't tell me you don't think so. You know? I'm starting to worry about you. Let's face it. You were whisked away in an ambulance by those hunky paramedics this past fall, some of the policemen who arrested us were on the hot side—I mean, who can resist a man in uniform? Swoon!" She let go of Kisrie and flopped to her back. "Then those guys today *plus* the paramedics." She let out a long sigh.

"That's creepy."

Jacque propped up on her elbows. "What? How so? Any warm, cold-blooded girl would see—"

"You mean warm. Humans and mammals have warm blood. Reptiles are cold-blooded." Tammie stepped over Jacque carrying tent poles and stakes.

"Well, aren't you the walking-talking Wikipedia Person." Another huff. "Anyway, Kisrie here doesn't seem to notice the fine specimens of masculinity that grace us with their presence. Unless..." Jacque trailed off and bolted to a seated position, legs straight in front of her. "Say it ain't so!"

Heat flashed through Kisrie's body. She knew where her friend's mind was going. "It isn't, and you know it."

"Jack, how can you?" Tammie threw the object in her hands to the ground.

"If you must know, I do notice when guys are cute, but why bother going beyond a simple notation in my head? Have you ever seen any guy show interest in me beyond calling me Cow Pie or Fatty or other names I don't want to think about?" She paused. Neither friend said a word. "What's the point of wasting my emotional energy on some guy who would probably moo or be mortified if I showed any interest? I don't need that kind of pain in my life." There. She said it. She tried maintaining a stern look on her face, but her chin trembled, and she felt the warm tears rolling down her cheeks cool in the night air. She *did* like boys. A lot. But they *never* liked her back.

Ever.

So the best way to avoid the heart shattering pain of rejection was to pretend they didn't exist, or that she was indifferent to them.

"All those guys from today are too old for you anyway. They were like old, old," Tammie said.

"I read a story on Facebook about a twenty-two-year old who is in love with some dude who was fifty-five. So there."

Tammie put her hands on her head and swiveled it side to side. "Kisrie, what do we say to that? I have no words. You know how rare it is when I cannot find words in my immense vocabulary to express my thoughts." She pointed a finger to the sky. "In fact, I cannot even form a thought about that."

"Hey, Joan, how old do you think those helicopter guys were?" Jacque yelled across the camp. It sounded like she had a bullhorn because the night was so still.

Kisrie slapped a mosquito that landed on her thigh. "I can't believe you did that."

Joan sauntered over, a lopsided grin on her face. "One-hundred and eight. That's my guess."

"Aw, come on, how old do you really think they are?" Jacque widened her eyes and made that stupid duck face all the pretty girls made when taking selfies.

"Why do you need to know?"

"She," Jacque nodded toward Tammie, "thinks they are older than dirt."

"I do not!"

"Oh!" Jacque squealed and flapped her hands. "If they're too old for me, they aren't too old for you. Whadda ya think, Joan?"

This was getting really embarrassing. What did it matter in the scope of all things? Miranda was hurt, her two best friends just dredged up painful emotions around boys, and now they were making utter fools of themselves in front of the whole guard. No wonder people tended to steer clear at times.

"I'm guessing you are forty-four. Those guys can't be much older." Jacque folded her arms.

Joan squeezed her eyes shut and grimaced as if she bit into something uber sour. "Wrong-o."

"Forty-three?"

"No."

"I'm gonna keep on goin' until you tell me."

"Please, for the love of all that is sanity, tell her your age so we can get this tent set up and eat." Tammie's voice had a gravely growl to it.

"Twenty-eight."

Tammie whirled to face Jacque. "See? I told you she was old."

"I'll have you young whippersnappers know that twenty-eight is *not* old." Joan folded her arms and stared them down.

"Would you all knock this off? Tam, Jack? This is

embarrassing! Leave her alone. Why does everything have to be about guys?"

Joan winked at her. "It's okay, Kisrie. They're just messing with me, and I'm messing with them." She stooped down to be eye-ball to eye-ball with Jacque and Tammie. "If you two busy-bodies must know, I'm still waiting to meet the right guy. It's kinda hard to find someone taller than six-three." She let out a deep guffaw.

"And that doesn't bother you at all?" Jacque asked, eyes wide.

"I'm pretty content with my life. It'll happen when it happens. When God wills." She tapped Jacque on the nose. "A lesson you need to learn, missy. The world doesn't revolve around boys."

As embarrassing as this was, the levity helped Kisrie forget her pain and the trauma of Miranda's accident. It could happen to any of them at any time. And didn't the leaders say this was the steepest descent on the whole trip? Maybe the risk factor would be much lower for the rest of the time.

A girl could hope, right?

The orange glow of firelight reflected off twelve pairs of eyes. Joan and Sharon commended the guard on how well they worked together and didn't panic when Miranda fell. Of course they did. When Keri went missing, they put aside differences and in-fighting that lost them a championship to try and find her. Sure, it resulted in Leigh Anne getting a ticket and losing driving privileges for a whole year, and a night behind bars, but the experience did make them get along. Kisrie shifted her weight from one butt cheek to the other. No matter how she sat, her body hurt. She hoped they'd wrap things up and send them all to bed.

"Now that we're in the Green River Valley, we need to have the bear and moose talk." Sharon leaned forward and rested her elbows on her knees. Her fingers hung toward the ground.

"Do we have to talk about bears in the dark? I mean, like, can't this wait until morning?" Zoe hugged herself and shuddered.

"How are moose dangerous?" Leigh Anne asked.

"Yeah. Aren't they just disproportioned deer?" Jenn let out a nervous laugh.

"Geeze. You people are so dumb." Sabrina sighed. "Moose can be more dangerous than bears."

"Enough of the commentary. If you all listen and abide by all the rules, the likelihood of an incident will be quite low. Now, it's nature we're talking about here. I can't make any promises. Animals are unpredictable, right Joan?"

"That's right, Sharon. I'm gonna demonstrate for youse guys, the use of bear spray. We have canisters for each of you. You want to keep it hooked to your shoulder strap or hip belt at all times. Take it in your tent and keep it within reach while you sleep." Joan proceeded to show them how to remove the safety clip, aim and spray. She didn't actually spray, but went through the motions several times.

"As we hike, we need to talk. We can't be mostly silent like we were today. If the bears hear us, they likely will veer away. But, if we don't properly take care of our food and smelly items, we will invite them into our camp."

"My dad and me, we heard about some hunters who were field dressing an elk outside of Dubois and a bear attacked them." Sabrina's voice had a ghost story quality to it. "They didn't have time to use the spray. All that was left was one guy's ribcage and a hand. The other guy was mostly in the bear's belly when the game wardens finally caught her."

"Oooh! Get me out of here!" Zoe hopped up and ran in

circles around the group, stumbling in the dark. "I can't! I can't do this!"

"Keep that up and you'll scare all the bears within a hundred-mile radius," Wendy said with a grunt.

Was she not afraid of bears? Kisrie felt all the hairs stand up on the back of her neck when Sabrina told her story.

Joan gave Wendy a stink-eye glare. "Zoe, we aren't going to be killing any game. We need to be bear-smart."

"That also means if any of you ladies are being visited by the lovely Aunt Flo, all of the hygiene products need to be double bagged and hung in a bear bag with all of our used toilet paper and such," Sharon added.

"Arrgh. Do we have to bring that up? Power of suggestion." Jacque put her hands on her throat and made gagging sounds.

"Grow up," Tammie barked.

"Now about moose." Sharon leaned back and stretched her arms toward the sky with a huge yawn. "Sorry. It's getting late. Anyway, moose *love* this river. We'll probably see them wading in it eating plants. They are amazingly beautiful creatures, but they can be deadly. Mama moose are super protective of their young. The female moose, or cow, doesn't have the antlers. When you see one, look for a baby. It's that time of year. If that mama feels her baby is threatened, she will charge you, front hooves a-flyin'. Your chance of survival is pretty slim. So, be aware of your surroundings."

Chrissy squinched up her face. "So, what do we do if we are attacked?"

Joan passed the bear spray from one hand to the other. "By a moose?"

"By a bear. Any kind of bear." Chrissy put her hands on her knees and leaned forward.

"For a grizzly bear you play dead. Put your hands over your head and play dead. For a black bear, you fight like hell.

Sorry about the word choice, but there is no other way to say it. For moose, be aware." Joan shielded her eyes with one hand as if gazing long distance. "If you see a mom and her baby, back away quietly. Try to be as unobtrusive as possible. When we are hiking through high brush, as we will, we will have to be extra vigilant. And sometimes, you just have to pray."

"Well, I'm prayin' we don't encounter any beasties." Jacque flicked her hair over her shoulder.

Sharon directed her fire-lit gaze at Jacque. "We all have to remember *we* are in *their* home. It's not the other way around."

Kisrie shot up a prayer asking to grow two extra pairs of eyes around her head.

"Bear, bear, bear, bear, can you hear me bear?" Zoe clutched her canister of bear spray against her chest as they descended from something Joan referred to as a saddle. It took every ounce of self-control for Wendy to not rip the red bottle out of the girl's hands and whack her over the head with it.

And then there were the songs. Tammie and Jenn started singing some stupid song about eating a baby bumblebee and puking that up. Then something about cute boys and sipping cider through a straw. Who comes up with these things? Whatever happened to good old conversation? Wouldn't that be enough to deter bears and warn moose?

Truth was, the more Wendy felt she was out of her captor's reach, the more she wanted to relax and enjoy the scenery. *And* the more she found the infantile behavior of the guard kids annoying. Even Sabrina and Brittany admitted themselves into Club Weirdo. There was no way Wendy was staying in this group when they got back. Hopefully by then Marcus and Jorge would be long gone and she could quietly finish school and go to college on scholarship as planned.

"Look! There's something in the river!" One of the girls up ahead cried out.

"It's a bull moose." Joan stopped and put her hands on her hips. "Isn't he a beauty?"

"He's not gonna kill us, is he?" Zoe asked, bear spray at the ready.

"No, he's just gonna keep an eye on us until we are out of sight. It's the females you gotta worry about."

"Hey!" Chrissy whacked Joan on the arm with the back of her hand.

Joan put her hands up as if in defense. "Hey, I'm a girl too! It's the don't-mess-with-mamma instinct we all have."

"It really is amazing out here," Tammie said. "Sharon, what river is this one?"

"The Roaring Fork."

"What about those mountains ahead?"

"That notch in the distance is Gunsight Pass. We'll be going up and through it today."

"Ohhh, not another climb!" Kisrie swayed on her feet, her face contorted as if in pain.

"It's not long, but it is quite an elevation gain. Cool thing is that when we are about two miles out from where we camp tonight, we should get a nice view of the Tetons."

Wendy'd never seen the Tetons. Because of geography class she knew where they were, but she'd never seen them. Had never really been interested in them until now. She wished she had her phone to capture the scenery all around. She found it hard to peel her eyes away from Squaretop Mountain. It reminded her of Devil's Tower as seen in that old-timey movie, *Close Encounters*. Being out in nature was doing something really weird to her insides. Like something deep inside of her wanted to be in awe of a higher power. But that would be stupid. There was no such thing as God. Scientists had all kinds of theories on how this stuff came to be, right? Ugh. These were not the kinds of thoughts she wanted to dwell on. She wanted to enjoy nature as it was in the present. Being present is what some of the counselors put an emphasis on.

Here she was, Wendy Wetz, in the middle of stunning Wyoming landscapes with crazy vibrant wildflowers, green rivers, thick forests, and rugged mountains to rival those in Colorado.

She inhaled deep through her nose.

She was alive.

She was going to get through this.

She was smart and could outsmart Marcus and Jorge.

Yeah, things were gonna work out fine. She was sure of it.

~15~

"Wakey, wakey! Rise and shine my darlings, we have another twenty-two mile day ahead of us." Sharon sang to a tune of her own making while running around camp scratching on tents. Kisrie rolled to grab the zipper.

Hmmm. That was odd...what happened to all the pain?

She unzipped and crawled out of her bag as Tammie stretched like a cat, and Jacque yawned like a hyena. There was a little stiffness, but Kisrie didn't feel like she wanted to die. In fact, the soreness in her body seemed to fade over the last three days of hiking. Hard to believe they only had two more days on the trail before they were in Yellowstone.

"Kiz, you gotta weird look on your face. You okay?" Jacque pulled off her sleeping T and fished around in her smelly clothes.

"I was just thinking. We're almost done, and my body is finally adjusting to all of this. I kinda sorta don't want it to end."

"Are you serious? Girl, I can't wait to slather myself in

moisturizer and wear enough makeup I'd need a chisel to take it off. And clean underwear?" She spread her arms and fell back, whacking Tammie in the back of the head on the way down.

"I miss flush toilets the most. I can't wait to poop and press the handle and see it go bye-bye." Tammie shuddered. "I am so sick of packing it out, even if we get to throw it all away every now and then. Trail hygiene is not my thing."

"Don't think I'm getting the results I was hoping for either." Jacque twisted to look at her rear end. "You'd think with all the steep climbs I would have achieved a Brazilian Butt by now."

"What is it with you and the Brazilian Butt lift thing?" Kisrie fished for the least offensive sock in her stash.

"High, round, and lifted. It's all over Pinterest and Instagram. You know I've decided I want to be an Instagram star, right?"

Kisrie and Tammie exchanged glances. Kisrie rolled her eyes until they hurt. Tammie folded her arms and cocked her head to the side.

"Oh. Really? And what if Instagram and Pinterest and the others are not around by the time you graduate?" Kisrie sucked her cheeks into her mouth to keep from laughing.

"This is a joke, right?" Tammie asked.

"No. I'm serious. Also, so you know, I don't have to graduate before I make millions on social media. I just need to go viral with my…idea."

Tammie looked away from Jacque. "Which is?"

Thump! Thump! Thump!

Kisrie nearly jumped out of her skin. A glance up told her someone was banging on the tent.

"Enough talking. Get out here. You three get to do breakfast with your feet tied together *and* two of you will be blindfolded." Sharon's voice penetrated the nylon of the tent.

"Look what you did, Jack. You made us late." Tammie scrambled into shorts and then yanked on mismatched socks.

"And I was determined to be the first out and ready." Kisrie huffed.

"Me? Hey, I'm trying to plan out my future here, and you two think it's some sorta joke. I'm gonna ask the group what they think."

Kisrie chuckled. "You do that, Jack. You go ahead and do that."

By the time they crawled out, the entire guard plus Wendy stood around the campfire pit looking hungry and irritated. Joan approached with rope and two bandanas which probably smelled horrid by now. Kisrie looked around for the food.

"It's still in the bear bag if you want to know," Joan said with a smirk.

"But...but—" Tammie backed away, hands up as if she were a criminal under arrest.

"We all agreed it would be interesting to add lowering the food bag to the meal prep."

"And," Sharon chimed in, "we thought pancakes would be a great breakfast before we embark on a twenty-two mile hike."

"Pancakes?" Kisrie's voice was barely a squeak. It was hard enough making them with all her limbs and vision.

Joan flipped what used to be a yellow bandana over Kisrie's eyes. It smelled of dirt and body odor. She gagged. "This thing reeks!"

"Have you seen a laundromat out here?" Joan paused. "Neither have I. And your fearless, all-knowing, all-loving, compassionate and kind leaders believe in natural consequences. You guys were *quite late* crawling out of that there tent."

"You're all best friends, right? So this should be a piece of cake," Sharon said.

"Ow! You got my hair." Jacque hollered from somewhere nearby.

Tammie must be the lucky one who didn't have to be blindfolded.

From all the elbowing, knee-wiggling, and jockeying around as both leaders tied them together, Kisrie wondered if their friendship could survive this ordeal.

Wendy picked a pine needle and some small rocks from the blackened blob that was *supposed* to be a pancake. Kisrie and her weird little friends messed up breakfast like no one imagined it could be messed up.

But it was all they had before a long, twenty-two and a half mile hike to some place called Fox Park.

As wondrous as the scenery was, Wendy was feeling quite tired. She didn't have the fat stores Kisrie did. It seems like as everyone else wore out, Kisrie grew stronger. Plus, she missed sleeping on a soft bed and taking showers. When she got back to civilization she planned on taking four a day—or however many it would take to get rid of this rank trail smell that permeated everything she had.

"I can't eat this." Chrissy balanced her bowl on a knee and waved her spoon in the air.

"Think of it as trail spice." Joan shoveled a whole blackened mass into her mouth and chewed with vigor. Her eyes twitched and she forced a smile. "Eelishus."

Jenn frowned. "It would taste better with some kind of syrup."

"Hey, it's not my fault the syrup powder spilled all over the ground. Kisrie knocked the skillet into the fire while I was trying to pour it *blindfolded* into a cup. So gimme a break." Zoe smacked her bowl on her knee.

"And the good news is that somehow, you three managed to pull off a…somewhat…edible breakfast." Sharon pulled a wad of dirt out of her bowl and flicked it into the fire.

"You guys are gonna have to scrape up that dirt with the powder in it and pack it out. Bears." Joan said before stuffing her face with more food.

"We hafta pack out dirt?" Jacque let out a squeal and tipped her head back as far as it could go.

"Bears are really active out here. There was a solo backpacker who got eaten on this trail a month ago."

"This trail?" Zoe's Scandinavian skin lightened a few more shades until Wendy thought she could see the girl's veins running like blue highways on a map under the surface.

"Haven't you been paying attention?" Leigh Anne finished her breakfast in one last bite and then followed it with a huge swig from her Nalgene bottle.

Zoe looked at the canister of bear spray tucked into her left arm pit. "I pay so much attention, I sometimes feel like my eyeballs are gonna fall out of my head."

"Well, we only have today and tomorrow for the big hiking, so as we pack up, I want you ladies to think on some things." Sharon set her cup, bowl, and spoon on the ground and brushed her hands on her pants. "I'd say, for the most part, we've all had what some call a peak experience. And you all need to know it's quite normal to feel a let-down after finishing an intense program such as this one. I believe you all are much closer than you were before this trip. I also think you work together much better…for the most part." She gave a sideways glance at Kisrie, Jacque, and Tammie. "It's true we will have several days in Yellowstone National Park to see the most amazing sites like Old Faithful, West Thumb, the Grand Canyon of the Yellowstone, Norris Geyser Basin, and more if we can fit it in. But it will be different than being on the trail. We'll be at an established campsite and there will be a van waiting for us when we get to Heart Lake tomorrow."

Brittany scratched her head and looked at Wendy who shrugged. She wished Sharon would just shut up and let them get on the trail. In some ways she was looking forward to being done, but in others, she wasn't. Even with bears and moose, Wendy felt much safer out here than back home in Denver where her former captors could pop up anywhere. She sure hoped Detective Arbuckle and the cops caught Marcus and Jorge by now.

"...such as depression are common." Sharon droned on as she continued her spiel about the letdown after the program.

What if things weren't safe in Denver?

What if they got away again?

What if they got to Zena while Wendy was out in the middle of nowhere?

If Zena was okay, Wendy decided she would convince the woman to come up here and stay in some isolated cabin like the one near Brooks Lake. If the pimps came up here, the bears could eat them.

"...important to recognize the signs of depression and have a plan..."

Did Yellowstone have phone service? Maybe someone at the campground would let her borrow their cell to call Zena and beg her to stay in Wyoming.

"...want you to think about ways you can help each other if someone in this group finds herself struggling with depression. Now, pack up!"

The hike started out in a sagebrush meadow. Wendy loved running her fingers through the gray-green leaves and smelling her fingertips. There was something refreshing about the scent. She also liked the way the sage smelled when the sun hit it. Wow. Look at her. Turning into Wilderness Wendy. She let a laugh escape. Been a long time since she did that for real.

"Hey, look at this print. That's a really big dog." Leigh Anne stood in the middle of the trail blocking traffic pointing.

Joan scooted through pack-laden girls to take a look. "That's no dog. It's a wolf."

"W…wolves?" Zoe pulled the bear spray from her pack strap.

"They were introduced to Yellowstone back in the late 1900s." Joan let out a short laugh. "Sharon, did you hear that? Late 1900s? We were born in that century. Makes me feel kinda old."

"Sorry to break it to ya, girlfriend, but we're both old."

"Anyway, the gray wolf was introduced into the ecosystem to help control the deer population and bring balance. Problem was and still is, that the original wolf was the timber wolf. A much smaller variety. These gray wolves are from Canada and have thrived beyond all expectations. They are now migrating out of the park and causing problems for ranchers. Now, before you guys get all twitterpated, wolves tend to steer clear of people. That's why seeing one in the park is so rare. But *how cool is this?*" She knelt and put her fingers in the print.

"We're walking among wolves," Kisrie said, her eyes sparkling in the sunlight.

"Think of all the stories youse guys will have when you get back to your school and band."

They trudged on. Wildflowers exploded in bright colors all around them. The leaders pointed out goldenrod, thistle, larkspur, fire weed and others as they came upon them. Until this trip, Wendy had no idea how many flowers could just grow. It wasn't like someone came out here and planted them.

"Hey, let's stop for a second. I want to point something out." Sharon motioned for the group to circle up. She waited until they were all in place, then pointed down toward another meadow. "See all those bare trees? It's from the massive fire in Yellowstone back in 1988. There were eighteen lightning strikes that were allowed to burn out because they assumed the average rainfall would put them out. Well, that didn't happen.

Instead, they had dry weather and high winds. It blew up out of control. Over ten-thousand people were involved in fighting those fires. My dad was one of them."

. "How much of the park did it burn?" Sabrina asked.

"They estimate a half a million acres."

Gasps erupted like geysers though the group.

"You'll be seeing evidence of that fire from over thirty years ago throughout the park."

"Now you guys know why we are so intent on dousing our campfires and making sure they are out, out, out."

Wendy couldn't help herself. "I thought you were being annoying."

"If it prevents forest fires." Joan flashed her a toothy grin.

"We need to keep moving." Sharon took off at a brisk pace.

Over the course of the day they crossed the Continental Divide and caught a mind-blowing view of the Tetons. Wendy assumed they'd be like the mountains she saw every day in Colorado, but she couldn't have been more wrong. These were so tall. So rugged. They had an imposing presence unlike anything she'd seen.

By the time they reached camp that evening Wendy could not wait to take off her boots and let her feet dry. There were so many water crossings her poor feet never had a chance to dry off.

"You know, it's kinda crazy that we can set up camp in like five minutes now, and we're almost done." Brittany set the last stake and pounded it in with a rock.

"I'm gonna miss this. It's more fun to be with a bunch of girls than with guys hunting," Sabrina said, tossing the stuff sack with her sleeping bag into the tent. "What about you, Wen? I'm kind of surprised you did so well."

Wendy felt her eyebrows rise up into her hairline. "What's that supposed to mean?"

Sabrina blushed and didn't meet Wendy's eyes. "Uh, well, I was thinking you'd be all mad like you usually are and, uh, sabotage things."

"I'm not always mad."

"Yeah you are." Brittany ducked out of the way as Wendy picked up a small rock and tossed it in Brittany's general direction.

"See? That was mean." Sabrina fished in the pocket of her shorts. "I hate not having my lip gloss with me."

"If you two must know, I like it out here. In fact, I want to stay here."

Brittany's jaw dropped. She used her hand to close her mouth. "How come? It's pretty and all, but there's no movie theatres, and restaurants, and malls. You know—all the important stuff."

"I have my reasons."

"You're worried about the kidnappers aren't you?" Sabrina moved closer. "It is! I know it. You're really worried they'll come back for you, aren't ya?"

"Can we drop this conversation?"

"No. Britt and I are your friends. We always have been, but you always hold us at arm's length. You've done stuff for us over the years, why don't you let us help you?"

Wendy gritted her teeth until her jaw ached. "I don't need your help."

"Look, Wen, this whole trip, it's all about trust an' all. Why don't you open up and trust us like we do you? It's only fair." Brittany swiped a strand of greasy hair out of her left eye.

"I got myself into this mess, I'll get myself out. Just like the other times." Wendy turned to leave.

"You mean Mr. Plank?" Sabrina's voice was a lasso that cinched around her, stopping her in her tracks.

She turned in a slow circle to face her friends. "What about Mr. Plank?"

"We lied for you."

"And I took that picture of Tammie when she was all naked after swimming." Brittany shuddered. "I hated doing that, you know."

A curse flew from Wendy's mouth. "Why are you bringing this up now?"

Sabrina stepped up until they were nose to nose. "Maybe because the whole Mr. Plank thing really messed with us? You act like it was no big deal. Heck, you practically got away with freaking *murder.*"

In a flash, Wendy's arms shot out and slammed Sabrina in the chest knocking her to her butt. She opened and closed her mouth like a fish out of water. Wendy leaned over her and hissed. "I didn't *murder* anyone."

"So you're pretty much sayin' you aren't sorry." Brittany stood behind her, arms folded. Eyes narrowed and glittering with a hardness Wendy didn't know the girl was capable of.

Was she?

Sorry?

"He might still be alive if... " Brittany tapped her wet boot in the dirt and let the end of the sentence hang.

"I don't need to listen to any of this. Just leave me alone." A fury bomb exploded in her chest. If she didn't do something she'd probably haul off and break Brittany's nose.

Run.

That was it.

Maybe running off this anger would bring her back to a functional state. She never actually tried it before, but it seemed like a good idea. Maybe now was the time to see if it helped for reals. She turned on her heel and took off toward the Snake River which lay below them. She just needed a few minutes, that was all.

"You forgot your bear spray!" Brittany called after her, but Wendy ignored it and kept going. The way she crashed through the brush and skidded down the incline caused more than enough warning for a grizzly.

And to be honest? They hadn't seen as much as a bear track.

She'd be fine.

~16~

Tears rolled down her cheeks as she thrashed through willows and other scratchy things. Red streaks covered Wendy's arms and legs but she didn't care. She didn't really feel it.

Her breath came in short bursts as her lungs ached from the effort. This was what she needed. Who would've guessed that after hiking over twenty miles, she still had energy to burn? Wendy let out a laugh as she used her arms to push through some thorny tree things.

Why did they have to bring up Mr. Plank?

Zena never brought it up, and she was his wife.

The word *was* hit Wendy in the chest like a cannon ball. She slowed to a stop.

It was suicide.

She wasn't in the car when he drove if off Lookout Mountain.

But did he do it because of her lies about him?

Wendy plopped to the ground and swatted at the swarm of mosquitoes that whined and buzzed all around her head. She thought back to the day it all started. The day he handed her that stupid paper. That paper with a bad grade and that bad grade threatened to jeopardize her ability to compete in a pageant for an academic scholarship.

It felt like a hundred years ago. Was it really this past fall?

Wendy wrapped her arms around herself and pulled her knees to her chest.

He refused to be reasonable about it.

What other recourse did she have?

Revenge and threats worked so well for her in the past. She always got what she wanted—always. So what changed?

"Wendy?" Joan's voice traveled in ribbons on the evening breeze. Great. Last thing she needed was to explain to the leaders what the fight was about and why she ran off into quintessential bear country without her spray.

She ignored her. Maybe if she didn't answer, the leader would go away.

Joan called a few more times, but all of a sudden, the tone changed. It went from a call to a warning.

"Wendy."

It scared her a little.

She cursed to herself.

If there was a bear, what would she do? Was she supposed to fight or play dead? Ugh! She couldn't remember.

"Wendy, if you're nearby and hear me, don't move."

Panic rose in her chest.

Stupid! Stupid! Stupid!

Despair filled her chest with an ache so deep she thought she would suffocate. Were her friends right about Mr. Plank? That he'd be alive if she kept her sorry mouth shut? She sucked in a stuttering breath. Maybe it was time for penance. Maybe she should let the bear have her. She'd rather a grizzly consume her for his dinner than Marcus consume her body in the most vile way.

Closing her eyes, she pushed up to her feet. She held her arms stretched out to the sides. *Come at me bear. Make me one with the nature around me.*

There was a snorty-grunt sound and sudden crashing.

This was it. She held her breath.

"Wendy!" Joan screamed her name so loud her voice cracked. In about five seconds something collided with her, knocking her to the ground.

"Joan! Wendy!" Sharon's voice called from not too far away.

Wendy squeezed her eyes tighter waiting for the first bite, but someone grabbed her arms and dragged her. She opened her eyes to see Sharon's face above her, then looked over her feet in time to see a giant moose without antlers rise up on her hind legs and box at Joan.

"No!" She wrestled from Sharon's grip. This was not what was supposed to happen. *She* was supposed to be eaten by a bear, but it was a moose, and Joan came after her and now she...she...

Joan put her arms over her head, but it was no use. The moose clocked her hard in the temple. There was a spray of red.

Sharon dropped Wendy and rushed into the fray, arms waving above her head. "Shoo! Leave her alone!"

A smaller moose appeared behind Wendy. It looked at her with liquid espresso eyes, then dipped its head to bite a leaf off a shrub thing.

"Wendy, get away from there. Get back to camp and get the first aid kit. Go!" Sharon's voice trembled, but was louder than normal.

Wendy crab-walked backwards away from the baby, her heart hammering at her ribs. As soon as she was about fifty feet away, she scrambled to her feet and took off running toward camp. There was no time to think. She had to get help. She hoped Sharon could scare the moose away.

Kisrie dropped an armload of wood next to the fire ring. She rubbed her hands together and looked at Sabrina and Brittany who sat back to back on a rock all sullen and silent. "Could you guys at least tell me what happened?" They confided in her before, why not again?

Sabrina shook her head.

"We don't want to cause no more trouble." Brittany traced circles in the dirt with her finger.

A crashing noise sounded a ways outside camp. The hairs on the back of Kisrie's neck stood at attention. "Do you hear that?"

"Grab your bear spray!" Zoe called, diving for hers which was never more than a foot away from her person.

The entire color guard scattered and armed themselves with the red canisters. They all pulled off the safety and stood in a line, spray pointed at the noises growing louder by the second.

"Hold 'em steady girls, and take aim." Jacque barked out the order then giggled a nervous giggle. "I've always wanted to say something like that."

"This isn't funny. We could all die." Zoe wasn't having any of it. If looks could kill, Jacque'd be dead a thousand times over.

"I've never known bears to sound like that," Tammie said.

"How do you know what sounds bears make?" Jacque widened her stance.

There was a yowl that sounded borderline human. Kisrie tightened her grip. Her pointer finger on the trigger.

Wendy burst from the brush at the edge of the meadow, her mouth open in a huge capital O shape. Tears streamed down her face.

Then she skidded to a halt. Her eyes grew super-wide and she raised her hands. "Don't shoot me, but bring those. Joan got attacked by a moose and Sharon is trying to fend her off."

Kisrie's stomach plummeted to her knees. A wave of nausea crashed over her. "Whoever is closest to Joan's pack, grab the first aid kit. Also, we need our head lamps. The sun is going down."

In less than a minute, the guard sprinted behind Wendy who ran like a bat out of a very hot place. Joan told them few people survived moose attacks. And how in the world did it happen?

Wendy stopped. Everyone piled up behind her. "I… I…it…they should be around here…somewhere."

"I don't hear anything," Jenn said.

There was a pause of about a minute. "I don't either." Leigh Anne's voice broke into a sob.

This was bad. Very bad.

Wendy cupped her hands to her mouth. "Sharon, Joan! Where are you? Please answer."

Nothing.

Each girl took turns calling.

Nothing.

"I think we need to split up and spread out like spokes on a wheel or something like that. I think we've made enough noise to scare any bears and we do have our spray. I hope it works on moose." Sabrina motioned with her hand for everyone to circle up. "Now let's all face out and go straight out from where we are."

"What do we do if we…" Jenn let the sentence trail off.

Kisrie switched the first aid kit from one shoulder to the other. "Stay put and call out until we all show up."

"Okay. On the count of three." Sabrina counted and they moved in their separate directions calling for Joan and Sharon.

About five minutes out, a blood-curdling scream split the

cooling evening air. Kisrie couldn't tell who it was, but from the frantic, hysterical tone, she knew it wasn't good. She turned, nearly poking her eye out on a branch, then jogged toward the cries.

When she arrived at the scene, her stomach heaved. Chrissy was on her knees keening at the sky. Wendy came up behind Kisrie and fell to the ground wailing. The others arrived one by one and each girl handled the grisly scene differently. But before she did another thing, Kisrie needed to know there wasn't a moose nearby. She scanned the brush.

Nothing.

She stood frozen, trying to make sense of the mess in front of her.

"Kiz, you have the first aid kit," Tammie whispered.

Yeah. She did.

But would it do any good?

Everyone kept a distance from the leaders laying on the blood-soaked ground.

"Zoe, you're one of the captains." She hoped the older girl would take charge, but instead she backed away from the scene, shaking her head.

Brittany and Sabrina knelt next to Wendy, rubbing her back, trying to console her.

Kisrie shot up a prayer asking for help, then took one step forward.

Then another.

Until she was next to the leaders. She had to force her eyes to focus. Joan wasn't recognizable from the trauma to her head. Sharon had a gash on her forehead and her right arm was at an awkward angle. "Sh...Sharon?"

A faint groan came from her lips.

"Oh, dear Lord, she's still alive!" Kisrie dropped to her knees and put her finger on Joan's wrist in search of a pulse. Could she have survived?

Nothing.

She put her fingertips to her own neck to find where the pulse should be, then took a deep breath and placed them on Joan's throat which was slick with blood.

Nothing.

Hot tears blurred her vision.

Dead.

The word sent a chill up her spine.

But Sharon was alive. Kisrie needed to act fast.

"I need help over here. I'm not really versed in first aid."

Tammie dropped next to her. "I'm not for reals, but I've read some books on medical stuff. I think we need to stop the bleeding."

"But what about getting help? We're over twenty miles from anywhere." Jenn's voice rose a full step in tone with every word.

"Oh, what are we gonna do? What are we gonna do?" Leigh Anne gripped her braids and wandered in circles.

"Didn't... didn't Joan say something about shock when Miranda fell a few days ago?" Chrissy wiped her face with her t-shirt. "Maybe we start there? I think he put something over her to keep her warm, and then you're supposed to elevate either the head or feet."

"I think it's the feet." Tammie pulled her shirt off over her head, rolled it up and put it under Sharon's feet.

Sharon opened one eye and looked directly at Kisrie. "J...J..." She couldn't get the word out, but Kisrie sensed she was asking about Joan.

Kisrie's chin trembled and a tear ran down her cheek and splashed on Sharon's face. Sharon closed her eye. Tears forced their way out onto her swollen face and traced a trail in the dirt and blood.

"We're gonna get you out of here." How? Kisrie didn't know, but isn't that what one says to someone who's been hurt in the woods?

"We need to make a splint for her arm."

"I see that, Tammie, but I think I need to stop the bleeding on her head." She opened the first aid kit and pulled out gauze and tape. What did Mom do when she or Keri got a cut? Put pressure on it and a band aid. But neither one of them ever had a cut this big. Kisrie leaned in closer. She could see bone. Her stomach bucked and lurched. This was way worse than anything she knew how to deal with.

It was something doctors needed to operate on. So what to do?

She looked at the gauze again. Something in her gut caused her to grab a few squares, tear them open and press them on the wound.

Now what?

"Tammie, can you hold this?" Tammie's hand replaced hers.

There was a roll of gauze. Maybe she should wrap that around Sharon's head to hold the bandage in place.

"It's getting dark." Chrissy shivered and looked around.

"Maybe we should send Brit, Sabs, and Wendy back to camp to get the fire going and dinner. We're gonna have to figure out what to do." Zoe somehow managed to pull herself together, yet stood far enough away to not have to take in the details.

"Can you get them to do that? We need to figure out how to get them," Kisrie nodded her head to the leaders, "back to camp.

Sharon opened her eye again. "L...leave...us."

"No. No way. Bears will get you both."

"Joan then." Sharon's breathing was shallow and labored.

The weight of what she said hit Kisrie like a wrecking ball to the chest. She looked at Tammie in the near darkness. Tammie looked away and sighed. A headlamp dropped into her lap.

"Figured you guys would need these," Jacque said in a small, high voice.

"She has a head injury for sure and those are bad." Tammie

166

grabbed her headlamp and put it on her head but didn't turn it on. She then reached for Sharon's legs and felt up and down each one. "I don't feel anything weird. Maybe with help she can walk."

"Well, let me finish wrapping her head, and we need to at least tie her arm to her body to keep it still. It looks broken."

"We need to move quick because bears will be drawn to the smell of all this blood, and I'm also getting really cold since I don't have a shirt on."

Jenn bent over Kisrie. "We all have our bear spray. We can make a defense ring around you until you're ready to try and move her."

All kinds of scary scenarios crowded into Kisrie's mind, but she pushed them away. A strange peace spread over her like a warm electric blanket. Her head was clearer than usual. "Sharon, I got your head all wrapped up. Tammie and Chrissy are gonna bind your arm to you and that may hurt when they move it. But I need to know if you can walk."

"Uh huh." Sharon's voice was weak, but she was still conscious. Kisrie remembered back to the fall when Wendy had those thugs beat her up. She suffered a head injury and the doctors were glad she didn't pass out. Maybe there was hope for Sharon if she could stay awake.

"Sharon, whatever you do, I need you to stay awake."

Sharon grunted in what Kisrie hoped was an affirmative reply.

Footsteps crunched close. "Those three are headed back," Zoe said.

"I think we're gonna need a couple more shirts. Kisrie, don't take this the wrong way, but yours would be great because it is kind of big." Tammie's teeth started to chatter.

Kisrie grabbed the hemline of her T and pulled the 2XL Santa Clara Vanguard shirt off over her head. The cold air hit her skin, and she erupted in goosepimples.

"Here's mine." Jacque flung hers down.

"And mine." Chrissy tossed her Blue Knights shirt into the mix.

"I need light." Tammie flicked on her headlamp.

"Would you look at us?" Kisrie could see the pale torsos reflected in the light. "We're in the middle of nowhere in our bras."

"Anywhere else, and we'd all be arrested." Jacque let out a short laugh. "Is it okay to make a funny when…when…"

"We'll have time to let it get to us when we get back," Tammie said while tying the shirts together. "I think this will go around her. I put Kisrie's shirt in the middle hoping it can kinda be a sling."

"You girls…doing good…job." Sharon licked her lips.

"I wish I had water. It sounds like you could use some," Jenn said from in the darkness.

"Alright, Chrissy and I are going to try and sling you. Kisrie's going to see if she can get you to sit up."

Sharon grunted.

"Just do it, Kiz."

The light flashed in Kisrie's eyes, blinding her for a moment. She had to feel around behind Sharon's shoulders. Once she had her hands on the leader's back, she pulled her up. Sharon yelped.

Tammie and Chrissy worked fast. "I think we can try to stand her up." Tammie got on one side and Kisrie the other. "Chrissy, spot her back and help Kiz and me if we need it. On the count of three…one…two…three."

Kisrie pushed up with her legs, hands wedged in Sharon's armpits. She hoped she didn't make the arm injury worse. In one fluid motion, they had Sharon on her feet, supported between her and Tammie.

"My head." Sharon slipped forward and dry-heaved.

"Let's move." Tammie took a step forward.

Kisrie matched her friend's steps. "Good thing we're guard girls and are used to being in step."

The rest of the guard made a tight circle around them, making sure the way was well lit and obstacles were moved out of their path. Kisrie tried real hard not to think of Joan's body lying where the moose attacked her. She hoped she didn't mind they had to leave her there.

But she wasn't *really* there. Kisrie knew that. Joan had the same faith she did. She was probably looking down from Heaven, praying for Sharon and the team. But the knowledge of that didn't make this any easier or less traumatic.

"I can smell the smoke from the campfire. We're almost there," Leigh Anne called from somewhere ahead.

Good. She and Tammie were practically dragging Sharon along. She was so weak.

Finally, they arrived at the camp. Brittany poked the fire with a stick as Sabrina stirred a pot of something that was dehydrated prior to having water added to it.

"I got Sharon's sleeping bag all set up in her tent." Sabrina lifted the spoon out of the pot and took a taste. "It's ready."

"Brittany, can you bring it out here? I think we should keep her somewhat sitting up and keep a fire going all night. I think I read somewhere that if a person has a concussion, they need to be woken up every hour or something like that." Tammie led them all toward the fire.

"Hey, you guys don't got shirts on." Brittany shielded her eyes with her hand and blinked against the light from the headlamps.

Once they got Sharon settled, Kisrie and the other shirtless guardlings ran to their packs to put on some warm layers. It sure got cold at night in Wyoming.

At first, no one said much. Kisrie was hungrier than she'd ever been before in her life, and it seemed that was the case with the others as well. No one said a word as the pot of reconstituted pasta was passed around. Kisrie decided it was best if she focused on her stomach and the food so she'd have the strength to do what needed to be done. She knew she couldn't think clearly on an empty stomach. And now that they were leaderless, they all had to be at the top of their game physically—and mentally. Kisrie whispered a prayer of thanks for the food and asked for help in figuring out the next steps. She dipped her food in and took a bite. The "lasagna" tasted better than she expected.

When the group finished eating, the pot was scraped clean as were all bowls. Tammie wasn't able to get Sharon to eat anything, but managed to get a sip or two of water in her.

In the glow of the firelight, someone sniffled.

Then someone else.

It wasn't long before the dam of emotions broke and everyone grieved the situation in a tearful, snotty mess. Joan was a great leader. She may have been goofy and eccentric, but she encouraged Kisrie in ways she longed for most of her life. Joan believed in her.

Like her cousin Meghan.

Like her Uncle Evan.

Who were also dead.

And Uncle Evan wouldn't have been dead unless...

Wendy.

Where was Wendy? Kisrie wiped her eyes with the back of her hand and peered around the fire ring. No sign of her.

Part of her was glad. It seemed like wherever Wendy went, destruction followed. Even poor Keri faced life in a wheelchair all because of Wendy.

Joan and Sharon wouldn't have gone into the brush near the river if Wendy hadn't run off.

To sum it all up, people Kisrie cared about died because of Wendy.

If Wendy stole away again, then good riddance! No one

would go after her this time. She could face the bears and moose on her own. Would serve her right.

～17～

They were all back now. Wendy could see the warm glow of the fire through the tent fabric. No one said much. She heard a lot of crying—something she'd been doing non-stop since she crawled into the tent. Never in her life had she shed as many tears or felt so much remorse.

Forget Mr. Plank, Joan's death *was* her fault. As were Sharon's injuries...and Keri's.

The girl who used to be in charge of her own destiny now flubbed up her own death which resulted in someone else's. Someone innocent and undeserving.

She really liked Joan.

She was honorable, loyal, and kind.

Everything Wendy was *not*.

Now what was going to happen? How were they going to get out of these woods? What about Sharon? They were far from anywhere.

Oh no. No. If they didn't come out at Heart Lake as

expected by the people who ran the wilderness program, they would be deemed missing.

A group of high school girls missing in the wilderness of Wyoming outside of Yellowstone in grizzly country would make the news—national news.

Which meant…Marcus…Jorge…Unique…any or all of them could see it and know where she was. And if they found her with the others—no. She could not bring any more harm to this group. Oddly, they kind of accepted her and treated her with respect. Her way of paying them back was to disappear in the night so no one would follow and meet the same fate Joan did.

Which meant she had to go out there and pretend she was part of whatever plan they came up with.

She unzipped the tent and crawled out.

"Kiz, are you okay? You're breathing funny and you have this creepy look on your face." Jacque asked, poking Kisrie in the arm. Wendy crept up on them.

"Has anyone seen Wendy?" Kisrie's voice was low—almost guttural. Her words came out slow and measured.

Wendy cleared her throat. "I'm right here."

Kisrie gasped and turned around. Orange light flickered on her face. Her eyebrows hunched low over her eyes, and her mouth was turned down in a fierce scowl. Jacque was right. Kisrie did look creepy.

"I'm so…c…cold." Sharon's voice was weak and trembly. Wendy pushed between Jacque and Kisrie to get to the leader. She dropped to the ground and pulled Sharon up against her, just like Sharon did for her a few nights ago.

"I'm here. I'll help keep you warm." More tears formed in Wendy's eyes, and the fire distorted and swam before her.

"Don't you think you've caused enough trouble?" Kisrie snapped.

"Kiz, stop. We don't have time for that. We need to figure

out what to do. It's what Joan and Sharon would want. Us to work as a team to get out of this wilderness alive." Jenn twisted her hair through her hand over and over again.

Zoe asked, "Sabrina, you've been hunting and stuff before. Do you have any ideas?"

"Uh, not really. We had ATVs and stuff. We weren't a hundred miles from nowhere like this."

"I think you guys need to get to Yellowstone as planned. Maybe you can get help for Sharon there," Wendy suggested hoping if they showed up as planned, it would keep them out of the news and off Marcus' radar.

Tammie held a book in her hands. She flicked on her headlamp, which illuminated the page. "According to Joan's trail guide, tomorrow's hike is over twenty-six miles." She let that sit for a few moments. "Today we did twenty-two. It would be shorter to go back. There's a campground not far from the trail. The book says it's the Turpin Meadow Campground and it's popular. We are sure to run into someone who can help."

"But can we get Sharon that far? Should some of us stay here with her while the fastest hikers go get help?" Chrissy asked.

Zoe put up her hands. "Stay here? Bears will probably be drawn to here because...you know."

"She has a point." Leigh Anne poked at the fire.

"Well, the twenty-six miles is an easier hike than the one we did today, according to this guide." Tammie held it up to show the elevation profile. "But, to be honest, I don't know if Sharon can walk twenty miles on a flat road let alone out here. And we can't carry her." Tammie paused and looked up at the sky. "What if we split it up into several days? Whatever route we choose to go, what if we take a couple days instead of one?"

"I...I don't know. Her head is hurt real bad and what if it gets infected, or her brain swells or something?"

Wendy thought Chrissy had a point. Get out and get out fast. "If the trail is easier to Yellowstone, then go that way. We can make a stretcher of some kind. If we take turns carrying it, we could make good time—especially if we leave a bunch of our stuff behind."

"But what if Heart Lake is far from roads or any kind of cell service?"

Tammie looked at Jenn then down at the book. "Says right here there is parking at the trailhead. But that doesn't help us if there's not cell coverage. I've heard there's only two places in Yellowstone where you can get service. Mammoth Springs and Old Faithful."

"But we don't have any cell phones," Chrissy said.

Tammie poked at the fire with a stick. "We can find someone and ask. We have an emergency situation here."

An idea struck Wendy. "What if the leaders have phones hidden in their packs, for emergencies of something? We can ask Sharon, or if she's sleeping, we can look through their stuff." They *had* to make it to the vans meeting them at Heart Lake tomorrow. "How far away are those places from where we come out? And won't there be someone waiting for us with a van?" Wendy couldn't hide the urgency in her voice. They *had* to keep on schedule.

Everyone looked around at one another. No one had been to Yellowstone before, it seemed.

It was settled then. She had to disappear.

"Given our circumstances, and the probability of bears coming near, I think we need to take turns staying awake all night. We need to keep the fire going, keep waking Sharon every hour, and sit with our bear spray at the ready." Kisrie looked around the group. "Maybe half of us can sleep while the other half stays awake and then we switch."

Panic fluttered in Wendy's chest like a startled crow. Not only were they not gonna exit the trail on time, now they planned on having some kind of night watch which would make it impossible for her to sneak away. Maybe *she* could volunteer to be on night watch and let the others sleep.

Tammie spoke next. "I agree with Kisrie, but we still need to figure out what to do in the morning."

It was decided that Zoe, Leigh Anne, Jenn, and Chrissy would leave at the crack of dawn and backtrack to that Turpin Campground place. Most everyone figured people in Yellowstone would be unwilling to help because they were on vacation and probably spent a ton of money to get there and stay there. Last thing anyone would want is to waste a day helping a bunch of teenagers and an injured adult. People at Turpin were probably locals and would know how to help.

The rest of the group was to backtrack as close to five miles as they could get. They wanted distance between Joan's body and bears and needed to find a place to set up camp where it wasn't so exposed in case they had to wait a day or two.

Wendy figured if and when she escaped, she would have to go sideways. When the news story broke about them all missing in the woods, Marcus would be able to start at Heart Lake and work his way backwards. He wouldn't anticipate her expecting him. She had to get way, way off the trail. She also needed to find a way to make sure she got a chance to go through Joan and Sharon's packs for extra food or gear she might need to survive in the wilderness for a bit.

"So, who's gonna take the first shift? Maybe we switch in three hours?" Kisrie twirled a curl around her finger.

"How're we gonna know three hours passed? We had to leave watches and phones behind," Sabrina said.

Wendy felt down Sharon's arm which was tucked in her sleeping bag. She was sure the leader wore some kind of watch thing. Aha! The leader had one on her left wrist. "Sharon has a watch."

Sharon shifted against Wendy. "Take…it." She pulled her arm out and held it up to Wendy. It was a simple watch with hands. Too bad it wasn't one of those Apple watches. Both Joan and Sharon seemed to prefer to do things the old way—guidebooks and maps instead of GPS devices and smart phones. Being the twenty-first century, Wendy figured there *had* to be an app for hiking the Continental Divide Trail.

"It's ten thirty," Wendy announced as she unbuckled the watch strap.

"Eleven-thirty, twelve-thirty, one-thirty…we will change at one-thirty and then again at…" Kisrie held up her hand and counted on her fingers. "…four-thirty."

"Why don't we go until two-thirty which will put the second shift ending at five-thirty which will put us close to dawn?"

"That's not a bad idea, Chrissy. Now who will stay up from now until two-thirty?"

"I will." Wendy looked down at Sharon. "I want to stay with her for a while." Maybe during the shift change she could grab some extra stuff.

"Britt and I will stay up with Wendy." Sabrina said.

"I'm not tired. I'll stay up. I'll rehang the bear bags." Chrissy stood up and brushed off her legs. "Zoe, you wanna stay with me and help?"

Zoe nodded and joined Chrissy. Kisrie and the others got up and headed to their tents to get a little bit of sleep.

"Come on Brittany, we need to get more wood if we are gonna keep this fire going all night." Sabrina switched on her headlamp and hooked her bear spray in her pants. Brittany did the same. Wendy found herself alone with Sharon.

"I'm so sorry," she whispered into Sharon's blood-matted hair which stuck up above the gauze wrapping Kisrie put on.

"It's not your…fault."

Wendy reached for a nearby water bottle and held it to the

leader's lips. Sharon took a small sip. Closing her eyes, Wendy took a deep breath to fight the swirling feelings of grief, anger, and panic. She had to stay in control. "That moose came after me. Joan knocked me out of the way…" Her control wavered. She couldn't finish her sentence. Death came at her and Joan took her place.

Why?

"Head hurts. Need sleep."

"Go to sleep. I'll wake you in an hour." Wendy put the watch on her wrist so she could keep track of time. She looked at the sky and wondered if she could count the stars shining so bright in the night. At least it would give her something to do to keep her mind from thinking about what happened.

Kisrie followed Jacque and Tammie into the tent. The circle of light from her headlamp passed over the dark blue fabric of Joan's sleeping bag. She froze.

"You okay?" Tammie turned her light off and looked at Kisrie.

She shook her head. She wasn't okay. If she opened her mouth she'd start crying—again. Images of Joan's wide grin, her sense of humor, her use of 'youse guys,' filled her mind.

Jacque stretched out next to her and draped an arm across her back. "I don't want to go to sleep. It's like every time I close my eyes I see..." Her voice trailed off and a sob rose from her throat. It was a few moments before she continued on. "I never saw a dead person before, and I don't know if I can ever get that image out of my mind. I want to remember Joan as she was before."

Tammie mirrored Jacque on the other side of Kisrie. "Same."

The three of them laid in silence for a while. Kisrie tried

to remember that first really hard day where Joan encouraged her over and over again. When she was with her she felt...human—like she was worth something. Joan showed her she could do far more than she imagined. "Joan was a Christian, you know." She hoped that would help her friends. It was the one seed of comfort she held on to herself.

"I figured she was." Tammie's voice was muffled.

"Me too."

Kisrie's back started to ache. She pushed up onto her elbows then rolled over. "Right now I'm really struggling with hating Wendy like I've never hated her before. I thought I was doing better since we came on this trip, but now...I mean, you guys, if she didn't run off like that, Joan would still be here."

"Kiz, being mad isn't gonna help you, or any of us in this situation. You're the one that keeps reminding us that Wendy and Keri went through some stuff we can't imagine. Don't people like that have PTSD? Wendy's had some moments on this trip where she wigged out over nothing. I don't think she meant for Joan to get hurt."

"Yeah. What Tammie said."

"But she got mad at Brittany and Sabrina."

"Still. It doesn't matter. It was an accident. She didn't have the moose on remote control."

Jacque snickered. "A remote controlled moose. Where do you come up with this stuff, Tam?"

"I'm also really worried about Sharon. I know what it's like to have a head injury. Mine wasn't half as bad as hers, and I had to spend days in the hospital. What if she doesn't make it? What if we can't save her?" Kisrie's heart beat faster and her breathing tubes seemed to shrink down to the size of the stir sticks her mother used for coffee.

Tammie propped up on an elbow. "We can only do our best. Hopefully those fast girls can get to the campground before nightfall, and even if it's later, there's got to be people there who can help. I bet we only have to stick it out one day at the most. I'm sure another helicopter will come for Sharon and she'll be just fine."

Something snapped about a hundred yards away. All the muscles in Kisrie's body tightened. "Did you hear that?" she whispered.

There was a snort and a low growl.

Jacque grabbed her arm and squeezed. "Oh my word, it's a bear!"

At the sound of the growl, Wendy felt as if all the air in the universe was sucked away. All the girls around the fire jolted to attention. Zoe's eyes grew big, and she began to shake.

"What do we do?" Brittany's voice was hoarse and near hysterical.

More twigs and shrubs snapped and popped as the large animal moved though the brush.

"It's going for Joan, oh, it's going for Joan. I don't want to hear this." Chrissy slapped her hands over her ears and sobbed.

"Everybody, just hold your bear spray at the ready. I don't think it will come over here because of the fire. I'm gonna add some more wood to make it burn brighter." Sabrina reached for the pile of sticks and twigs, grabbed a fistful, then arranged them in the blaze. The flames licked around the wood, sending sparks into the chilly air.

"Ah, I can hear it!" Leigh Anne squealed from inside her tent.

"One hundred bottles of Sprite on the wall, a hundred bottles of Sprite," Kisrie, Jacque, and Tammie sang out into the night.

Sprite?

"It's beer, you guys!" Wendy called to add to the noise. Maybe if they were loud, the bear or bears would leave.

"Ninety-nine bottles of SPRITE on the wall..." Kisrie and her weird little friends screamed the name of the soda at the top of their lungs.

"What's going on?" Sharon murmured from her cocoon.

"We're having a singing contest—hey you guys, we need to out-sing them. What songs do you know?" She hoped they knew something because she didn't know anything except the beer version of the song being sung.

"Baby shark do do dodododo," Brittany began.

"I don't know that one."

"Oh, Wen, just follow along, it's super easy." Sabrina and Chrissy joined in.

"That's the dumbest thing I ever heard."

"Daddy shark do do dodododo."

"Eighty-five bottles of Sssssspprrrittte on the wall..."

"I guess if I were a bear, I'd run from us as well," Wendy admitted before joining in on the end of the daddy shark verse of the song.

It took the baby shark song, the alphabet song, and a song about a bear going over the mountain before Kisrie and gang finished their dumb Sprite song. After the last echo of voices faded, the campsite fell quiet. Wendy strained her ears past the crackle of the fire to see if she could hear something.

A cricket chirped.

Then another.

Water from the Snake River burbled and bubbled over rocks.

A slight wind shooshed through the grasses in the meadow.

But nothing more.

It sounded like the bear or bears were gone—for now.

"I think we did it ladies!" Wendy clapped her hands together and cheered. The others joined in.

Whoah. Was this what it felt like to *really* be part of a team?

It felt good—real good.

The last thing Wendy wanted was to add onto the trauma everyone was feeling. What if she was honest with them and told them what was going on and told them she was going off on her own for their protection? Would they let her go? She'd be saving them. She'd be doing something heroic to make up for all the death and destruction that floated in her wake. Plus, they'd know the danger lurking in the woods and be on the lookout for more than just bears and moose.

Yeah. That's exactly what she'd do.

In the morning.

A slash of crimson appeared in the eastern sky. One by one the stars faded as the light expanded into a wash of orange, pink, salmon, and yellow. Kisrie hunkered deeper into her fleece jacket. She didn't realize how cold the nights were until she had to sit out in one. Tammie sat with Sharon who was struggling more and more to string words together. That wasn't good. She worried about how they were gonna get her a few miles back on the trail to a safer spot. "What time is it?"

Tammie looked at the watch. "Six."

They'd gone longer than the three hours. "How's she doing?"

"I'm a little worried. She's not moving around as much."

"Jacque, can you wake the others up? We really need to get going. Zoe, Jenn, Leigh Anne, and Chrissy are gonna have to get moving and move fast."

"Yes sir!" Jacque flipped her canister of bear spray in a

circle on her trigger finger. She then jogged to the tents and pounded on the fabric.

Everyone gathered at the fire pit in record time.

"What're we gonna do for breakfast?" Jenn asked with a yawn and a stretch.

"I think I saw some more Pop Tarts in the bear bag when we hung it last night," Zoe said.

"We can take those and eat on the way." Leigh Anne sat down and pulled off her boot, then gave it a shake. "We should probably make sure we have stuff for lunch as well. We'll need to have some fuel to keep us going for over twenty miles."

Ten minutes later, they were off at a brisk jog.

"I hope nothing happens to them. There are those hills." Sabrina bounced up and down rubbing her arms.

"We should eat something, then figure out how to move our camp a few miles away." Kisrie turned to the bag of food Zoe fetched a while ago.

"Um. Can I talk to you guys?" Wendy picked her way to the middle of the group. "There's something you need to know, and I'm asking you to hear me out before you say anything."

Tammie glanced at the watch. "This better not take long. We need to get out of here before the grizzlies come back."

"What? You have a better idea than us?" Jacque folded her arms and pressed her lips into a firm line.

"Your lives may be in danger beyond the bears and moose and you need to know about it." The former Queen of Mean shifted her weight from one foot to the other as she made eye contact with everyone, then landed on Kisrie.

Weird prickles skittered up Kisrie's spine until her shivers had shivers. There was something to the tone of Wendy's voice that clued her in this wasn't another dumb ol' stunt. "Let's sit down." Kisrie sat. The others followed her example. "Okay, let's hear it."

"Um, well, you all know that Keri and I were kidnapped

this past spring." Wendy licked her lips and swallowed hard. "The guys who took us were pimps. They ran, and still run, a pretty big prostitution ring. After I was rescued, they crashed the RV they kept us... kept us in." Her voice broke and she swiped at her eyes. She looked at the ground and brushed her toe back and forth. Wendy then looked up, eyes overflowing with tears. Pain was etched in every line in her forehead. Her voice was barely audible. "Kisrie, that's when... when Keri..." She put her face in her hands and her whole body shook.

Jacque elbowed Kisrie with a look of concern on her face.

"Go on," Kisrie said softly.

"The pimps, Marcus, Jorge, and Unique must've gotten away. And right before you guys left for this trip, I saw Marcus following me in the mall. Somehow he'd been watching me. I knew I had to do something to get him away from Keri. I decided to come on this trip." Wendy stopped and took a few breaths before continuing. "You all wondered why Mrs. Plank wasn't at the send-off ceremony since this trip was her idea. Well, on the way, we both saw Marcus following us." The tears flowed hard. Wendy wiped her nose with the back of her wrist. "She lost him and went to meet with the police." She stopped and looked each person in the face. "I don't know if the pimps were caught yet, but I can't take that chance. I don't want anything bad to happen to you."

Jacque cupped her chin and twirled a finger in the air. "I don't get it. If you guys lost him, why are we in danger? We're in the middle of freaking nowhere."

"Remember how I pushed so hard for you guys to go to Yellowstone as planned?"

Everyone nodded.

"You... you... realize when we don't show... we're gonna be reported missing. And a group of teen girls lost in the Wyoming wilderness full of bears and other dangers will make the news." Wendy's voice cracked on the last two words.

"So...you're sayin'...." Sabrina slapped her hands over her mouth. Her eyes grew wide until her eyebrows disappeared under her bangs.

"What you all don't get is that these pimps are evil in ways you can't imagine. They don't let anyone get away from them. They 'tie up' loose ends." Wendy held up her fingers and made quotey-gestures with them. "I...I'm a loose end," her breath grew choppy, "and so is Keri."

"So you're pretty much saying those guys are gonna see on the news that we're missing because our names and photos will be put out there and then those guys will go to Heart Lake and try to trace the trail back to us?" Tammie stood up and started pacing back and forth, wringing her hands.

"That's why I'm leaving you. I have to get as far away from the trail as I can—and you guys need to get off the trail as well."

"How's that gonna help us? If you're gone and they find us, we can't outrun them, not with poor Sharon like this. Those guys are gonna kidnap all of us and leave Sharon to die! Why'd you do this to us? What were you thinking?" Sabrina jumped to her feet, fists clenched at her sides.

"And if we need to get off the trail too, then what's the point of splitting up?" Tammie cocked her head to the side.

Wendy's face contorted and twisted. "I was trying to get him away from Keri. She's suffered enough because of me, all right?" Wendy wrapped her arms around herself and howled. "Last...night..." She choked and gasped between her words. "I...ran off hoping...I didn't intend to come back. That moose...was meant for me. I was supposed to die, *not Joan.*"

Wendy dropped to the ground and curled into a ball. Kisrie put a hand over her mouth. Wendy's intent was to commit suicide by wild beast. Not once did Wendy let on she was that desperate, or was the desperation a reaction to Joan's death? Aunt Zena was the psychologist, not her. Kisrie wished she could call her aunt and get advice—actually she'd first find out the status on the bad guys. Maybe they were in jail and all this panic was for nothing.

"So now what do we do?" Brittany pulled her pony tail. "I'm scared."

Wasn't everyone? Wendy's revelation put a wrinkle in everything. Not only did they have to worry about hungry wildlife, they had to evade kidnappers—maybe. And Wendy insisting on going off by herself? Not gonna happen. It seemed like Wendy was full of remorse and felt like her only penance was ending her life for the ones lost.

A thought popped into Kisrie's mind.

She rolled her eyes because this wasn't her first experience of such things.

She needed to insist Wendy stayed with the group. They would go sideways off the trail *together*. Yes, it would be much harder to bushwhack with Sharon, but they had to try. However, a few months ago, Kisrie would've jumped at the chance to let Wendy fend for herself in such a situation. But something changed. *She* changed. Sure, she was super angry at Wendy last night, but Tammie was right, Wendy wasn't responsible for the moose. It was a terrible, terrible *accident*.

Kisrie hopped to her feet. "You're staying with us. We will all go deep into the woods together."

"What? No, no, Kiz. How're the others gonna find us with the rescuers? We have no way to tell them where we went!" Jacque grabbed her arm and pulled at her to sit back down.

"The girl just admitted she wants to die." Kisrie pointed to the still sobbing Wendy, who lie on the ground, Brittany huddled with her. "Didn't you *listen?* We can't let her go alone."

"But...but we're gonna leave marks! What if the bad guys track us?" Sabrina's voice rose to a near squeal.

Tammie walked over to her and put a hand on her arm. "We'll be fine. There's enough of us to wipe any tracks. We don't have to go terribly far. Besides, I think we'll be out of here sooner than later. Those girls are determined to reach Turpin by evening. Help will be on the way in the morning at the latest. We'll be okay."

Kisrie ran over and hugged her friend. "I knew someone would see the sense in this plan."

"I still need to know how the rescuers are gonna find us if we are a ways off the trail." Jacque crossed her arms.

Kisrie scratched her head. That was a hard question. "We may need to take turns watching the trail in pairs in case someone comes along—hikers, paramedics—or the bad guys. Maybe Wendy and I will be the ones to keep an eye on the trail. We'll lead the rescuers to you guys when they come."

"But what if we get separated and we never see you again? What do Tam and I tell your parents? That you went on a double suicide mission with Wendy?" Jacque threw herself at Kisrie, wrapping around her like a tight fitting jacket. "What if she sacrifices you to save her own skin?"

Kisrie opened her mouth to tell Jacque she was being ridiculous, but she stopped. She couldn't promise everything would be okay. She had *no idea* what she was getting into.

None.

Tammie sniffed and pulled Jacque off Kisrie. "I guess all we can do is pray."

"I think that's the best thing you can do." Kisrie nodded. "But how hard can it be to find you guys once you set up camp a ways off the trail? Anyway, we need to pack up. We should probably travel light and hide what we leave behind so it doesn't look like anyone was here."

~19~

"What have I gotten myself into?" Kisrie whispered to the tall pines as sweat poured down her forehead while she scrambled up the side of a steep hill far behind Wendy. It took the group way too long to pack and hide stuff, then they had to make it look like no one camped there. *Then,* it took them another few hours to get roughly two miles down the trail.

By the time the group went sideways, it was pretty late in the afternoon, and there was a good chance the runners had made it to the campground—or would soon.

Moving off trail was slower and harder than anyone anticipated. It took a lot of effort to move Sharon and then go back and hide the trail. The group would be lucky if they made it to a decent camping area before dark. But someone needed to keep an eye on the trail in case rescuers came. Then there was the fact they should've been in Yellowstone by now. Who knew how long before they were officially reported missing?

After a brief group meeting during a rest, it was decided the group keep heading deeper into the woods, while Kisrie and Wendy would go back to the trail and keep watch. If they stayed on a straight line, they shouldn't get lost—right?

So now Kisrie scrambled after Wendy who was determined to keep a pace bound to kill them both from exhaustion. "I'm alone in the woods with a honkin' mad woman."

"You need to keep up with me." Wendy's voice bounced off the trees and boulders. She was nowhere in sight.

"I would if you'd slow down a bit." Where that girl's sudden burst of energy came from, Kisrie had no idea.

"Think of me as your personal trainer. I'm getting you out of here thinner and stronger than you came in."

Since when did Wendy care about her physique? "So, you mandated yourself as my own personal Beachbody coach?" This was nuts. Irrational. Not long ago, the girl had a death wish. She was curled up in a ball on the forest floor. Now she was running through the woods like a deer.

"Just keep up, will you?"

"You are psycho!" Kisrie's foot slipped on a rock the size of her fist. She went down hard on her hands and knees. Pain seared her palms. She rolled over onto her butt and looked at her hands. They were scraped. Great.

She felt a trickle on her shin. Looking down, there was a rivulet of red sourcing from a tiny gash on her right kneecap. At least it was small and didn't hurt too much.

"Where are you?"

This was not a safe pace. The more tired Kisrie got, the harder it was to maintain balance. Her pack was so heavy—heavier than Wendy's. Wendy insisted Kisrie carry more because duh—she weighed more. "I just fell. I'm bleeding. I'm taking a rest." Ooh, she wished they could've made it to camp and unloaded the weight, but in her gut, she knew the group had to find a campable area and someone needed to watch the trail. That would be her. With crazy Wendy. "And I'm hungry. I need a snack." That was true. Her stomach rumbled and twisted. Never in her life had she felt such deep hunger as she did out here. It was like her body could never catch up on calories. She snorted. What a position to be in! Not being able to get enough calories.

But man, it sure hurt.

Wendy appeared through the trees. Extrapolating from the look on her face, Kisrie could imagine steam blowing from Wendy's ears. "No snacks. You will not eat beyond three meals as long as we have something to eat."

Kisrie ran a hand down her face and sighed. "Do you have any idea how dumb this is? I thought this was about survival—about making sure we can lead help to the group and stay away from bad guys." Kisrie imitated Wendy's tone and speech cadence. "Not about my weight."

"You're the one that insisted on coming with me."

"Because I was afraid you'd do something stupid and get yourself killed! You weren't exactly in the best of moods last night and a few hours ago."

"Oh, so *you* want to be the hero? You want to say you sacrificed to keep the poor orphan Wendy alive so you could be a hero like your cousin, Meghan."

Wendy's words cut deep. They weren't all true, nor were they all false. Kisrie did wish people spoke of her with the same admiration they held for Meghan. And her last attempt at being heroic? It landed the entire color guard in jail for a night *and* put them on this trip where Miranda got hurt and...and Joan got killed.

"Well? Am I right?" Wendy crossed her arms and her nostrils flared.

Kisrie didn't want to have this conversation now. "Let's keep moving." She got up and brushed dirt and rocks off of her skin.

"We'll keep moving when I say."

"I don't get you. First, you yell at me for not keeping up.

Now, when I'm ready to move on, you want to stay? What is it Wendy?"

Wendy stood there and breathed heavy.

"Do what you want. I'm moving on." Kisrie continued her plod up the hill. She had no idea where she was going. They should have reached the trail by now. But she didn't remember the terrain being this rough when they came in with the group. They were *supposed* to be moving straight back from where they came. But in a forest full of trees, it was hard to tell what direction "straight" was. Maybe when they got to the top of whatever they climbed, they could get a feel for where they were. At some point, they needed to find the Continental Divide Trail.

Every muscle ached in Wendy's body. Never in her life did she ever push as hard as she did now. She was sure she could've covered more ground if she didn't have that dead-weight with her.

But she had a point to prove, and she was gonna prove it no matter what. A few hours ago Kisrie called her suicidal. Okay, maybe she was, but the *way* it was said made Wendy seem weak. She was surprised the group didn't assign her a twenty-four-seven body guard—or did they? Kisrie.

Wendy groaned. She did not want or need a babysitter. She was perfectly fine.

"Don't you think we should've been to the trail by now?" Kisrie called from too far behind.

The sky had clouded over, and the wind was ripping through the trees sending a chill through Wendy's outer layers. As much as she wanted to keep going, she didn't feel like getting caught out in a storm. But on the other hand, stopping would mean having to spend time in a tent cooped up with

Kisrie. And that blob would probably force her to talk about her feelings.

Could things get any worse?

And how should she respond to Kisrie's question? Yeah, they were supposed to go straight. But when she took off from the group, everything looked the same. Truth was, and she wasn't about to admit it to Kisrie, they were lost. If they were lost, they needed to stay alive until they were un-lost.

She stopped and waited for Kisrie to catch up. Kisrie's face was all shades of red, and her breathing sounded like the chugging of a steam engine. She plopped onto her bottom and looked up at Wendy. "You know, I think a storm is coming. I'm already chilled. Maybe we should put the tent up around here."

"We gotta be close to the trail by now."

"I think we're lost."

Kisrie was right. They were, but Wendy couldn't let her façade of control slip. She had to show the puffing dough girl she was *not* weak. "I'm not seeing anywhere flat enough for the tent, and if the wind blows more, we could be crushed by a dead branch or something."

Kisrie rolled her eyes and let out a sigh. Didn't seem like she was buying it.

So what?

"We are not stopping until we find us a flat spot." Wendy took off at a brisk pace, forcing her muscles to move. She couldn't let Kisrie see any weakness in her.

Thunder rumbled and growled in the distance. The wind bit deeper and colder.

"Wendy, I think we need to just stop and put up the tent and at least ride out the storm."

"Whatever. Let's put it up…there." She pointed to a spot that was somewhat flat and not under a dead tree.

By the time the tent was up, they were both sweating from

fighting the wind. And when that wind hit Wendy's damp skin, she felt the cold seep deeper toward her bones. And she did *not* want to be in a position to share body heat with Kisrie. She'd rather die.

As soon as they pulled their packs in, the sky opened up and the rain pounded the tent as the wind whipped so hard the dome flattened to a point where they had to lie down to avoid being suffocated by nylon.

"I wonder how long it will last," Kisrie shouted over the noise.

"Do I look like a meteorologist to you?"

"I'm just trying to make conversation."

"I don't feel like talking."

"This is gonna be a long, who knows how many days, if we can't carry on a normal conversation."

"The door's right there. You're more than welcome to use it."

Kisrie propped up on an elbow and looked at Wendy. "There you go. You're being duplicitous."

Wendy rolled onto her back to avoid Kisrie's gaze and put her hands under her head. "What's that supposed to mean?"

"It means you're being a psychotic ping-pong ball."

"My, don't you sound like your aunt."

"I mean, one moment you're all like, 'It's my fault Joan's dead! That moose was meant for me', then the next you're all like, 'I'm a gonna be the hee-row and make sure Kisrie doesn't die', and now you're all like, 'don't let the door hit you in the butt'. Which is it, Wendy? I can't deal with this. I won't."

Duplicitous. Who used words like that?

However, the word stung. Kisrie was right. Wendy's emotions had been—and still were—all over the place. Joan's death caused something to snap. God, if He even existed, knew Wendy had been through more than her fair share of horrible things. A whore for a mother who abandoned her last fall. The whole thing with Mr. Plank. The abduction. Keri. Joan. Now she was lost in a place where there were things higher than her on the food chain.

And Kisrie wondered why she was acting *duplicitous?*

Cow Pie didn't deserve an answer. It was none of her business.

Wendy told Kisrie what she could go do to herself.

Kisrie rolled away and stayed silent.

Darkness crept on them and the rain didn't let up. The thunder crashed so loud Wendy was sure she felt the tent shake. She bit the insides of her cheeks to hold back a scream.

"That was close," Kisrie muttered.

Ah, now ol' Cow Pie was trying to scare her. *Play it cool.* "How do you know?"

"After the flash you count one-one-thousand, two-one-thousand, and so on. For each five, it's about a mile from the lightning strike."

Wendy broke out in goosebumps and shivered. "How far was that one then?"

"I got to seven-one-thousand. So a little more than a mile."

That couldn't be good. That meant they could get struck, right? Wasn't lightning attracted to metal? The tent poles were metal. The stakes were metal. The lace hooks on her boots were metal. She was doomed. They were gonna die. After all this…*she* was going to die.

And then what?

Did anyone *really* know for sure what happened when the heart stopped beating?

"Wendy? You okay?"

"Of course." Liar. But she couldn't let Kisrie know she was scared.

"I don't think we'll get hit if that's what you're worried about."

"Who said I was worried?"

"You're breathing funny."

"I am *not*." Wendy sucked in air until both lungs filled. Pursing her lips, she let it out slowly. She had her breathing under control, or hoped it looked like she did.

"Lots of trees higher than us."

"Would you leave me alone. I'm going to sleep." Wendy dug in her pack and pulled out her sleeping bag. She needed to stop all the thoughts about death from running through her mind.

"We can't yet. As soon as the storm is over, we need to eat something and hang a bear bag a couple hundred yards from us. We're still in griz country."

"Who's in charge here?"

"You sure aren't making good decisions right now, Wendy."

Staying in control of the situation with Kisrie around was a lot harder than she thought. She figured Kisrie'd still be afraid of her and she'd defer to her so-called Queen of Mean persona to keep it that way. But that wasn't the case.

"I'm pulling out some peanut butter and tortillas. Let me know if you want some." Kisrie sat up and started rummaging through her pack in the dark. "Wish I could find my headlamp. Can't remember where I put it."

The smell of peanut butter made Wendy's stomach rumble. She was starving, but last thing she wanted to do was admit it to Kisrie. Maybe she'd get up in the middle of the night and get something to eat from the bear bag. "Why do you have to be so gross when you chew?" Kisrie kept smacking her lips and tongue in her mouth after every bite and it got on Wendy's last nerve.

"I offered you some," Kisrie said around her food which was even grosser.

Wendy clenched her jaw.

"We also need to discuss what to do now that we are officially lost which means Chrissy and them aren't gonna be able to find the others—or us."

"Are you blaming me?"

Kisrie took another obscene bite and chewed like a cow. She didn't even bother to swallow before talking. "You're the one that took off running when we were supposed to head back to the trail."

"I was trying to be efficient. I didn't want to miss the rescuers in case they came in on ATVs or something like that."

"If we moved slower, we probably could've backtracked to the trail. The fact we *haven't* found it means we're still on the same side as the others, but how far up or down?"

"It's not far."

Kisrie paused mid-bite. "How do you know? You have a map?"

This was getting ridiculous. "I just know." Liar. She didn't know. But she had to hold it together.

"Why didn't we think to take the guide book?" Kisrie spoke more to herself it seemed than to Wendy.

They left the guide book with the others. Getting back to the trail wasn't supposed to be hard. It didn't seem hard. And Wendy had to admit to herself, she didn't pay attention because she just wanted to run. Running felt good.

"Look at it this way, Cow Pie—"

"Don't call me that."

"*Kisrie.* Marcus and Jorge can't find us.

"Well then. I feel so much better." Kisrie's voice dripped with sarcasm.

By the time the storm passed, it was night. Kisrie and Wendy were supposed to have been back with the others before dark, and Jacque and Tammie were to be the next trail watch. Wendy burrowed deeper into her sleeping bag. They probably thought something terrible happened. If that group split up, more lives would be in danger. Way to go. She did it again. Lost control and yeah. Who knew how many—if any of them—would make it out alive?

A faint snort in the distance jolted Kisrie from her sleep. She rubbed her eyes. The sun was already up, and water dripped from the trees onto the tent. Wendy lay on the far side of the two-man tent snoring up a storm. Was that noise from Wendy? Or was it from something else?

A few twigs snapped and there was a grunt and a huff. It wasn't super close, but it was in the direction of the bear bag. All of the *Reader's Digest* stories of people surviving bear attacks rushed from her memory into her present consciousness. Several stories were about how the bear slashed through the tent with its massive claws, then chomped down on the camper's head, dragging him or her off into the bushes to be eaten. Then, by some miracle, they'd escape with an arm and half of their face missing.

In most cases the person had something in the tent that attracted the bear. Kisrie made sure all of the smelly things were in the bear bags. She even put the packs away from the tent under a tarp.

After what seemed like a small eternity, the sounds disappeared. The only growling she heard was from her tummy.

Sharon's WhisperLite stove was in her backpack, as was Joan's Jetboil. Oops. Probably should've left one for the others—but then again, they were supposed to *be* with the others.

They had to find the trail today. Once found, the hard part would be figuring out which direction to go. She rubbed her stomach. All this thinking made her hungry. Maybe she could make breakfast. She really wanted something more than PopTarts. They had a few packages of egg scrambles and pancakes. Hmmm. What did she feel like eating?

Eggs.

Protein sounded good.

Careful not to wake Wendy, Kisrie slid out of Joan's sleeping bag and crawled to the entrance of the tent where her boots and socks were. She pulled them on, then carefully pulled the zipper.

No matter how fast or slow she pulled, the zipper was *loud*. Wendy needed the rest. The girl was so distraught, Kisrie feared she'd go crazy and get them both killed. Another tug and a loud *zip*. Kisrie feared her zipper could be heard all the way to Yellowstone.

She glanced at Wendy. But Wendy didn't move. That was good. Maybe a good breakfast would also calm the Queen of Mean down a bit.

Leaving the tent flap open, Kisrie crept outside peering into the thick trees and foliage to make sure a bear wasn't hiding nearby. Then she hiked through the wet ground cover to where she hung the bag the night before. The sun's rays cut through the high boughs of the evergreens and occasional aspen trees illuminating droplets of water. In a few cases, the sun hit the water just right to create a prism effect. Ugh! How she wished she had her camera! The lighting was amazing.

About thirty yards farther on she saw a spider's web—a

perfect orb—dotted with thousands of droplets. It was like every strand was covered in micro fairy lights. Her hatred of all things arachnid didn't deter her from examining the web and storing it in her memory. Really, if she had her camera, this would be the kind of photo all those outdoor magazines would buy. Oh well. Maybe someday she could spend time in the wilderness—just her and her camera—and shoot all the amazing things most people don't notice.

When Kisrie arrived at the spot where she hung the bear bag, her sense of wonder evaporated in an instant. She ran a few steps and stared in horror at the remains of what had been their food supply.

She looked up into the tree from which she hung it. The branch was intact.

So how?

She did everything right.

There was no way a bear could've gotten that bag…unless…

Wendy!

That had to be it.

Kisrie vaguely remembered the zipper in the middle of the night but thought it was part of her dream. It was probably Wendy getting up to get something to eat. She likely took the bear bag down, ate something and didn't hang it up right.

Kisrie dropped to her hands and knees and pawed through the mess. There was nothing edible left. The animals had even licked all the powdered stuff from the chewed up containers. She rocked back onto her haunches. At least the bears in this area had a full belly and wouldn't be interested in eating people.

But what would she and Wendy do? They had *zero* food. They didn't have a way to hunt, and even if they did, Kisrie knew nothing about hunting or what to do with a dead animal to eat it. She was sure Wendy was even more clueless.

This was fantastic. They were going to starve to death out here.

Using the trunk of a nearby tree, Kisrie pulled herself to her feet. She jogged back to the tent and pounded on the fabric. "Wake up." Her tone was sharp. She was kind of mad. Hangry, to be precise.

"What is it?" Wendy's voice was muffled from sleep and being buried in her sleeping bag.

"Thanks to you, we have no food."

There was a rustling of nylon against nylon and a few seconds later, Wendy poked her head out. She squinted in the bright sunlight. "What're you talking about? I rehung the bag."

"Well, obviously, it wasn't high enough. I went up there to get it and make us a nice breakfast, and guess what I found?" She paused, hoping their new reality would sink into Wendy's thick skull.

"I don't know, you tell me."

"Nothing. I found *nothing left*. Something, probably a *bear* got into our food supply and it's all gone."

"It can't be all gone."

"It is. And now we're stuck out here with nothing to eat." Kisrie tried, but failed at controlling the volume and pitch of her voice.

"For you, that's probably not such a bad thing, you're sure to lose some weight from—"

"What is it with you and my weight? Food is energy. I'm feeling a little sick right now because I need something in my stomach."

"I've skipped breakfast for years and it never hurt me."

What was wrong with her? Now wasn't the time for a stupid standoff. One minute Wendy was all life-and-death freaked out over these killers coming after her, and now she wanted to lie around and argue over weight and skipping breakfast?

Kisrie tapped her finger against her lips. There was no way she could hike all day long without food. Heck, she wouldn't be able to make it halfway to what *should be* lunch. Maybe there were some kinds of berries in the woods? But what if some were poison? A twisted thought popped into her mind. She could always have Wendy test them out first.

No. She shook her head. That would be wrong on so many levels.

Her hand fell to her side, and she felt her eyes stretch wide. On the other hand, what was stopping her from walking away? She could leave Wendy to her own devices. Her nemesis didn't seem to want her around anyway. If the worst should happen to Wendy, Kisrie wouldn't be to blame. Not one bit.

But then there was the fact bears and other creatures higher up on the food chain liked to go after solo prey. Argh! What to do?

She looked back down at Wendy who still squinted up at her. "You know what? I'm heading back. You don't seem to want me here. I think I can find the trail." She gestured to the tent with a sweeping motion of her hand. "And you can keep that. Less weight for me. Now move aside so I can get my stuff and be on my way."

The moment she crawled in the tent, a realization hit her: She was *two* days from potential rescue *if* she didn't get turned around in circles. That meant no food or shelter for two days. And if she couldn't find the trail? She could be out here for weeks, and months, and years. She'd become like the beasts of the fields. Would she resort to eating bugs?

Ugh. She couldn't back down now. She stated her ultimatum to Wendy and had to stick to it. She couldn't let Wendy see any vulnerability in her. Those days were over. Kisrie was in charge of her life from now on. She would not allow Wendy to derail her any longer.

She grabbed a fistful of sleeping bag and shoved it into the bottom of the stuff sack. On the second grab, she felt fingers close around her arm.

"You can't go."

Shaking her arm free, she turned to face Wendy. "*What?*"

"You...you can't go." Wendy's eyes were wild like those of a caged animal. The girl was certifiably crazy.

"Seriously, Wendy, what's the matter with you? I'm not gonna bother ticking off the list of contradictions you've made over the past few days. But losing the food was it for me. All you do is treat me like scum—which is what you've done since we were little kids. I don't have to take it anymore. You're on your own."

"No! Please don't go." There was a note of desperation in Wendy's voice. Kisrie wished she paid attention to her aunt when she talked about mental illnesses or trauma or stuff like that. Heck, she didn't even pay much attention when it was her they talked about. She sure suffered quite a bit of it at Wendy's hand.

But why?

Why did Wendy draw a target on Kisrie's back so long ago?

"I'll consider staying if you answer a question for me. If I don't think you're being honest, I'm leaving. And as much hell as you've put me, my family, and my friends through—not to mention this group and Sharon and...and Joan, I *want* nothing more than to leave you here to have your guts eaten by grizzly bears. So. You tell me, Wendy Wetz, why have you hated me so much all these years and tried to destroy me every chance you got? What did I *ever* do to you in Kindergarten?" Kisrie didn't realize she was yelling until she heard the echo of the last word bounce off the hard surfaces nearby.

Wendy blinked a few times and cleared her throat. Her lips curled in and out of her mouth. She looked down at her hands and fidgeted with her thumbs.

"Yeah. Just as I figured. You don't have a reason other than you're just plain mean." Kisrie started stuffing the sleeping bag as fast as she could.

"I've hated you because you have everything I don't." Wendy's voice was quiet and unsteady.

Kisrie froze. She stared at the yellow nylon wall of the tent. "I don't understand."

"You have a family, Kisrie. You have parents who love you and care about how you turn out. You have friends who like you because…they like *who you are*. My friends only were my friends because of what I could get them, or what I could get from them. And then there's…there's…"

"Go on." This was all new to Kisrie. Hearing that Wendy Wetz, the most beautiful girl in Mountain Ridge High School was jealous of *her* was the last thing she expected. She turned and sat.

"It's your innocence." Wendy put her face in her hands and broke down.

"My…innocence?"

Wendy looked up at her with reddened eyes and a tear-stained face and a vulnerability Kisrie didn't know was even possible for someone like Wendy. "When your mother sells herself for sex *in your own apartment* you…learn things." She looked away. "And when you're thrown in as part of the package deal as a little girl—"

Horror wrapped taloned tentacles around Kisrie's heart. "You don't have to say any more." It all made sense now. All of her breath rushed out as if she were punched in the gut.

"I felt it was unfair. The worst part of it was, from that first day in kindergarten, I saw what you had and that you didn't seem to appreciate it. And that's why I hated you so much. And I tried to rob you of that innocence so we'd at least have some common ground."

"Hated. You just said that in the past tense."

"Because right now I can't seem to make myself hate you if I try. Please don't go. I'm sorry."

Kisrie closed her eyes and breathed deep through her

nose. How long had she waited to hear those words? Maybe she didn't wait because she didn't think she'd ever hear them. And now she had a choice to make. Ever since the stuff with Uncle Evan and the weird urge to pray for Wendy, she wrestled with hating her in return or forgiving her. Now it was up to her to bring everything from the past together in this one moment.

Forgive or stay mad?

Wendy caused so much harm—irreparable harm. Keri would forever be in a wheelchair because of Wendy. Two people were now dead. Reputations were ruined. Wendy deserved the fallout from her actions. Staying angry felt natural.

But if she were to forgive? That meant she couldn't dredge any of this up and hold it against Wendy. She couldn't use it to manipulate her. Forgiveness meant Kisrie had to give up her right to be angry. Could she? What if once they got out of the woods, Wendy went back to her old ways?

"Kisrie? I said I'm sorry...for all of it." Wendy *sounded* sincere. She'd been through so much. And here they were out in the middle of nowhere with no food and possibly bad guys after them. There was no guarantee they'd make it out alive. Did she want to die and face Jesus with bitterness in her heart? She heard so many stories about people who died and the regrets of the living for not forgiving. Kisrie made up her mind. And what might letting go of the past violations do for Wendy? Who knows? Maybe Wendy was so mean because no one ever forgave her for anything.

"I forgive you."

Silence hung suspended between them for several moments.

As of this moment, Kisrie no longer had a mortal enemy. Her enemy was now her ally.

Now that she wasn't leaving, they needed to make a plan of what to do from now on—especially since they didn't have any food.

~21~

Wendy pulled the collar of the jacket higher up against her neck as she sat on a rock waiting for Kisrie to finish filling up her water bottle from a small stream using a filter pump. A weird calm washed through her after Kisrie accepted her apology about the food and forgave her. Never in her life did Wendy imagine the two of them could get along. They had to in order to survive this ordeal.

They decided they would keep looking for the trail, and then they'd take a parallel route toward the campground. If they came across another backcountry traveler, they'd ask if the person had food to spare. She would explain that they were taking a course on orienteering through the backcountry and that bears got into their food. But they'd been hiking for about five hours and had yet to see the trail or a single sign of human life. How could she be so stupid about the bear bag?

"Hand me your bottle. I'll fill it for you since I'm already down here." Kisrie tossed hers on the ground and reached for Wendy's.

"I wonder if the others were rescued yet."

"I'm hoping and praying so."

"Oh no." Wendy slid off the rock and paced back and forth along the stream.

Kisrie stopped pumping and looked up at her. "What is it?"

"How could I be so *stupid?*" She cursed and saw Kisrie cringe. "So a rescue team comes in for Sharon and the others."

"Well, yeah, isn't that what we wanted?"

"But we're not all there! You know your parents and Zena aren't going to sit back and let us stay out here. They're gonna demand the search and rescue teams search for *us*. Two missing girls out alone in the vast wilds of Wyoming…Kisrie, it'll be all over the news." She wrapped her fingers in her hair and pulled until her scalp stung. "How could I miss that?"

"Wait. You sound like you *want* us to stay lost." Kisrie's eyebrows pressed downward to match the corners of her mouth.

"Come on Kisrie, you gotta know we've been reported missing by now, and like I said, if the others were rescued and *we* were gone…Marcus and Jorge are gonna know it. They're gonna come out here and try to find me—us." Wendy pointed a finger into Kisrie's face. "Don't you think for a moment that they will only take me. No, they'll be excited to get a two-fer. We need to go deeper into the wilderness and hide. Maybe find an old cabin or something."

Kisrie threw her hands up in the air. "You've got to be kidding me. We're more likely to die from starvation or freezing or animals long before anyone finds us."

Could that girl be any dumber? Wendy slapped a hand to her forehead and let it rest for a moment before reaching out and grabbing Kisrie by the front of one of her stupid color guard shirts. "You just don't get it, do you? Trust me when I say this." Wendy lowered her voice to almost a growl. "Death by bear or hunger—or whatever—would be better than what those guys would do to us." She gave Kisrie a shake. The girl's eyes were like two huge blue marbles stuck in her face.

"Maybe they aren't smart enough to find us?" Kisrie squeaked in a question more than a statement.

Wendy shoved her away. She'd had enough of the body odor. "But they are! Kisrie, I knew Marcus for a long time. He was one of Iona's clients. He was one of the nicer ones, or so I thought. He was smart and funny. And he's built a huge trafficking empire that stretches across the country. He may be a bad man, but he's not dumb."

Kisrie stared at her, slack-jawed.

"You seeing how serious this is?" Wendy shivered and wrapped her arms around herself.

Kisrie nodded, her face as white as fresh snow. "But if the rescuers find us, those bad guys can't get us…" Her words trailed off.

"They wouldn't think twice about killing anyone to get to me—us."

"But the others?"

Wendy broke eye contact. What about the others? What if Marcus and Jorge came in on the heels of the search and rescue team and killed them, and Sharon, and took the rest? They wouldn't pass up an opportunity to make more money. And then they would be looking for her. Either way, she and Kisrie were in a bad situation. She looked over at her now partner. Kisrie's eyes were closed and her lips moved. "What are you doing?"

"Shush. I'm praying."

"Lotta good that's gonna do us." Wendy rolled her eyes and grabbed her water bottle. She dipped it into the icy water.

"Maybe you should give it a try. I feel a lot calmer now."

"Whatever."

"I'm guessing helicopters might be used to look for us. We

need to avoid open areas and stay under the trees. Probably should avoid bright colors."

Wendy looked down at her hot pink t-shirt. She was sure there was a gray one in her pack—one that used to be white at the beginning of the trip.

"It also means no fires." Kisrie tossed a pebble into the stream. "Which makes things even harder for us because it keeps getting colder at night. And also, fires keep animals away."

Wendy pulled the bottle out of the water. Things sure got a lot more complicated.

Marcus slapped a couple of Slim Jims, a can of Monster, and a package of Little Debbie Swiss Rolls on the counter of the convenience store. While the clerk made change, a headline on the *Oklahoman* caught his eye.

Teen Trip Turns Tragic: One Dead, One Injured, Two Still Missing

Below the headline were photos of two girls. One had a very round face and blond curly hair whereas the other was…Wendy Wetz! He grabbed a paper and threw it on top of his purchases while fishing out more money to pay. This was too good to be true.

Once in his motel room, he locked the door and made sure the security chain was in place. He popped the can of Monster open and peeled the wrapper off the Slim Jim. The paper lay in front of him on the Formica table.

Western Wyoming, huh? The group was reported missing when they failed to show up as scheduled in Yellowstone National Park at Heart Lake. A search team was sent out from

YNP, but two days later, four girls stumbled into a camp-ground asking for help to call 911. The rescuers brought out four girls, an injured adult and the remains of another. Two teens were still missing. One was Wendy. New search teams were being assembled. Volunteers were welcomed.

Volunteers.

A smile crept onto Marcus's face. He could easily alter his appearance by shaving his head and dying his brows a much lighter color. Fake glasses, knit hat, fake beard...no one should recognize him when he signed up to volunteer.

He shoved the short piece of Slim Jim in his mouth and jogged to the bathroom, flipped the light switch and examined his reflection. Oh yeah, his idea would work. He just needed to go to a Sally's Beauty Supply and a costume shop and he'd be good.

But what if they asked for an ID?

Good thing he had contacts. He knew a guy in Arvada who could hook him up with a new identity in twenty-four hours.

He went back to the table and picked up the paper and studied Wendy's picture. "You can try to run and hide all you want, but I'm on your trail. I'll find you. And you'll make me rich."

~22~

Wind whipped the tent fabric all around them. Wendy couldn't stop shivering despite the layers and layers of clothes she had on inside her sleeping bag. It was still summer, so why did the temperatures drop so low at night up here?

In the dark she could make out the lump that was Kisrie. The lump wasn't moving. Maybe she wasn't freezing. All those extra layers of fat were good for something. Wendy wished she had a little extra, or that Kisrie could share.

"K...Kisrie, you awake?" Wendy hated what she was about to ask because it was something she swore to herself she wouldn't do.

"Unnnngh."

That had to be a yes. "A...are you f...freezing like I am?"

"Nuh uh."

"I th...think...I'm getting hypo...th...thermic."

"Layers?" Kisrie's speech was weak. As the day wore on and hunger gnawed at them both, Kisrie grew slower and more listless.

"All of th…them."

Kisrie grunted and rolled over. There was no hinting her way to what she desperately needed—body heat.

Frustration built inside. Too bad it didn't produce heat. "I need help getting warm." If her teeth chattered any harder, they were gonna crack.

"'Mere."

Wendy slithered like a nylon serpent to where Kisrie lay on her side of the tent. It took several awkward maneuvers, but finally Kisrie figured out what was needed. They needed to get out of the bags and zip them together, then crawl inside and share body heat. Kisrie was out in a flash, but Wendy couldn't bring herself to move.

"C'mon, Wendy, you need to get out so I can put these together."

Wendy writhed out into the night air. She didn't think it was possible, but her shivers got shivers. Kisrie worked fast and before any of Wendy's teeth shattered, Kisrie was trying to get the bags over them both.

And oh, they both smelled so bad. But bad smells were worth putting up with for some warmth. Kisrie felt like a freakin' space heater.

Eventually the shivering subsided and Wendy closed her eyes. Next thing she knew, light streamed through the tent and birds were out in full force singing their morning songs. Her stomach knotted, reminding her it was empty. Maybe Kisrie knew of edible plants or how to fish, or something like that.

What time was it? Maybe she could make a sundial in the dirt with a stick…but how would she know where the twelve went?

Kisrie moaned, stretched, then went still. Shouldn't she be waking up?

Wendy unzipped her bag and sat up. "Kisrie, we should pack up and get going."

"Too tired."

"So am I, but we need to stay on the move."

"I can't move if I don't eat something. Maybe we should stay put and figure out how to get food."

Wendy laughed. "Well, I was kinda hoping you knew of berries or something like that. Edible plants? Or do you know how to fish using shoelaces? We can find a lake."

Kisrie opened both eyes. The blue stood out against the blood-shot whites. "I'm not a walking Wikipedia. I don't know what grows up here in Wyoming."

"Fish?"

"Never been fishing in my life."

"What if we find a lake or pond or something and tie a worm onto a shoelace?"

"Do you know how to de-gut a fish or whatever one does to it before eating it? Because I sure don't."

"I'm at the top of the class, and you're…not at the bottom, so between the two of us, I'm sure we can figure something out…right?"

"All's I know is that I want a large pepperoni pizza from MC's. With a side of heaven bread. And cannoli. They have the best homemade cannoli—"

"Kisrie, you're not helping. I thought you'd be all over this idea. All you do is complain about how hungry you are." Now that they were no longer mortal enemies, they needed to figure out how to work together to survive for however long the universe allowed.

Kisrie sat up and pulled a knit cap off her head. Static caused her curls to stand on end. She looked like Einstein with his finger in an electric socket. Wendy couldn't help but giggle.

"What?" Kisrie's mouth dropped into a frown.

"Your hair."

Kisrie reached up with her hands to feel around. "So? It

does that. By the time we get out of these woods, I'll probably have dreadlocks. And besides, yours doesn't look much better."

Wendy reached up to touch her own mane. It was matted and dry. Tangles abounded. She was too tired to bother with combing it out.

"So now what?" Kisrie let out a huff of air.

Another hunger pain stabbed Wendy in the gut. Maybe Kisrie was right. Maybe they needed to stay put to see if they could find a way to get a few calories.

"We stay here and figure out how to eat."

Mile after mile of sagebrush plains with the occasional rock formation flashed by as Marcus hooked his wrist over the steering wheel. The cruise control was set at seventy. No need to get pulled over for speeding.

He looked up into the rearview mirror and laughed out loud. He didn't even recognize himself. Shaved head, hipster styled beard, black-framed glasses, and a hemp necklace. Even drove a Subaru Outback to complete the persona.

While filling up in Casper, where he needed to get onto highway 20/26 to Yellowstone, an idea struck him. What if he was a long-lost estranged uncle? If he showed intense interest in the well-being of Wendy and her future, maybe he'd be alerted when they were on her trail.

He and Iona had a thing going for a few years. He knew enough about the family history—or lack of—to create a plausible connection. He was Wendy's mother's brother. Wendy knew him when she was younger, but he lost touch. When he saw the headline in the paper, he couldn't believe his luck! He didn't know his sister flaked out on her daughter. What a reunion it could be to rescue her and take her as his own.

Kisrie wiped the sweat off her forehead with the back of her wrist. She hoped against hope that Wyoming was bursting with wild blueberries. But, sadly, that wasn't the case. She found some dark blue or purple berries on juniper trees, but didn't know if they were edible. Wendy found some white berries on a plant growing out of rocks, but what if they were some kind of deadly nightshade?

Why didn't they teach a class on how to survive in the woods at high school? Seriously. She could've used such a class.

"Hey Kisrie, I found a small stream!"

Kisrie headed in the direction of Wendy's voice. Wendy knelt along a small mountain stream flipping over rocks. "There's crayfish in here! Not very big, but I saw a couple of them."

"And?" Kisrie didn't like where this was going. She hated any and all kinds of fishy creatures when it came to eating.

"I'm trying to steel myself up enough to catch a few. We can boil them and eat them."

Kisrie peered over Wendy's hunched form. Wendy slid her fingers under a decent sized rock and turned it so as not to stir up the muck on the bottom of the stream. Sunlight illuminated and rippled over a creature that looked like a mini lobster. Emphasis on *mini*. "What is there to eat? It's not much larger than a cockroach."

"I read people in the south eat them all the time."

"Yeah, but aren't things like bugs and crayfish much bigger in the south?"

Wendy glanced up at her. "I have no idea. Never been."

Kisrie dropped to her knees next to Wendy. "Neither've I."

"We're both very hungry, and we haven't found anything

else we know for sure we can eat without it killing us. I don't know about you, but I need something." Her hand flashed into the water and she pulled back squealing. The brown crayfish glistened and sparkled in the sun, it's pinchers reaching for Wendy's flesh and its *eight* nasty little legs wiggling with fury. "I need something to put it in! Hurry!"

Kisrie looked around. Camp was probably a few hundred yards away. They did have the big pot. "Can you hold onto it that long? I will run for the pot."

"Ow!" Wendy screeched and opened her hand. The crayfish hung for a moment from its claw then let go.

"If you caught one, I'm sure you can get some more. I'll be back with the pot." Kisrie tried to hide her shudder. Eight legs. Were those things related to spiders? And how were they gonna kill it before cooking it? Or were they like lobsters that had to be boiled alive? If Keri were here, she'd probably know kingdom, phylum, class, order, genus, and species. She'd also probably think it was cute and want to keep it for a pet.

"Would you go already?" Wendy slapped the backs of Kisrie's calves with her fingers.

Kisrie jogged there and back, amazed she wasn't as winded as she usually was after such a run. Boy, cymbal laps would be nothing after this trip. "Here." She set the pot next to Wendy.

"Where's the lid?" Wendy's eyes narrowed.

"Lid?"

"Duh. If we don't have a lid, they'll crawl out."

Kisrie rolled her head back and moaned.

"Stop wasting time. We need a *lot* of these suckers if we're gonna get past our hunger."

With a loud sigh, Kisrie trotted off again.

Whump! Whump! Whump!

Uh. Oh. Helicopter. She didn't know if it was a search and rescue team or not, but she figured she better take cover. She hoped Wendy heard it and did the same.

Whumpwhumpwhump!

The beating of the rotors got louder. Kisrie crouched lower under the cover of a tree. She knew movement was something they looked for. She watched enough of those survival shows on Discovery Channel to know about that.

Hiding from help felt really weird. In any other scenario, she'd strip off her shirt and be out in the open waving it around and dancing a jig. But if Jacque told the cops Wendy feared bad guys were after her, wouldn't they catch the bad guys? Hiding from search and rescue seemed so backward, but from what Wendy said about her captors, they couldn't take any chances.

Would a couple of missing girls be interesting enough for headlines all over the place? Weren't there more important things going on in the world like terrorism and the fight against socialism? But Joan was killed. In a most gruesome way. News people liked gross because gross sold stories. Maybe it was best to hide.

The helicopter was gone, but Kisrie knew she needed to pay attention in case it circled back around.

She ran to their camp and grabbed the lid. Wielding it as a shield, she grabbed a stick and thrust forward. "Take that evil kidnapper man!" She sliced and slashed at her invisible foe. Maybe she and Wendy could fight those guys off. Maybe they needed to have sword practice after they ate those nasty bug-looking crustaceans.

"Kisrie?" Wendy appeared from the thick forestation. "What. Are. You. Doing?"

Kisrie let her shield fall to her side and lowered her makeshift sword. "Uh, I was imagining what I would do if the kidnappers found us."

Wendy strode over and knocked the sword out of her hand and grabbed the lid. Her face was twisted into a dark scowl. "You really did come from the stupid farm, didn't you? Those guys aren't a joke." She broke the stick over her knee and tossed the pieces into the groundcover. "These guys will have real weapons—like guns. You think your freaking *stick* will scare evil men with guns?"

Kisrie shook her head. She really didn't know. She didn't even think of that. Most of the evil she faced in her life was dealt by the girl standing in front of her.

"If I could've fought my way out, I would've. And I would've died trying to save your sister. You need to know that."

Never did Kisrie imagine she'd stand chastised by Wendy Wetz of all people. Best tactic now was to change the topic. "You see the helicopter?"

"Of course I did. Why do you think I'm here? I had to make sure you didn't do anything to blow our cover."

"I mean, did you *see* it? To like, know what kind it was?"

"It wasn't worth the risk. Let's get back to the creek and catch food."

Kisrie followed Wendy like a dog with her tail between her legs. She couldn't comprehend what her former nemesis and sister went through those weeks they were gone. And Wendy probably wasn't gonna tell her.

~23~

Wendy set up Joan's Jetboil stove to be used with the large pot full of crayfish she caught, along with plenty of water. She grabbed the pot handle, lifted it up, and set it on the stove. She put her finger on the ignition button.

"Wait! Won't that hurt them?" Kisrie curled her hands under her chin and made a hideous grimace with her face.

"You're really concerned about a bunch of pin-brained mud bugs?" Wendy kept her voice flat.

"I've heard people say lobsters scream when they're put in boiling water."

"These aren't lobsters."

"They look like mini lobsters."

"Kisrie, they're not lobsters." Wendy turned on the ignition and the flame leapt to life, licking at the bottom of the pan. She figured she'd boil them for a good fifteen minutes to be on the safe side. Surely they didn't require much more than that.

"I can't believe we're eating these." Kisrie plopped down next to her with a thud. "But I don't think I can go another day

without food. My stomach feels like it has a knife stuck in it."
Kisrie chuckled.

"What's so funny?"

"I was just thinkin'." She laughed again and scooped some dirt into her hands then tossed it in the air. "If Keri could only see us now. You know her obsession with dung beetles and all."

Wendy looked sideways at Kisrie. A stray hair hung across her field of vision. "So tell me something." She shifted her position to take the pressure off her right leg. "Has Keri ever eaten those things for real?"

"Oh, no. No. Mom wouldn't allow it. She was horrified at how sincere Keri was about being a bush baby and all. You know," She met Wendy's eyes. "I really miss being startled in the middle of the night by shrill whistles and shrieks. I miss…the way she was." Kisrie dropped to a whisper. "All these years I took her for granted and flat out even resented her. She was everything I was not. Thin. Smart. A prodigy. Talented…more prodigy stuff there. Mom and Dad seemed to favor her in ways they didn't me."

Wendy looked at the pot on the stove. She could hear the water bubbling. How was she supposed to know when fifteen minutes were up? She'd just have to guess. "Kinda like how I felt about you."

"I still don't get that. *You* jealous of *me*."

"Back it up. I wasn't jealous of *you*, I was jealous of what you *have* that I don't. Just like how you feel about Keri."

"I may have been mean to her a few times, but I never tried to destroy her entire life."

Ouch. That hurt.

But it was true.

Wendy did go out of her way to destroy Kisrie so she could feel better about herself. It brought a twisted sense of justice.

"You know, Kisrie, I never had anyone in my life tell me how to behave until your aunt took me in. Or how to cope with all the horrible things life threw at me. I only had myself to rely on. I had to find my own way…and yes, I probably didn't always make the best choices in that." Oh dear god, she sounded like a counselor. And why dear god? She didn't believe in any god. Big G or little g.

The lid on the pot skittered around, releasing the pressure built up by the boiling water.

This was awkward. Sitting here, spilling her guts to the girl she used to hate more than life itself. Funny how fate slapped them together in a real life and death situation. The Universe must have a sick sense of humor.

"I haven't heard any screaming."

"I told you they don't scream."

"Maybe it's because that Jetboil stove is so loud."

"I'm gonna check and see if they're done." Wendy didn't know how to tell. She was going to assume that any lack of motion meant they were dead and edible. She put a pot holder on her hand and lifted off the lid. Steam assaulted her in a full facial attack. She jerked back. Better take this off the stove, away from camp to let the steam escape before pouring out the water a safe distance away. Didn't need to invite any wildlife to dinner. "Turn that off. I'm going to go dump out the water a ways from camp."

"Okay," Kisrie said.

Wendy heard the burner go silent. She adjusted her grip on the handle and watched where she put her feet. Stumbling with a pot of boiling water in the middle of nowhere would be a disaster—not to mention deadly.

She ventured out to what she thought might be the suggested two-hundred yards. She couldn't see camp anymore. She took off the lid and let the steam dissipate. The crayfish were still. Must be done. She put the lid back on, then slid it back a little to act as a strainer. This was gonna be interesting. Pouring it out with only one hot pad.

A rock, tall up to her shin, caught her eye. What if she balanced the pot on the rock and tipped it so the water poured from under the lid?

Setting the pot on the rock, Wendy squatted alongside it and slid the lid back just a little bit so she could pour the boiling water onto the ground. Slow and steady...no splashing...

The water poured out nicely.

Snap!

Wendy jerked, losing her grip on the pot. It fell to the ground and splashed all over her legs and hands. Searing pain climbed up her skin and she let out an ear-splitting scream. Four mule deer thundered by. Frantically she looked around for any cold water source.

Nothing.

The skin turned a bright red. She was sure blisters were going to form soon if she didn't cool it off. She looked to where the pot and all the crayfish were scattered on the ground. At least they were all dead and not crawling away.

Another scream burst from her lips as the burn intensified.

"Wendy!" A breathless Kisrie appeared through the trees. Her intense blue eyes doubled in size when she looked at Wendy's legs. "Oh!"

Wendy gritted her teeth to try and keep from losing control. "Some deer startled me and I spilled the pot."

"We need to get you to the stream and put those burns in the water."

Wendy glanced at what was supposed to be dinner. "But what about—"

"We'll have to take our chances and hope it's still there after we soak you."

Pain trumped hunger right now. Wendy hobbled to Kisrie who put an arm around her to steady her. The stream was a good way from where she spilled the pot. She hoped she could make it. "Ow, this hurts so much. I can't stand it." The tears came unchecked.

It felt like forever before they reached the little stream filled with crayfish. It was narrow, but Wendy was able to sit in the stream with ice-cold water from the glacier capped mountains. Using her burned hands, she splashed water over her legs. The burns looked angrier than they did at first, and blisters pushed up through the layers of her skin, adding to the pain.

Before long, the parts of her that were in the water went numb. A chill shot through her body. She shivered. Her teeth chattered.

"Your lips are turning blue. Maybe it's time to get out and warm up a bit."

As uncomfortable as the chill was, it wasn't as awful as the pain of the burn. "No. I...I'm s...staying here."

"But you don't want to add hypothermia to the burn."

"Burn is worse."

Kisrie took a wide stance and put her hands on her hips. "You need to get out of that water now. Adding complications to your injury will put both of us in more danger. You yourself said we need to keep moving. How are you gonna move if you're sick on top of having these burns?"

"Y...yes...M...Mommy." Who knew Kisrie could be so bossy? Wendy got out of the stream and stretched out on the ground in the golden sunlight. The sun wasn't as intense as it was earlier and an evening chill crept into the air. And they couldn't have a fire because it would give away their location.

Back at camp, Kisrie helped her get into some dry clothes. The burns looked uglier than ever. They looked in the first aid kit and found a very small bottle of ointment, but it wasn't for large area burns. The little booklet that came with the kit said burns should be covered with dry, sterile, loose bandages. They'd used up most of the gauze bandaging for Sharon's head wound.

And what was she gonna do all night if she couldn't stand to get in the sleeping bag? A sense of failure set in. "We're doomed."

Kisrie dug through her backpack looking for the cleanest possible shirt to use as bandages. "What do you mean?"

"These are pretty bad." Wendy held her hands in front of her face and turned them a little bit from side to side examining the burns. "I don't think I'm gonna be able to tolerate the sleeping bag on my skin, so I will freeze to death tonight."

"Pffft. You're not gonna die. I won't let you." Kisrie dropped what she was holding. "Look, why don't I go back and see if I can salvage our dinner. Hopefully critters didn't beat us to it. We'll both be a little more rational with some food in our stomachs—no matter how gross it is."

"Whatever."

Kisrie jogged off. In the past few days, Kisrie moved faster than she ever had in her entire life.

What seemed like fifteen minutes later, Kisrie trotted back to camp with the pot swinging from her hand. "I beat the critters! Dinner is served…cold." She dropped the pot in front of Wendy. "So. How do we eat these nasty things?"

"First step is that you have to stop thinking of them as nasty, or you'll never be able to get it down." Wendy reached in and scooped one into her hand. She couldn't move her fingers a whole lot due to the pain and swelling. She held her palm up so Kisrie could see the crayfish. "You ever have lobster? Like *real* lobster?"

"Nope."

"Well, since these look like lobsters, I'm assuming we eat them like one. That means the meat is in the claws and tails."

"But they're so tiny."

"Which is why I caught so many. We won't get full from all this, but it should give us energy." Wendy stared at the lifeless creatures then looked up at Kisrie. "I'm gonna need your help. I can't use my hands."

"You mean I have to…touch one?" Kisrie squeezed her eyes shut, pressed her lips, and the left corner of her mouth pulled down toward her chin.

Man, that girl was stupid at times. "You expect it's gonna jump in your mouth?"

"I hate things with more than four legs."

"They're dead, Kisrie."

"I know."

"I thought you were hungry."

"I am."

"Then take one of these, pull the tail off for me, then pull the meat out and put it in my mouth. I'll eat one first, and if I die, you know they're poison."

"What? These are poison?"

Wendy rolled her eyes. "I'm trying to make a joke you idiot." She thrust her hand toward Kisrie. "Here."

Kisrie used her pointer finger and thumb to pick one up by a claw which then broke off, causing the rest of the creature to fall back into Wendy's hand.

"Just grab it, would ya?" Patience was wearing thin.

"Ew, ew, ew, ew, ew." Kisrie picked it up by the body, grasped the tail and pulled it off. "Oh, yuck! Oh, man, that's so gross!"

A little bit of whitish meat could be seen peeking out of the tail. "Pull that out and give it to me."

"I don't think I can. I'm so grossed out."

"You eat fried chicken and you touch chicken, don't you?"

"Yeah."

"Pretend it's chicken."

"But it's not! It doesn't have a beak!"

Wendy let fly enough foul words to peel paint off the side of a boat. "Neither does your Kentucky Freakin' Fried Chicken!"

Kisrie pulled out the meat and dropped it in Wendy's

hand. Wendy picked it up with her lips and worked it into her mouth. Not bad. Not something she'd order on purpose at a restaurant, but it wasn't bad.

"You're turn." This should be hilarious.

Kisrie reached down, then paused.

"Go on. You can do this."

Picking one up, Kisrie pulled off the tail and tossed the rest of it on the ground. She wiggled it back and forth before finally pulling it out and popping it in her mouth. At first, Kisrie looked like she bit into a moldy lemon, but as she chewed, her face relaxed a tiny bit. "Okay, not my favorite. Definitely doesn't taste like chicken—"

"I never said it did."

"Well, *they* say everything tastes like chicken. Like, on all those shows I watch on Discovery, they say squirrel tastes like chicken. Rattlesnake tastes like chicken—even alligator is supposed to taste like chicken and did you know Chinese restaurants that use cats and dogs do so because it—"

"Would you shut up already and get me another one?"

It was dark by the time they were done. Kisrie cleaned up the campsite and took the remains of the crayfish far away from camp. By the time she got back, Wendy was freezing, wishing she could get into her sleeping bag.

"We gotta figure out how to get you in the sleeping bag, huh?" Kisrie took one of Wendy's hands and studied the burns. She then knelt and looked at her legs. "I think your legs are worse. I'm thinking we can use a T shirt to cover them. Mine are pretty gross. What about yours?"

"Mine are filthy, too."

"I guess I'll have to see which one is less icky."

Wendy won the least icky award and had the pleasure of watching Kisrie tear one into strips. Kisrie tore the shirt like it was made of paper. The girl was strong, quite strong. Wendy'd never noticed that about her before.

It took every ounce of self-control to not punch Kisrie in the face while she wrapped Wendy's legs. As soon as the cotton touched her skin, Wendy screamed and arched her back. Her legs shot out, nailing Kisrie in the chest. Kisrie fell back. Wendy felt like her legs were being held against a grill.

Recovering from the shock of getting kicked, Kisrie moved in again. "I'm trying to put the ends on the backside of your calves because you're not burned there. I need to press a bit for the tape to stick well. Please don't kick me again."

At least Kisrie seemed to try to work as fast as she could. Wendy gave her credit for that.

"Done." Kisrie wadded up the rest of the T-shirt and tossed it to the tent. She then put the medical tape back in the first aid kit. "Let's get you in the tent and in the sleeping bag. I'm thinking I need to unzip it all the way and you can lay down in it before I put it over you and zip up."

Even though the bag was a down fill, the weight of it on Wendy's legs was too much to bear. She couldn't sleep and tried not to move a muscle all night long. Then there was Kisrie's snoring. It wasn't fair that Cow Pie could sleep and she couldn't.

By morning, she was in the foulest of moods.

And in even more pain than the night before.

Marcus couldn't believe how trusting the folks were in Northwestern Wyoming. They bought his estranged uncle story like it was a BOGO on Grade A steak at the grocery store.

He was assured if anyone found a clue, or a sign of the missing girls, they'd contact him and get him to that search area. The leaders of the search believed the group only made it as far as Fox Park since four of them asked for help at Turpin Meadow Campground. It was supposed the two missing girls would've headed west from the Fox Park location. A helicopter was going up to do a search. The ground team would follow a grid pattern from where the girls were last known to be.

A faint braying caught his attention. Someone was bringing in scent dogs. Apparently the girl with Wendy used her shirt as a bandage on the wounded leader.

This was almost too easy.

The sound of a helicopter aroused Kisrie from her sleep. Something in her gut told her it was searching for them. She looked over at Wendy who was on her back, staring at the roof of the tent, hands folded over her chest. Her hands were bubbly and oozing. That couldn't feel good at all. She wondered what the legs looked like but figured it was best to leave the makeshift bandages alone. The cotton was probably stuck to the burns by now. "I think we should pack up and get moving. I'm sure there are a force of rescue people out there looking."

Kisrie wondered what her family was going through about now. First Keri, now her. She wished there was a way to let them know she was fine and doing the right thing by making sure Wendy wasn't re-kidnapped.

"I need help."

"Oh, sure." Kisrie scooted out of Joan's sleeping bag, unzipped Wendy's, then peeled it off. The bandages were still in place. That was good. They just needed to stay put when Wendy hiked.

While Kisrie took down the tent, she heard the faint thwaping of the rotors again. It grew louder and louder as she rolled up the fly.

"Kisrie, that thing is coming in low, you need to get that tent wadded up and hidden. It's like a bright yellow beacon." Wendy sat propped against a tree.

Scooping it into her arms, Kisrie dashed for cover as the helicopter roared overhead. "That was close."

"I bet they will be passing over this area again and again. We need to watch what direction it flies, and go perpendicular to that."

Kisrie dropped the tent on the ground. "Are you up for this?"

"What choice do I have?" Wendy was pale. Her eyes hung at half-mast most of the time, and her voice was flat. She had to be hurting pretty bad.

"Here it comes again." The helicopter had circled around and was heading back toward them. The sun was high enough in the sky, but Kisrie couldn't quite tell which way it was going. The helicopter seemed to fly from the direction of the sun. That had to be east-ish. It was headed west-ish. So that left north-ish and south-ish as possible ways to go.

"I bet they can see that we're here." Wendy used the tree to help her stand. She yelped and grunted as she pulled to her feet. "Forget the tent. We need to get moving."

But what if it rained? They'd already been through a few storms. Getting wet up here was no joke. Hypothermia was no joke. "I don't think that's a good idea. I can get it rolled up and in our packs real fast."

"I'm not taking my pack."

Kisrie bowed her head for a moment to collect her thoughts. Wendy was panicking and making some stupid decisions. A thought struck her. "You promised to return me safe and sound to my friends and family. You want to be the hero? Then I'm packing the tent all in my backpack. You can have all the credit *if* you let me take all the essentials."

Wendy wobbled toward her on unbending legs. She struggled to keep her balance as it was without a pack. "Time for purge four-point-oh, or is it five?"

"Maybe six?"

At least Wendy had a little humor in her. That was a good sign.

"We gotta make sure what we leave behind is well hidden out of sight. Wendy, can you grab that stick over there and start raking up some pine needles?" Kisrie dumped both backpacks under the cover of the trees so the helicopter couldn't see them. All their clothes were dirty. No use in taking extras.

Warm layers were a yes. Waterproof layers…yes. That extra pair of underwear? Nah. It didn't matter now.

Socks? Yeah, probably a good idea to have a dry pair in case they had to cross some boggy areas again.

It wasn't long before Kisrie had two sleeping bags, the tent, both stoves and fuel with clothing layers crammed into her pack. The pot hung on the outside. She grabbed it by the top loop and tugged to hoist it onto her thigh. Holy sheep on a metal pole that thing was heavy! But what could she do? Wendy couldn't carry anything. It would take every ounce of strength for her to propel herself. Kisrie bit down on her lower lip and thrust up with all her might. She caught one of the shoulder straps and pushed her arm through. Got it!

Bending at the waist, Kisrie got the load where she wanted it and pulled the hip belt as tight as she could. Hm. Fancy that, she was a few inches smaller than when she started. The Wilderness Diet was effective, yet brutal.

She stood and took a tottering step. This…was gonna be a challenge, but she was up to it. She was a guard girl. And she had to get herself and Wendy back alive. But how would she know when it was safe to leave the woods? Ugh. "That way." She pointed using her whole arm so Wendy could see. They set off. Going was slow as they had to push through thick undergrowth and climb over fallen trees. The helicopter sounded more distant after a while which meant they were moving either north-ish or south-ish. How she wished she paid attention in geography class!

"Kisrie." Wendy's voice was soft.

Kisrie was trying to figure out how to get around another downfall at that moment. She stopped to face Wendy. Wendy looked at her and pointed to her legs. The bandages were wet with what looked like a mixture of blood and ooze. All of a sudden something shifted in Kisrie's guts. Her stomach had lurched and churned all morning, but she chalked it up to being near starving. An urge hit in her undercarriage. "Oh no!" She unclipped her belt, dropped the pack and made it out of sight of Wendy before she tore down her shorts and nearly rocketed into orbit. Pain slithered around her belly like a boa constrictor and squeezed. Her forehead beaded with sweat as she was overcome with a prickly and weak sensation.

Another explosion.

And she left behind all the "clean" clothes!

"Kisrie?"

"Stay away." Her voice was weak.

Not wanting to be left out of the propulsion, her stomach heaved, and what little was in there flew into daylight.

The crayfish.

Maybe they were poison after all!

"Oh, what's that smell?"

"Stay...back. I'm...sick."

"Way to let the entire world know where we are." Wendy's voice took on an edge.

"C...can't help it." Kisrie's body became a human blow torch from both ends. This was so awful. She'd never been so sick in her entire life. Was this it? Was this how she was gonna die? Covered in her own nasty, smelly, mess?

~25~

"Mr. Jaramillo, we just got word from the chopper that they spotted some movement under the canopy about four or so miles from here." The team leader re-attached the radio mouthpiece to his vest. "He gave me the coordinates. I can plug them into my GPS and we can head over there."

Marcus smiled at the man and put a hand on his chest. "I'm game. Let's go."

"We're gonna die out here. I know it. They'll find us. And don't think it's just me they'll take. There are men out there who have a thing for fat girls."

Kisrie groaned. Her body purged itself of all it held. Now she was expelling bile and probably gizzard juice. No kidnapper would want her smelling like this. Maybe this was how God was going to keep the kidnappers away. But she seriously doubted it. "I think it...was the...crayfish."

"So it's food poisoning? Why didn't I get sick?"

Kisrie didn't answer as another dry heave turned her inside out.

"Maybe I'm immune to it? But you'd think you'd stop being sick once it's all cleared out and from the looks of it over there, you put out enough vomit and diarrhea for a small village."

Intervals between episodes *were* increasing. Kisrie felt like a sponge that'd been wrung out several times. Maybe she would get through this, and when she did, first thing on the agenda was finding a stream or a lake—or something for her to soak all this off.

"Is there any way you can—?" Wendy froze mid-sentence with a swollen hand in the air. "Did you hear that?"

Kisrie strained her ears. She heard her shallow breaths and her pulse. That was it.

"I thought I heard shouts in the distance."

"I don't hear any—"

"There. There it is again! Oh, God, Kisrie, they're not too far away. We have to get out of here." Wendy came close and prodded her with a foot since she couldn't' bend her hands in any fashion. "Get up."

"The...the pack."

"Forget it. We need to get out of here and hide—after we clean you off."

Kisrie pushed up to her hands and knees, then stood up. She was shaky, but nothing came up or out when she stood. She pulled her shorts back up.

"Man, you stink."

"And you don't?"

"Not like that."

Wendy took off in the direction they had been heading, yelping and gasping. Kisrie followed, stumbling along like she imagined a drunk person might. She was so tired. She wanted to lay down and sleep.

But it wasn't an option.

Not now.

She heard a shout echo in the distance.

Wendy wasn't imagining things.

Someone was on their trail.

Wendy glanced behind her. Kisrie stumbled along trying to keep up. What a pair they made. Her with bad second-degree burns, and Kisrie covered with her own excrement. They needed to find some kind of water and quick, or Wendy was sure she would be the next one getting sick.

They were climbing now. The going was steep and hard. Wendy hoped taking these hard trails would throw off whoever followed them. She looked up. She believed she saw the top of the ridge. There seemed to be an awful lot of daylight and less trees. She forced her body onward despite the pain. As long as she kept moving she could tolerate it some. It was when she stopped—when things stiffened up and she tried to move again—that made her wish she were dead.

It had been a while since she heard the shouts. Maybe the searchers went another direction. She got closer to the top, or clearing, or whatever it was. Just a little farther…ah! Oh, yes! There was a small pond. "Kisrie." She whispered as loud as she could go. "There's water up here. You can go for a swim."

Kisrie looked up at her with red-rimmed eyes. The corner of her mouth lifted. "I can hardly stand myself."

When they reached the shore of the pond, Kisrie didn't hesitate to march on in. She covered her mouth to muffle the squeals. Wendy saw the goosebumps erupt on Kisrie's skin. It had to be cold. Should she go in?

The brown scum floating away from Kisrie's body helped

her make up her mind. She had open wounds. There was e-coli in them there waters.

"Well, I sure feel invigorated and alive now." Kisrie waded out up to her chest, then disappeared under the water for a few seconds. She popped up and shook her mangy mane.

"Don't stay in there all day." Just because they couldn't hear anyone following them at the moment didn't mean they could stop for long.

"I just want to make sure I get all of this nastiness rinsed off." Kisrie scrubbed at her arms, then splashed water on her face before plunging her hands below the surface to rub all the stuff underwater. When she was done, she did a side-stroke until the water was too shallow. "I'm not sure I got it all out, but it's way better, and I feel better myself."

They took off at a faster pace. Nothing mattered now except staying away from Marcus and Jorge.

"Now that we left *everything* behind, what're we gonna do for food and sleeping?"

Wendy moved a branch out of her way. "We will probably have to huddle under a tree or something and use leaves as a blanket."

"What about spiders?"

Seriously? "Don't tell me you're afraid of little bugs."

"Spiders aren't bugs…they have eight legs."

Wendy stopped and faced Kisrie. She felt like it took every ounce of energy to remain standing in one place. "We are in a life-and-death situation and you are worried about spiders?"

Kisrie shrugged.

"It's probably too cold for them anyway." Wendy braced herself for the pain as she started moving again.

"If we need to build some kind of shelter, we should probably stop and do that soon. The sun is getting low and I really don't know how long we have until it gets dark. Hard to tell with all the trees and mountains in the way."

"That sounds like a good idea, but I want to make sure we are super well-hidden so nobody could ever find us, even if they stand right in front of us."

"Which means we need to camp in an illogical place. People expect to camp where it's flat, and there's water and all."

Kisrie had a good point. But there wasn't anything around them in the moment that was a good hiding place.

"What if we spend the night in a tree?"

"You've got to be freaking kidding me. What if we fall out? And how will we stay warm at night?"

"Yeah. You're right."

"I'm thinking we need to find a rocky area with lots of nooks and crannies."

"And snakes."

"Would you quit it with the creepy-crawly critters?"

"You realize we left our bear spray with my pack?" Kisrie asked in more of a statement than a question.

Kisrie was more tolerable when she felt sick and hardly spoke. Now she was being a pain.

"About leaving the pack there—what if they find it?"

Wendy turned as fast as she could without spiking her pain level. "And what if they don't? Things are what they are and we just need to deal. Okay?"

"I don't see any rocks or cliffs nearby, and I don't know how much farther I can go."

There were some pine trees whose branches were close to the ground. "What if we burrow under one of those—and I don't want to hear a word about spiders."

"It could work. We just have to make sure if someone comes by, there is no evidence of us crawling under. We may have to get a branch from another tree and sweep the ground where we went. But how are you gonna manage with your burns and all?"

"Let me tell you something, Kisrie, I would rather feel the pain from these burns a hundred times over than be in the hands of Marcus and Jorge again."

"Let me at least get it ready so all you gotta do is get under there."

"That's fine. I'll keep watch."

Kisrie got on her belly and used her elbows to pull her upper body under the tree. There were a whole lot of dead, dry branches. She'd have to break a lot of them off to clear a space big enough for the both of them if they laid on their sides pressed together wrapped around the trunk. As far as insulation went? She had no idea. There wasn't much room. They'd have to share body heat and hope for the best.

A dull ache invaded Kisrie's head. Her mouth felt like it was full of wool. No matter how hard she tried, she couldn't make spit in her mouth. Great. She was probably dehydrated from being sick. And they didn't have their water bottles anymore. Note to self: don't make decisions when in terrible pain or very sick.

"How's it look in there?"

"It'll be rather tight, but we can manage. I think it will hide us if a night team comes through."

"Let's just hope they don't have sniffer dogs."

Kisrie backed out and rubbed her temples with her fingers. "Let me ask you this. Now that we have no food, no water, no shelter, no bear spray—where does this end? You're assuming the bad guys are still at large? What if they were caught while we've been out here? What if this is us taking a huge risk for nothing?"

"It's not for nothing." Wendy drew in a deep breath and

blew it out. "And…I…maybe we'll come across an old cabin that has hundred year-old beans in cans and a fireplace. We can live there until Marcus and Jorge think I'm dead."

"But what about me? My family? They've already gone through Keri missing, and now me." Kisrie blinked at the tears pooling in her eyes. "I can't bear them to go through that kind of pain again—especially my dad."

"If Jacque grew a brain and did her job, she'd tell them we just got a little lost, not *missing*."

"In these woods." Kisrie gestured with her arm. "As we've already experienced, these are some hostile environs."

"Look at you all sounding smart. Environs? Who uses words like that?"

"Tammie would. C'mon Wendy, we need to go back and tell them what's going on and maybe you can go into a witness protection program or something."

"I'm not going back! Not now, not ever. If you want to go, fine. Go. I'm not holding you back anymore. I don't care about being a stupid hero. It's not like I have much to live for anyway. My life is pretty screwed up."

What to do? Walking away would be the easy thing, but she probably wouldn't make it out alive at this point. She didn't even know which way was out anymore. Plus, she didn't have bear spray. Kisrie figured they both had a better chance at survival now if they stuck together. But they really did need to find their way back to civilization. They didn't have what it took to live for long in the wilds. And there was the fact Wendy seemed depressed.

"Your life isn't worthless."

Wendy glared at her. "What do you know?"

"You're smart. Pretty—"

"Would you just shut your pie hole? You have *no idea* what went on those weeks I was gone. Hell, you have no idea what my life was like *before* all this happened. I told you what my *mother*—if she could even be called that—did for a living. Look at me, Kisrie Kelley. I'm the daughter of a common whore. I had to spend my whole life making up stories about her being some hot-shot lawyer just so I could feel *normal*. Would you look at me?" Wendy grabbed Kisrie's face and made her look. "Can't handle the truth, can you?"

Kisrie forced herself to hold Wendy's gaze. She thought back to the time when she saw Wendy's mom when Wendy accused her of attempted murder with a sabre. Her mom wasn't dressed as Kisrie imagined a lawyer would be, but what did she know?

"I know I said this a few days ago, but all my life, from the time I was a little girl, she brought her *clients* into our apartment. I had to lay in my bed…" Wendy stopped for a moment, then barred her teeth when she continued. "…listening to her bed banging on my wall. All the *sounds*. Then there were the times I was part of the package deal. I won't bore you with the details. Use your imagination."

"I…I—"

"Then, after Iona walked out on me and your aunt took me in, I thought I had a shot at life. But now Marcus, a former *client* of my mother's, had to grab me and force me into his *business* of human trafficking. And you know what the worst part of it was?"

Kisrie felt her chin tremble. She sucked in her lower lip and bit down.

Wendy squeezed Kisrie's face harder. She tried not to wince from the pain. "It was watching them beat your sister up and threaten to torture her in order to control me."

A sob escaped Kisrie's throat. She had *no idea* what things were like for Wendy and…Keri.

"There were times they tied her up." Tears flowed down Wendy's face. She didn't seem to notice. "And they would kick her and punch her. She would scream and beg for them to stop. I tried to make them stop, but they took it out on her worse.

"Then there were the drugs and rapes. This is why I resented your innocence so much, if you must know, but they shot me full of universe knows what before handing me over to some john who did unspeakable things to me.

"These are *bad* men. Evil, if you want me to use your god-speak language." She gulped, let go of Kisrie's face, and wiped at her own with the heel of her palm. "Let me put it like this, Kisrie, if those men find me, they will then go after Keri. They leave no loose ends. They can't leave anyone alive to testify against them in court if they are ever caught. Now do you understand? This isn't about just me and you—it's about Keri too."

Kisrie blew out. She must have been holding her breath throughout Wendy's monologue. And her face hurt. A lot. No wonder Wendy was the way she was. Some of what she said before about being jealous made a little sense, but now? It made a lot of sense. "Then I'm staying with you." It seemed like in the past everyone Wendy hoped would give a rip about her left her. Kisrie refused to be one of those people. And she knew Aunt Zena wasn't going to be either. She was arranging to adopt Wendy.

By then, it was dusky. Wendy seemed spent and lost in her thoughts. Kisrie, headache ten times worse than before, went to work on clearing out their shelter slash hiding place.

Hopefully search parties went back to some town and rested for the night.

~26~

"Hot chocolate?" One of the fellow volunteers held out a foam cup and thermos to Marcus. He thanked the woman and took it.

They were getting close. Some discarded clothes and two backpacks were found. The journals indicated they belonged to Wendy and that girl with the stupid name. Why'd they leave their stuff behind? That was a mystery—especially in bear country.

No indications of a bear attack had been found, but now they had more for the hounds to sniff.

He was sure Wendy suspected he'd be able to find her when things went wrong on that little outing. She was out there hiding from *him*.

Of all the girls he managed, she was by far the brightest. If she'd just stop fighting him she could make more money than she imagined possible. Wendy Wetz was a high-dollar commodity.

He poured some hot drink into the cup and walked the thermos over to another group of searchers.

"…say she's afraid of a sex trafficker who's after her. That's why they are hiding."

Ah, so word got out. He had a plan for this. "Hey, I couldn't help but overhear what you were saying. Wendy? She's my niece. Her mother was my sister. We lost touch a long time ago. Wendy and me were tight when she was little." He took a sip and swallowed. "What was that you were saying about a pimp?" He then held out the thermos.

Taking it, one man answered. "Did you hear? Maybe it was only on the news in Colorado, but she was abducted by some men who are believed to head up a fairly large trafficking ring. Amazing she got out. That's so rare."

Marcus conjured up what he believed to be a horrified face. "My little Wendy?" He put a hand over his face. "I don't…I have no words."

"Well, we're glad you're here. Story goes, her mother abandoned her and she was living in some kind of foster care with a school psychologist. Poor thing's been through a lot." The man swayed his head side to side.

"When we find her, I will make sure no harm ever comes to her again." This was too good. And too much fun. "She'll be so surprised to see me. Maybe I'll adopt her and she can put all that awful stuff behind her."

Another man put his hand on Marcus' shoulder. "You're a good man, my friend. A good man."

Marcus lifted his cup of hot chocolate as if to offer a toast. "To finding Wendy."

On top of the burns, Wendy felt like she'd been hit by an RTD bus. At first she assumed it was because the night was so cold, but when all of a sudden she felt as though she was bursting into flames, she knew something was wrong.

Fever.

Which meant infection.

"My word, Wendy, all of a sudden you feel like a hot light bulb."

So Kisrie noticed.

"And I feel like I'm about to die of thirst. I haven't peed since before I got sick."

Great. They were both in compromised health. There was no way this could end well.

Neither one slept much through the night. Wendy vacillated between freezing and sweating, and Kisrie whimpered from the pain in her head.

Then there was that heightened sense of listening for anyone approaching them.

But no matter how ill either one felt, Wendy determined they had to keep on moving. Moving targets were harder to hit than static ones.

"Maybe we should get up and get moving and try to find some water."

"But you have a fever."

"I'll manage." Wendy hoped.

With great care, Kisrie slithered out from under the tree, then helped pull Wendy out. Once in light of the dawning day, Wendy looked at her hands. They were covered in blisters oozing with pus. No wonder she had a fever. She hated to think about her legs.

And the scars they'd leave.

Any hopes of winning Miss America or even modeling vanished. She felt her shoulders slump.

"I'm dizzy," Kisrie muttered, holding her head between both hands.

"Me too." Wendy was. When she took a step, it felt like the ground shifted underneath her foot. "Maybe we can lean on each other."

Kisrie didn't say a word, but stumbled toward her and they put their shoulders together. Wendy couldn't help but chuckle in spite of everything. "Who would've thought way back in the fall that we'd be leaning on each other like this?"

"Crazy, huh?"

"Yeah. And Kisrie, I'd rather this than the way things were. You're not a horrible person."

Kisrie let out what sounded like a nervous laugh. "You know, you're not so bad yourself. I'm really sorry about all that you've been through. And if I'd've known…"

"We need to focus on staying alive right now."

"Right."

Together they took one step forward.

Then another.

Marcus picked his way over a fallen tree. How in the world did they cover so much ground out here? This place was a mess.

Shouts of the girls' names were suddenly drowned out by hysterical barking. The dogs must've picked up a scent. Marcus imagined giving himself a high-five. No one could escape dogs.

No one.

"I don't think this is a false alarm." The handler called out to the group. "Shouldn't be long."

Marcus made his way to the team leader. "Hey, since we're closing in, do you think when we find them I can go in alone? I can't imagine how scared she is. A familiar and favorite face from the past may be just what she needs to feel safe."

The leader looked at him with gray-blue eyes surrounded by wrinkles and crow's feet. This man looked as if he'd spent years of his life in the elements. "Don't see why not. I'll let the handler know."

Marcus shook the man's hand. "Thank you so much. It means so much to me that you all are putting in so much effort to find my niece."

Walking away, Marcus grinned and patted the Glock in his pocket. Wendy would have to play along.

~27~

Progress was slow and painful. Every step sent shockwaves of pain through Wendy's body to the point she wondered if she'd pass out. And Kisrie wasn't doing much better. She was listless and often muttered nonsense to herself. Sounded like she was praying to some imaginary guy in the sky.

Their main priority was to find water. Kisrie was badly dehydrated, and Wendy was well on her way. She was still baffled over the fact that Kisrie refused to leave her.

"Wendy?" Kisrie's voice was rough.

"Yeah?"

"I hear dogs."

"Dogs?" Oh no, were they being tracked by a pack of wolves?

"Like hound kind of dogs you see on TV."

They stopped moving. Wendy held her breath. The wind shooshed through the trees all around them. Every now and then...yes. A bark. Two. A whole chorus of barks.

Because the sound was carried on the wind, it was hard to

tell what direction they were coming from or how far away they were. Her heart rate jumped, causing the throbbing pain to worsen. "Kisrie, we hafta hide. I bet those are search dogs."

"Then we need to find a tree. Dogs don't climb trees."

Did either one of them have enough strength for that?

"I wish we could find water. They'd lose our scent if we went in water or walked down a stream."

The braying started to get louder. "Kisrie, they're closing in! What if they find us? Marcus will know where I am if they take us out of here. For all I know, he's in some town waiting for me."

"Maybe he's not. He may not even know about any of this." Kisrie's words were slurring.

"I see a tree we can climb." Wendy pushed on Kisrie to guide her.

The dogs were closing in. It was only a matter of minutes now. "Hurry, hurry."

The pine had branches like a ladder. Kisrie shoved into the foliage and started climbing. Wendy pushed through her own pain to follow.

As soon as they were about four feet from the ground the first dog arrived at the base of the tree and let out a long howl. Five others rushed in and joined. All the stress and fear Wendy'd been stuffing burst out. "I don't wanna go back. This can't be happening."

A few moments later the figure of a man appeared. "Wendy."

He reached into a pocket in his jacket and pulled out a gun.

All the air left her lungs. She felt a stranglehold on her throat. She *knew* that voice.

Marcus!

"Kisrie, it's him. Oh, God, it's him. We're gonna die. He'll kill us both."

"Wendy, calm down. What if I get out of the tree and create a diversion causing the dogs to chase me and catch his attention? That way you can go the other way. I'm sure there are more people in the woods looking."

Wendy couldn't believe what she was hearing. "He has a gun! You could and probably will *die,*" she whispered.

Kisrie started climbing down the tree. "I'm not afraid to die. I know where I'm going. You don't. It has to be me." With a massive cracking of branches, Kisrie let go and dropped out of the tree. Somehow she landed on her feet. The dogs stopped for a second. Kisrie took off running, the dogs in pursuit.

Crack!

Marcus spun around to see the dogs take off after someone running. *Wendy!* He had to keep up his charade for the rest of the rescue team. "Wendy, it's your Uncle Alfonso! Hey, you're safe now." He raised the Glock and kept it centered on her back.

The girl wove through the trees, dogs on her heels. "Wendy, I need you to stop running." Keeping the gun pointed in her direction, he took off in a sprint, hurdling over rocks and stumps and pushing through trees that tore at his jacket.

She didn't slow down.

Fine. If she wanted to play hard to get…

He put pressure on the trigger. The distance between him and Wendy closed. He didn't plan on killing her, just stopping her. A gunshot wound would make for a tantalizing sales pitch.

He fired.

He saw a spray of red and the girl went down.

"Noooo!" A female voice screamed. "Kisreee!"

Marcus turned in time to see Wendy drop out of a tree ten

feet behind him. He looked back at the still from lying on the ground ahead of him. He lowered the gun. "Kisrie? What the—?"

Just then several members of the search team poured into the small area. Marcus looked down to see the gun still in his hand.

"What's going on here?" The leader of the group pulled a handgun from a holster on his hip. "Drop it."

"I thought I saw a bear—"

"I said, *drop it.*" The man stepped forward. His vest shifted and Marcus saw the badge. He was a sheriff from one of those po-dunk Wyoming towns.

Marcus zeroed in on Wendy, about a hundred yards away. With one smooth motion he lifted his Glock.

Wendy saw Marcus's gun pointed at her, but before he could shoot the man behind him fired and Marcus dropped. The man then rushed toward the kidnapper.

"No! No, over here. He shot her! He killed Kisrie!"

The man put a mic of some sort to his mouth and yelled something. He sprinted to where Wendy pointed. The dogs sat in a circle around Kisrie and whined. Wendy fell to her knees, wound her fingers in her hair and yanked until some tore loose. "He killed her! Oh, my God, he killed her." A woman came alongside and draped a blanket over her shoulders.

"Shhhh. Let the sheriff take a look."

"I...I...saw it. There's no way. It should've been me. It was me he was after. It should've been me." The woman pulled her into her arms and rocked her.

Moments later a helicopter hovered over them. A wire dropped and some guy slid down to the sheriff and Kisrie. Another man came and called the dogs away. The first man, probably a paramedic, pulled a stethoscope from somewhere on his uniform and listened to Kisrie's heart. He nodded and made hand signals to the sky. A stretcher came down.

Wendy hiccupped and wiped at her eyes. They weren't putting a sheet over her. Did that mean...? She twisted against the woman who held her. "Is she alive? Does that mean she's alive?"

"Yes, honey, for now."

It was amazing how fast they got Kisrie on the stretcher and hoisted her up into the chopper.

Lips trembling, Wendy did something she'd never done in her entire life. "Dear God, if you are real, please let her live."

Men on horses appeared after a while, and behind them was a group of medical type people with another stretcher—for her. The men on horses were all kinds of law enforcement.

As she was loaded on the stretcher to be carried out, the sheriff from Fremont County asked her a few questions regarding Marcus who would never bother her again. But where was Jorge?

The sheriff informed her a body was found floating in Chatfield. He was identified as Jorge Ramirez. And a woman named Unique turned herself in for fear she'd be next on Marcus's hit list.

Wendy felt a prick in her arm. Warmth and peace washed over her. The world went black.

~28~

Wendy stood in the hall outside Kisrie's hospital room in Idaho Falls, IV pole in one hand, the other occupied with holding her gown closed. The person who came up with the design—probably a guy—should be prosecuted for committing a crime against humanity. No one should have to live in perpetual fear of butt exposure.

Channels on the TV in Kisrie's room flicked on to Discovery Channel. *Man vs. Wild.* What a weird choice considering all they'd been through the past few days. She took a deep breath and knocked, hoping the ties would keep her nether regions covered.

"Hey, can I come in?"

Kisrie muted the TV. "Sure."

Wendy wheeled the pole in. She sat in the recliner next to Kisrie's bed. "I'm glad to finally see you alert and with it."

"Me too. But considering the...what was it? Two surgeries I had, I'm happy I was out of it. The doctors are pretty amazed the bullet missed all my major organs. It did a lot of damage to my insides, but it could've been a lot worse."

"Yeah. About all that." Kisrie's willingness to *die* haunted Wendy day and night since they were rescued. The girl ran in front of a man with a loaded gun without hesitation. What did Kisrie know that she didn't?

Kisrie turned the TV off and faced her.

Wendy took a deep breath, turned her head, and looked out of the window. "When you jumped out of the tree, you said you weren't afraid to die because you knew where you'd go. You also said you had no idea about me. What did you mean by that?"

"Are you just curious? Or do you really want to know?"

"I really want to know." She faced Kisrie, blinking tears out of her eyes. She didn't want emotions to get in the way of this conversation. She wanted to be rational. "You ran out there and took a bullet for me without giving it a second thought. Just like how Joan…when that moose charged me…she threw herself in harm's way while knocking me out of it. I don't get it. And I want to."

Kisrie closed her eyes. Wendy feared her former nemesis would fall asleep without answering. Then, all of a sudden, those brilliant blue eyes popped open. "What I have to say is about God—Jesus, to be exact. You said you don't believe in Him."

"No. I…didn't." Wendy leaned forward and grabbed the rails on Kisrie's bed. "But God is the thing you and Joan had in common. Normal people don't do what you both did. Nobody is willing to die for anybody else. And in a matter of days, it happened to me twice."

"Actually three times."

"What?" Wendy sat back in her chair. Her bandaged hands fell to her sides. Who else did she inadvertently kill? Did someone else in the group die while she and Kisrie were away from them?

Sharon?

"Wendy, you look like you're gonna be sick. Do I need to

call a nurse?" Kisrie reached for the call button wrapped on the opposite rail of the bed.

"Who…else? Sharon?"

"Sharon's fine. She's here in another room."

Wendy's heart beat faster, harder. "Then who else died?"

Kisrie's eyebrows disappeared into the mess of curls on her forehead. "Oh, you think someone in our group died." She shook her head. "No, this happened over two-thousand years ago. You see, Jesus, Son of God, died for you."

"That's stupid. I wasn't even born yet. I can believe he died and all, but not for *me*." She scoffed. "He doesn't even know who I am. Or you for all that matters."

"That's where you're wrong, Wendy. He's God. When he died, he died for everyone in the past present and future. All you gotta do is realize he died for your sins and ask Him to forgive you."

"Oh, come on. There's got to be more to it. Like, what about praying the 'Our Father' a hundred times a day or beating yourself with a stick? No religion's stuff is simple."

"But it is."

None of this made sense. Muslims had to wear those black robe things and hide their faces. Jehovah's Witnesses didn't celebrate holidays and were required to knock on doors. There had to be *something* required of her. *Something* beyond her reach. And besides, she was far from a model citizen. "I've been a horrible person, as you know. You've been the target of most of it."

Kisrie sighed. A spasm of pain seemed to flash across her face. "Go read about King David. He had an affair and tried to cover it up by murdering the woman's husband. But the Bible still says he was a man close to God's heart."

"The Bible? Really? Science has proven it's not true. You can't totally believe all that? What if it's all a bunch of fairy tales—like *Aesop's Fables*?"

Kisrie toyed with the TV remote, flipping it end over end in her hand. "I believe it's all true."

"I...I don't know what to think."

Kisrie dropped the remote and grabbed the bed controls. She lowered the head part a bit.

No, no, no. "You can't sleep until you answer my question." Wendy's voice rose in pitch. She didn't want to sound desperate, but wondering what would happen to her if she died gave her nightmares. "You and Joan weren't afraid to die. I mean, *both* of you must know what happens afterwards? Right? Tell me, Kisrie. Tell me."

Kisrie's eyes fluttered. A low moan escaped her lips. Her skin was almost translucent. "I chose to run because I knew if I died when I ran in front of Marcus, I'd go to heaven and you wouldn't."

Wendy rocked back as if slapped in the face. What kind of thing was that to say? Anger flared in her gut. But then it sputtered out. She knew if the roles were reversed she would *never* be willing to die for anyone. Sinking into the recliner she thought through her next question before speaking. "So, where exactly would I go?" Did she want to know? Something in her told her what she was about to hear was truth.

"Hell."

Wasn't she already in hell? Life so far had been nothing but hell. And everyone said that was a tactic Christians used to scare people into going to church. Kisrie's calm expression as she sprinted in front of Marcus flashed in her mind. Joan's absence of fear when she put herself in front of the moose *knowing* it would kill her...

These were more than words or fairy tales. People weren't willing to die for nothing. The fact neither Kisrie or Joan were afraid clung to her like super glue.

"Let me ask you this. If I were to believe whatever it is you believe, would my fears about death go away?" It was no use.

The tears rolled down her cheeks and splashed onto her hospital gown. What would it be like to sleep at night and not be tormented by nightmares?

"If you really for really believe, yes. I'm not gonna lie to you and tell you your life will be easy." Kisrie laughed. "Just look at my life. Aunt Zena's. Keri's. But what I can promise you is that I would rather go through the worst life has to offer with Jesus than without him. I was only able to do what I did because He gave me the strength."

Wendy let it all sink in. She felt like she had to make some kind of decision then and there. "I want what you and Joan have. I want peace. I want to know I'm going to heaven when I die." Sobs wracked their way up through her chest. It was like some dam of emotion ruptured and years and years of pain and anger spilled out.

Kisrie reached out a hand. "Come here. I'll pray with you so you can be sure."

Wendy dove at the bed, and her IV tore out of the back of her hand. But she didn't care. Kisrie's hand rested on her head. Wendy did something she never did before in her life.

She talked to God. Big G.

The peace she craved flooded her soul.

Several weeks later Wendy sat in the passenger seat of Zena's car outside the high school. A kid carrying a tuba walked by as if the thing weighed only three pounds. Across the parking lot flags went up and down, some flew into the air. "I can't believe I'm doing this."

Zena patted her on the knee. "I think you knew deep in your heart, for quite a while, that this was where you belonged."

There was a moment of silence before Zena spoke again. "Wendy, before you get out, I want to tell you something. While you were in the hospital I filed all the necessary papers to adopt you." She shifted in her seat to look directly at Wendy. "I already think of you as my daughter, but I want it to be official. I want you to be Wendy Plank."

Wendy felt hot tears fill her eyes and roll down her cheeks. Her chin trembled. Despite the fact that Iona gave birth to her, Wendy didn't ever remember the woman calling her daughter.

"I realize it's not a perfect situation. I would be a single mother, but—"

Wendy unbuckled her seatbelt and leaned over the console to wrap her arms around Zena—soon to be mother. Never in her life did Wendy imagine she'd feel this way. She'd tried so hard to keep the Plank woman out of her heart. But after all she'd been through, after asking Jesus to forgive her sins, *she* changed. "Does that mean I get to call you Mom?" Tears flowed freely now.

"You can call me whatever you want, but I'd really like it if you called me Mom." They pulled apart and Wendy swiped at her face. Zena fished in her purse and handed her a tissue.

A group of girls carrying flutes ran past.

"Dr. Morgan likes to start on time." Zena dabbed at her eyes with the corner of a Kleenex.

Wendy stared at the kids milling around on the practice field. This was the *last* place she ever imagined she'd be. In spite of the excitement over her adoption, she was a little nervous about joining the color guard. "What if I break my face? Or, worse yet, break someone else's?"

"Gavin and the others will make sure you learn how to spin properly."

A rifle spun high into the air. In spite of the heat, a shiver skittered down Wendy's spine. That looked hard.

"I think you need to get out of this car and head over there."

Wendy sighed and unclipped her seat belt. "You're right…" She opened the door and slid out. "… Mom."

Color crept into Zena's face. She laughed and rubbed her hands along the sides of the steering wheel. "Oh, Wendy, I love you so much. I can't wait to see what the future holds for our little family."

Wendy paused, hand resting on the top of the door. She looked Zena square in the face. "I love you too." Her voice cracked. Emotions like a warm blanket filled her entire soul— from the top of her head to her toes. Never in her life did she say those words to Iona, let alone anyone else. But ever since she decided Jesus wasn't one of those whack-a-doodle mythical prophets, her heart had been full of nothing but.

"Again, I love you too, Wendy. Now go! You have three minutes before rehearsal starts."

As Wendy made her way across the field, members of the band stopped what they were doing and stared. Some even whispered to one another wondering what *she* was doing there. Others had terror-stricken looks on their faces.

Tammie saw her first and called out to the rest of the guard. They all stopped what they were doing and ran toward her. The whole group encircled her, breathing heavy. Kisrie held out a tall metal pole with some fabric on one end.

"Here. This is for you. I put it together myself."

Wendy took the offering and turned it fabric end down, then up. "How'd you know I was coming?"

Brittany and Sabrina grinned at her. "Aw, Wen, we figured back in the woods that you'd be here. You're one of us."

"One of us," Wendy repeated, letting the words sink in.

Zoe flipped her sword thingy—sabre—in a small flip. It landed in her hands with a *smack!* Wendy flinched.

"Don't worry about this just yet," Zoe waved it at her, "you gotta learn flag first."

Kisrie took the flag from her hands. "It's pretty simple, actually. All's you need to do is spin..." Kisrie made the flag go around and around so fast the brightly colored fabric was a blur. "Then you stick your hand in like this and toss." The flag launched into the air and turned around a few times before landing at an angle in Kisrie's hands. "Finally, you catch. That's all there is to it. Spin. Toss. Catch."

About the Author

Darcie Gudger spends much of her time dodging the Wyoming wind ducking into historical museums and archives imagining life on the frontier prior to modern comforts. When not in a library or at her computer, Darcie can be found paddling the river in her kayak, hiking, walking her psychotic freak-biscuit of a dog, or in the pool determined to hit her two-mile goal. Her ridiculous love of books almost flattened her son when over-burdened shelves collapsed on him during his birthday party. Her husband implemented an immediate ban on physical books. Undeterred, Darcie finds creative ways to sneak books into her home and pushes her Kindle to its limits.

Visit her website: www.djgudger.com

Visit the Mountainview Books, LLC website for news on all our books:

www.mountainviewbooks.com